Also by Ruth Rendell
Published by Ballantine Books:

TO FEAR A PAINTED DEVIL

VANITY DIES HARD

THE SECRET HOUSE OF DEATH

FROM DOON WITH DEATH

SINS OF THE FATHERS

WOLF TO THE SLAUGHTER

THE BEST MAN TO DIE

A GUILTY THING SURPRISED

DEATH NOTES

RUTH RENDELL

MASTER OF THE MOOR

BALLANTINE BOOKS • NEW YORK

Originally published in Great Britain by Hutchinson & Co. (Publishers) Ltd.

Copyright © 1982 by Kingsmarkham Enterprises Ltd.

Library of Congress Catalog Card Number: 82-47871

ISBN 0-345-30273-7

This edition published by arrangement with Pantheon Books

Manufactured in the United States of America

First Ballantine Books Edition: September 1983

5¢

For Nan and Maurice Romilly

It was the first dead body he had ever seen. At first it had been a shock and had made his heart beat faster. Now he knelt down and looked at the dead girl curiously. Something unpleasant had happened to her face; it was swollen and a greyish-blue colour, and her eyes protruded under strained shiny eyelids. She had been very fair, a blonde, he could tell that by her pale brows and lashes, though not by her hair, for someone had clipped all that off very close to the scalp.

She lay on her back on the grass within the avenue made by the great standing stones, between the ninth and tenth of them on the northern side. It was still early in the morning, 8.30 or so, and he supposed she had lain there all night. The sun was shining and there was an east wind blowing which set the clouds tumbling and their shadows rushing across the shallow hills and the craggy outcroppings. The shadows of the perpendicular stones lay parallel to one another like the teeth of a giant's comb. It was very cold, the biting brilliant cold of April in the middle of England. The girl was dressed in jeans, a thick sweater and a thick quilted jacket. She had been a slender, tallish, very young girl. He had known at once that she was dead. Now for the first time he touched her skin, the skin of her forehead, with his fingertips. It felt like marble, like the angel on the Tace tomb in Chesney churchyard, as cold and as unyielding.

His instinct was to lift her up and carry her down the hillside to the village. He was strong enough to do that without effort. But memories came to him of books he had read and films he had seen. She must be left there for the police, he must get the police. What a climax to a moorland walk! He had left home a little before eight, having put a cup of tea on the bedside table next to Lyn, walked through the village and climbed the fell. An ordinary walk on the moor, such as he had taken two or three times a week for years and years. What had he been thinking about? A kitten, of all things. He had been thinking about buying Lyn a kitten for her birthday, and as he came up to the great dolmen, had paused to look at it for the thousandth time, he had seen the bundle on the ground. An incongruous coloured speck among the green and the grey. A patch of red and blue with the head of a damaged doll.

After a while he got up from his knees. He had a strange sensation that for many minutes he had been holding his breath, though he couldn't of course have been doing that. The girl's eyes were exactly like the turquoise blue marbles he and Peter Naulls had played with as children. He took in deep breaths of the clean, icy moorland air. High above him a hawk hung like a pendulum. The wind had torn open a rift in the clouds and the sky revealed was as blue as those dead eyes. He turned his back abruptly and walked away. He walked back the way he had come and let himself out by a gate in the railing where a metal notice planted in the earth read: *Department of the Environment. Ancient Monument. The Foinmen.* The hawk dropped to the ground, rose again in a flurry of striped feathers.

In those parts where they call hills foins and mineshafts soughs, the paths that ascend the hillsides in hairpin bends are crinkle-crankle paths. He made his way down the crinkle-crankle path that traversed Chesney Fell. He took long strides and he walked fast but he walked easily too and without great exertion. His body was a strong vigorous machine which the moor had developed and sustained. He wore an anorak over a wool sweater with a polo neck and he wore tough cord jeans and walking boots. He was twenty-nine but he looked younger because his hair was fine and very dark and his skin a fresh white and red. On the cold air as he made his way down his breath blew like smoke.

The clock on the tower of St Michael-in-the Moor chimed nine as he came onto the road. The milkman's van was on the green; Mrs Southworth from the Hall was at the pillar box, posting a letter. He walked on away from the green and the houses up the bit of the Jackley road from which Tace Way turned off. The council houses, of fudge-coloured brick, stood in two rows and a horseshoe shape with a screen of Leyland's cypress hiding them from the village. The moor was all round the saucer in which Chesney lay but the best views of it were from his house, the last house before the road curved round.

Lyn's mother, still in a dressing gown, was watching

from her downstairs window. She waved and he waved back. He waved too at Kevin Simpson who was getting his car out. He waved and grinned as if nothing had happened. The wind came whipping off the moor and bent the cypresses as if they were blades of grass.

Lyn heard his feet in the sideway and opened the back door to him. Though she was dressed, her long fair hair was still in pigtails, the way she wore it at night. She looked like a tall little girl.

'You weren't long.'

'I hadn't got far. Oh, Lord, darling, there's something pretty ghastly up there. A girl and she's dead. I found her lying among the Foinmen.'

It occurred to Lyn — fleetingly, to be gone in a moment — that most men would have broken such a thing more gently to their wives. She spoke steadily in her soft, low voice, 'What do you mean "dead", Stephen? Do you mean she's had an accident?'

He shook his head. 'Her face is all blue. And her hair's gone, someone's cut off all her hair.'

These days when Lyn had a shock it made her shake. No matter how controlled and calm she might sound, her hands would shake and sometimes her whole body. Her mother said it was all nerves, but what had she to be nervy about? Her body began its trembling.

'Oh, Stephen, no!'

'Pretty frightful, isn't it? She's been murdered. Strangled, I should think. I'd be willing to bet she's been strangled. Oh, Lord, now I've upset you.'

'I'm all right,' said Lyn. 'Are you going to phone the police?'

'I certainly am. Straightaway. I came back at once. I came back as fast as I could.'

'Oh, Stephen . . .'

They were standing close, looking at each other. She

put her arms round him and held him tightly. He allowed her to hold him but it was an effort, he was impatient to act, to get to the phone. She let him go.

'Where?' the man on the phone said.

It amazed Stephen how little local people knew of their countryside, their heritage really. Those Simpsons, for instance, who knew the Foinmen no better than they knew Stonehenge, Dadda who bragged he hadn't been on Vangmoor these twenty years. 'At the Foinmen,' he repeated, 'between the ninth and tenth stones on the north side.'

'The best thing'll be for you to show us, Mr Whalby. You stay where you are and we'll come to you.'

Stephen wasn't having that. 'I'll meet you on the green. I'll be waiting for you on Chesney Green.'

While he was on the phone Lyn's sister had come in, big-boned, yellow-haired Joanne, only nineteen and married six months. Her voice was as strident as Lyn's was gentle.

'I don't reckon I ought to have shocks like that in my state of health.'

Lyn said worriedly, 'I wish you hadn't listened.'

'Come on, love, don't you know when I'm kidding? I'm going to dash back and tell Kev. Does Mum know?'

Stephen went out again. Joanne and her mother were talking on Joanne's doorstep. He didn't stop. He walked back down to the green and waited out of the wind on the churchyard side. Between the lychgate and St Michael's ancient oak door was the Tace tomb, white marble, black bronze and Giacometti's agonized angel with wings like fishbones. Stephen leaned over the gate, waiting for the police. The square tower of the church was built out of the dun-coloured limestone called foinstone and so were all the cottages and Ches-

ney Hall itself. Long ago it had been quarried out of a
deep pit called Knamber Hole. You could see Knamber
Foin from here, a bleak mass of rubble rising out of a
plain that was grey, smoky-looking with the leafless
boughs of ten thousand little birch trees. Clouds shad-
owed densely those south-eastern parts, but the north
and west were broadly lit by the sun, the higher hills
gleamed in sunshine, and a flock of birds flew across
the expanse of blue sky above Big Allen.

The wind was like a blade that just skims the skin.
Stephen saw the police cars coming a long way off,
three of them in a convoy coming up the white road
from Hilderbridge. An army of police — well, enough
to show they believed him. The cars parked one behind
the other in a row on the road that crossed the green
from the Hall to the church. Already there were a couple of people watching, Kevin Simpson's mother and
an old man whose name Stephen didn't know, hungry
for excitement on an empty April Saturday. He said to
the police, 'This way. We have to go up over the fell.'

There was a detective inspector, a thickset man of
about his own age, athletic-looking but red in the face
and with reddish hair, and a detective sergeant, a bit
younger, dark with a wedge-shaped rodent face, a
beanpole of a man. Then there were officers with particular functions, one whose job it was to be at the
scene of the crime before the body was touched or
moved. Stephen took them up the zig-zag track. If he
had been on his own he would have gone straight up
but he was more used to walking and climbing, no
doubt, than these policemen. He fancied too that he
felt the cold less than they did. They had stamped their
feet and rubbed their hands while they were waiting
about. The inspector said to him suddenly, 'Are you the

Stephen Whalby that writes that nature column for the *Echo*?'

' "Voice of Vangmoor?" Yes. Yes, I am.' No one had ever asked him that before and Stephen felt pleased. It was seldom, of course, that he met people who didn't already know. 'Are you — ' he tried to speak as a real writer would ' — one of my regular readers?'

'On and off,' said the inspector. Stephen now remembered he had said his name was Manciple. 'You must know the moor like the back of your hand.'

'I know it pretty well.' Stephen couldn't resist boasting a bit. 'I daresay I'm actually the greatest living authority on Vangmoor.'

Stephen said this very seriously but for some reason it made the wedge-faced sergeant guffaw. He had an unpleasant grating laugh and Stephen felt anyway that it was unseemly to laugh in these circumstances. He compressed his lips in silent offence.

The inspector gave no sign of noticing. 'You'll be watching "Bleakland" on the telly, I expect. They say that chap Alfred Tace who wrote the books, he knew the moor inside out.'

'Alfred *Osborn* Tace,' Stephen corrected him, and said after a little hesitation, 'He was my grandfather.'

They were both impressed now. 'Is that a fact?' said Manciple, and the sergeant said, 'You'll maybe be getting a bit of money out of this series, then?'

'Good Lord, no!' He wanted to laugh, though it would have been a bitter laugh. 'Actually, it was through the female line,' he began, wondering how much he meant to explain, but they had ceased to listen to him. They were at the top of the hill and Foinmen's Plain had unrolled itself before them. The wind scored shivering channels through the ling and bilberries, the growth of fine, dry grass. Against the bright, con-

stantly changing sky the dolmen stood stark and black.
'Look, over there.' Stephen pointed.

They went forward slowly. They could all see it
now, there was no need for hurry. The scene-of-crimes
man stumbled as one of his feet went into a rabbit hole.
Stephen liked to make a ceremony of his visits to the
Foinmen, walking slowly the length of the avenue up
to where the Giant stood, but there was none of this
now. They didn't even bother to use the gate but swung
their legs over the low railing and walked straight in
among the stones to where the girl was.

A small green insect with folded wings had settled on
her forehead. They looked at her and for a time no one
said anything. Then Manciple said, without touching
her, without even bending down, 'She's dead all right.'

One of the men Stephen had taken for another policeman in plain clothes came closer, looked at the girl's
open blue eyes. The sergeant called him Doctor. 'Of
course she's dead,' the doctor said, and then, 'A moors
murder, my God. Sooner or later it had to be.'

A gust of wind roared across the plain and the insect,
blown by it, took wing.

He was most of the day at Hilderbridge police station.
Manciple disappeared and Stephen was questioned by
a chief superintendent called Malm. Why had he been
out on Vangmoor so early? Wasn't it very cold to be out
on the moor at that hour? Had he ever been to the Foinmen before? Dozens of times, maybe even hundreds?
Then why had he gone this particular morning?

It was impossible to make Malm see that one might
love the moor, enjoy walking, have become accustomed to the cold. The sergeant, whose name was
Troth, came back and sat next to Malm. They were
perfectly polite, curious, baffled. After an hour or so of

that Malm changed his tack and wanted to know whom Stephen had met on that morning walk, everything he had seen.

'I didn't meet anyone. I hardly ever do.' Stephen tried irony. 'I saw a hare and after I'd found the body there was a sparrowhawk, a kestrel.' He saw he had made Malm think him of unsound mind and he said quietly, earnestly, 'There was nothing, nothing but what I've told you.'

After that they went back to why was he there and didn't he mind the cold. They didn't tell him the girl's name or where she came from. He had to find that out from the television when he got home. Lyn jumped up when he came in.

'That's what you get for being public-spirited.' Stephen forced a laugh. 'They're acting as if they think *I* did it.'

'They can't be, Stephen. It must be just their manner.'

'I feel worn out, much more than I would if I'd been for miles on the moor. D'you know, that was the first dead body I've ever seen. It's a strain on you. Have you ever seen a dead person?'

'My grandmother, my mother's mother. She just looked as if she was asleep. Would you like a drink, love? A proper drink or just tea? I've made supper, we can have it whenever you want.'

'Put the box on, shall we? It's time for "Bleakland".'

Lyn brought tea in and then supper on two trays. She sat beside Stephen and held his hand. Vangmoor came up on the screen as if they were looking out of the window, but Vangmoor in summer without the wind and with leaves on the trees. Stephen had watched some of the film-making, the scenes they had shot in the Vale of Allen. It was a strange experience to see Lady Irene in her Edwardian dress, Alastair Thornhill in Norfolk jacket, Big Allen behind them, and then, when the romance was over, the episode ended, the real moor of today come onto the screen with the news. It was as if the moor were the whole world and there was nothing anywhere but the moor.

The announcer said that the dead girl had been called Marianne Price and that she was twenty. She had been stopped and killed while cycling home from Byss to Hilderbridge late on the previous night. A picture of her as she had been in life came up on the screen. A round face with a high forehead, blue eyes, short straight nose, a mantle of shining, fair hair. Stephen's name wasn't mentioned.

Police were searching for the missing bicycle, but the announcer said nothing about the missing hair. Stephen switched off the set. He went to the window and drew back the curtain. There was a bright, nearly full moon. The silhouette of Big Allen stood out densely black against a lustrous, opaque sky.

'When I was a child I used to imagine the moor belonged to me, that I was a young prince or the heir to an estate or something. It was after Mother left that I started thinking like that.'

'You needed something to make up for it,' Lyn said.

He shrugged. 'Yes — I suppose Freud and people like that would say I was compensating for losing my mother. I don't know. I used to think of the moor as all my property, my kingdom, I suppose, and I'd decide where I was going to build my capital city and where I was going to have my hunting forest. And the Reeve's Way, that was where I was going to march my army. You'll laugh, but I was going to have a coronation. I was going to be crowned at the Foinmen, standing on the Altar.'

Lyn didn't laugh. She had heard it all before but he always seemed to forget he had told her. His voice went up in pitch.

'Good grief, when I think of some creature coming onto the moor and doing a vile thing like this! It makes my blood boil, it's sacrilege!'

But Lyn said quietly, 'I wish it hadn't had to be you who found her.'

2

There were Sundays when Dadda didn't come to lunch, when depression kept him from stirring out of doors. His depressions were an illness, not merely a feeling of lowness or irritability. They dragged him down into horrors he said no one could imagine. But between bouts, in a precarious euphoria that to others seemed like dourness, he drove up from Hilderbridge in Whalbys' van.

The depression of last week had lifted like a fever passing when **the** patient sleeps or asks for food. Dadda looked shattered by it, though, bruised under the eyes. He wore his one good suit, grey with a white chalk stripe, and he had brought with him Lyn's birthday present in an unwieldy brown paper parcel. He didn't kiss Lyn, he never touched women, or men either for that matter, but he seemed to make a principle of shrinking from the touch of women.

Lyn unwrapped a small round table, high-polished, with curved legs and a top carved in a design of a chestnut leaf and cluster of spiny fruits.

'It's beautiful, Dadda. You are good to us.'

'Don't go ruining it with hot cups.'

'What a lovely piece of work!' Stephen exclaimed. 'Early Victorian, isn't it?'

'Late,' said Dadda. 'You ought to be able to see that with half an eye. You're supposed to be in bloody trade.'

Lyn's parents and Joanne and Kevin always came over on Sunday afternoons. Mr Newman was a small quiet man, half the size of Dadda, probably literally half his weight. He ran a finger along the carving.

'We shan't be able to compete with that.'

'It's not a question of competing,' said his wife. 'Lyn knows she's getting a cardigan, anyway. Have to wait till Wednesday.' She had brought two Sunday papers with her. Everyone had a paper except Dadda who never read anything. Mrs Newman's face was round and healthy and high-coloured like Joanne's. 'It's a funny thing,' she said, 'but in a place like this, a sort of open space, forest, moors, anywhere that's National Trust, you always get killings. It's a wonder we haven't had them before.'

Joanne said, 'What d'you mean "them", Mum? There's been one young girl killed so far as I know.'

'So far. You get one now and another in a couple of weeks and folks are scared to go out or we women are. It'll be one of those pathologicals.'

'Psychopaths.'

'Whatever they call them. Maniacs, we used to say.'

'A proper ghoul, isn't she, Tom?' said Mr Newman.

Dadda didn't answer but gave his awkward humourless grin. He sat with his huge shoulders hunched up. He was used to company but hopeless in it, he never improved. Many men are as tall as or taller than their fathers and Stephen was six feet, but Dadda still towered above him. He filled his armchair, all long, gaunt, bent limbs, that somehow suggested a cornered spider. All but he wanted to know how Stephen had got on with the police.

'I'm their number one suspect. No, it's a fact.'

'He's exaggerating,' Lyn said.

Dadda spoke. 'Beats me why he had to stick his neck out.'

'Once I'd seen her,' Stephen said, 'I had to report it.'

'I'd have shut me eyes and carried straight on. It all comes of this traipsing about the moor.'

'Good grief, you sound just like the police! Can't anyone understand a man can love the countryside? It's a simple enough pleasure in all conscience, harmless enough, I'd have thought.'

Kevin winked. 'I tell folks Lyn's not a grass widow, she's a moor widow.'

A grim smile moved Dadda's mouth.

Mrs Newman said, 'I should think this'd put you off anyway, Stephen. You won't want to be up there with this maniac about. I don't like that word widow, Kevin, that's not very nice.'

Joanne and Kevin held hands on the sofa. 'I knew that girl, that Marianne Price, Mum, did I tell you? Well, you must have known her, Stephen. She was at the cash desk in the Golden Chicken.'

'The Market Burger House they call it now, Joanne.'

'Whatever they call it. Don't you get your lunch there, Mr Whalby?'

'Me? I keep me feet under me own table. Stephen goes out for his dinner, he's young.'

'There you are, Stephen, like I said, you must have known her, you must have seen her hundreds of times.'

'Good Lord, Joanne, how would I know? She'd have looked a bit different, I can tell, from what she was like lying up there with her hair all cut off.'

Joanne gave a little scream and put her hands up to her own abundant blonde hair.

'She won't be there tomorrow,' said Mrs Newman. 'I shouldn't be surprised if they were to close tomorrow out of respect. I remember when you and your brother were little, Lyn, Joanne wasn't born, old Mr Crane over at Loomlade got killed in his car and they closed the electric shop two days out of respect and the branch in Byss.'

But next day the Market Burger House was open for business as usual. Stephen took particular note of it after he had taken Lyn to the Mootwalk and parked the car in the market square. The restaurant was the only one in Hilderbridge, in the Three Towns probably, that served breakfast. People were breakfasting, some were just having coffee. An Indian girl in a blue sari was at the cash desk in Marianne Price's place. Stephen went across the square to Whalbys.

Dadda lived alone in the three-storey house in King Street, a narrow foinstone house, one room deep and heated with oilstoves. The workshop was the coachhouse next door and the room above it. Over the double doors, painted dark brown, was a sign in gilt lettering that said: *Whalby and Son. Restorers of fine furniture*. The sign was peeling and you couldn't read it from the other side of the square but the Three Towns knew who Whalbys' were without that. A Whalby and his son had been there for as long as anyone could remember and Dadda used sometimes to boast on his good days that Alfred Osborn Tace had himself been a customer and that Whalbys had recovered the seats of the Hepplewhite chairs at Chesney Hall.

Stephen said hallo to Dadda before going upstairs to start work on the three-piece suite they had brought in on Friday. Dadda was smoking. Between his nutcracker lips was one of the thin twisted little cigarettes he made himself. The frames of the furniture were sound, a lot better than the kind of stuff they manufactured nowadays. He began tearing off the old, almost ragged, tapestry and prising out tacks. The scent of tobacco was wafted up the stairs. Dadda only smoked when he was contented and then he would get through forty or fifty a day, bringing on a cough and staining his fingers yellow-brown. Dadda might have been a lot different, Stephen thought, if his wife hadn't deserted him. Or was it because he was the way he was that she had walked out one day when Dadda was at work and he at school, leaving a note on the kitchen table and the remains of the week's housekeeping money? He had been too young to read the note but he could still remember how that table had looked when he came in, its top at the time the height of his own shoulder. He could still remember the piece of folded exercise book paper, the three pound notes and the pile of coins at eye level.

Dadda never spoke of her directly. When, a long time ago now, Stephen had tried to call him Dad or Father and drop the babyish name, he had shouted that Stephen was all he had in the world and couldn't he have a little bit of kindness and call him by the one name that meant something? And sometimes he had clasped Stephen to him, almost crushing the breath out of his body, muttering his tortured affection. It was only in such oblique ways that he referred to his state of deserted, now divorced, husband. There were no photographs of her in the house in King Street, and the photographs Stephen had seen he had wrested out of old Mrs Naulls. He guessed she had been named after Lady Irene Nevil's daughter in *Wrenwood*. She had Tace's colouring. She was slender and very fair with long golden hair and as unlike as possible any Naulls that had ever been.

The wind had dropped and a cold whitish mist from the river lingered in patches. Lyn walked across the cobbles and over the Old Town bridge. This morning the water was clear and silvery, chuckling a little as it lapped over the smooth, oval, brown stones. A pair of swans drifted down towards the town centre.

She was early for work as usual because Dadda liked Stephen to be in soon after nine. She whiled away time walking along the Mootwalk, an ancient wooden cloister that faced the Hilder and under which was a row of shops: an optician's, a hairdresser's, a wine shop, a jeans and sweater boutique, a newsagent, the pet shop. There was a pale green sweater in the window of Lorraine's she thought she might buy. That sort of green, a clear, pale jade, was her colour. The newsagent's Sunday paper placard was still outside: 'Local Girl in Moors Murder'.

A few cars passed along the cobbles or parked, a few people on foot were on their way to work, not many. The great influx would be north of the river, the other side of town where Cartwright-Cageby's mill employed 60 per cent of the working population of Hilderbridge. Down here it was always quieter, it was older, it was peaceful. The ramparts of the moor could be seen in the distance, its peaks blurred against a leaden sky, their lower slopes wrapped in mist.

Lights came on in the Mootwalk shops as one by one they began to open. Out of the pet shop window a cat looked at Lyn with champagne-coloured eyes. It was in a wire pen on top of some tortoises and under a pair of lop-eared rabbits. The cat looked at Lyn and opened its mouth in a soundless mew.

Lyn didn't much like the old man who kept the shop. He ogled her and once he had come out and asked her if she would like a dear little puppy dog to keep her warm in the night. He wasn't there this morning. Instead, there was a man of about her own age, no older, tidying up the cartons of fish food on a shelf behind the counter. She pushed the door and went in.

'I've been looking at the cat in your window.'

He came out to her. 'Attractive colour, isn't it?'

'I wanted a ginger kitten, but it's not exactly ginger.'

'More beige, wouldn't you say? Or even peach. It's not a kitten either, it's more than half-grown. Someone brought it in on Saturday and said she had to go to Africa and would I take it.'

Lyn was indignant. 'That's awful, taking it to a pet shop. You wouldn't know who might buy it. It would be kinder to have it put down.'

'Oh, come. Not this pet shop. Not under my management.'

Lyn glanced up at him. She had trained herself not to look at men, a restraint that wasn't difficult to practise in this case. He was rather nondescript, not very tall, thin, mousy-haired, as unlike dark handsome Stephen as could be. But what on earth made her compare them?

'Are you the manager? What's happened to Mr Bale?'

'In hospital, having a hernia operation. I'm his nephew. I'm looking after things for him.' The cat mewed, not soundlessly this time. He opened the pen and lifted it out in his arms. 'He's a fine healthy cat, a neutered tom. I'd estimate his age at around nine months.'

'I wanted a kitten,' Lyn said. 'Isn't it strange the way everyone's got kittens to dispose of when you don't want them and none when you do?'

'Have this one and save him from a fate worse than death.'

Lyn held the cat. It felt tense and afraid. Its eyes seemed to her full of tragic puzzlement. She made up her mind quickly, the way she always did. 'I will have him,' she said. 'I can't take him now, though. I have to go to work, Gillman's the optician's. I'll come back at one when I finish.'

She phoned Stephen.

'How much does he want for it?'

'D'you know, I didn't ask.'

'Never mind, darling,' Stephen said, 'as long as it's what you want. You're to have just what you want.'

He went back to the armchairs. Dadda wouldn't have a phone extension upstairs, preferring to summon him with a shout when it rang. He got his way in most things, had despotically guided Stephen's life, had chosen Lyn for him, before that had picked him out of this school, pushed him into that, as soon as he could removed him altogether from academic threat. Stephen would have liked further education, though he hadn't expected Oxford or Cambridge or even, say, Nottingham. He would have settled for Hilderbridge College of Technology. If he had fought Dadda, with the backing of the school and the rumblings there had been about court orders to override parents, if he had struggled, he could have got there. But he never fought Dadda. He had left school willingly, or very nearly, glad to be pleasing Dadda, rewarded with a second-hand motor bike and next year a car, and had learnt Whalbys' trade. Or learnt some of it. He would never be able to do what Dadda could, those exquisite inlays, that delicate carving, achieving that mirror polish, and all with hands like a gorilla's paws. His heart wasn't in it. He could drive the van and upholster a settee.

He had started on the second chair when Dadda shouted up the stairs.

'Stephen!'

'What is it, Dadda?' The phone again?

'Some woman says she's from the paper. You can bloody come down and see to it.'

Stephen felt embarrassed that this woman, a *Three Towns Echo* reporter presumably, should have heard him call Dadda by the shameful name. He went down quickly. Dadda was back at his polishing, making figures of eight on the already brilliantly lustrous surface of a mahogany dining table with french polish on a knob of wadded lint. He had turned his back. The reporter was a young girl in denim dungarees and a bright red knitted coat. She had a red woolly hat pulled down round her ears.

'Mr Whalby? You're the Mr Stephen Whalby who writes "Voice of Vangmoor" for us, aren't you?'

Stephen had thought of describing his discovery of Marianne Price's body in this week's column. It was due in tomorrow and he planned to write it tonight. The girl reporter said this wouldn't really do. What they wanted was a news interview with him. He felt disappointed because writing 'Voice of Vangmoor' was the only money-making activity he did that he enjoyed, and this would have been more enjoyable than usual, a piece of real journalism as against the usual pedestrian stuff about the view from the top of Big Allen or hearing the first cuckoo. But this girl who couldn't be more than twenty-two or twenty-three was going to do it, not he. It was rather indifferently that he described to her his walk, his find, his leading of the police to the spot.

The girl took it down in speedwriting, not proper shorthand. 'When she didn't come home on Friday night,' she said, 'her parents thought she was staying with her boyfriend and the boyfriend thought she was at home with her parents.'

'A bit too permissive, those sort of parents,' said Stephen.

'Oh, well. He was her fiancé. They were going to get married in June.'

'Maybe if they'd postponed living together till they *were* married, she'd be alive now.'

'That's a bit hard, Mr Whalby. Anyway, you can't say that, you can't know. If her parents had reported her missing the night before she'd still have been dead, wouldn't she?'

The girl was getting belligerent. She probably lived that sort of life herself, Stephen thought. 'What's the fiancé called?' he asked.

'Ian Stringer. He lives in Byss.'

'I was at school with an Ian Stringer,' said Stephen. 'I wonder if it's the same one.'

'He's about your age.' The girl put away her notebook. 'We'd like to send a photographer to take your picture. Will that be okay? Around twelve?'

Stephen said it would, though Dadda's mood wouldn't be improved by it. He saw the girl out and put the bar up across the double doors.

'Bloody keep off the moor in future,' said Dadda. 'Keep your feet under your own table.'

* * *

The receptionist who took over from Lyn in the afternoons came into the cloakroom where she was putting her coat on.

'There's a man who says his name's Nick Frazer asking for you. The girl with the beautiful hair, he said.' She giggled. 'He's brought you a cat.'

Lyn reddened at the description of herself. She took off her scarf and tied it round her head, and then thought better of it — why allow herself to be provoked? She put the scarf back round her neck and went through to the shop. Nick Frazer was standing just inside the street door, holding a wicker basket with a barred opening in it.

'I thought you'd like to have this basket to take him home in.'

Between the bars wary golden eyes stared out.

'It's very kind of you.' She undid the lid of the basket. The cat made no attempt to get out. She stroked the soft, thick fur which felt warm, though the cat was trembling. Like me, I shake like that sometimes, Lyn thought. 'He's very afraid,' she said.

'He'll be all right with you. You'll bring the basket back, won't you?'

The way he said it, it was as if he was only lending it to her in order to have her bring it back again, but she was forced to agree. 'How much is he?'

'I'd like to give him to you. I didn't pay the Africa lady anything but I ought to make a bit for Uncle Jim. Shall we say two quid?'

Lyn gave him two pounds. She closed the lid of the basket.

'Do you have a long way to go?'

'Not really,' Lyn said, then briskly, 'Goodbye.'

The Hilderbridge to Jackley bus was three-quarters empty. Lyn took the cat out of the basket and held it against her. I shall call you Peach, she thought. The trembling had stopped, though the cat didn't yet purr. It occurred to her that the way she was holding Peach was the way a woman holds a baby and she lowered him gently into her lap.

Taking care not to swing the basket, she got off outside the gate of St Michael-in-the-Moor and walked across the green. Police cars and police vans were parked everywhere. Just inside the gates of Chesney Hall was the lodge where Stephen's grandmother had lived. Police had taken it over as an emergency headquarters. She could see lights on inside and men moving about, and as she stood there a policeman in uniform came out of the front door. Pinned to the gate, poster-sized, was a blown-up snapshot of a blonde girl not unlike Lyn herself, a girl with a vulnerable face, tender and a little melancholy, a girl who wore her long fair hair like a cloak.

Lyn put her free hand up to touch her own hair. When she realized what she was doing and that those policemen might have seen her, she felt her face grow hot. She turned away and carrying the basket with great care, walked on up the road to Tace Way.

3

'*Bumble bees* are appearing in large numbers,' Stephen wrote, beginning his fourth paragraph, 'due, most probably, to the exceptional mildness of the past winter. Few, however, will escape the predatory beaks of our Vangmoor songsters, bent upon feeding their young. Let us hope that this year we shall see an increase in the butterfly population, notably that rare member of the family *Lycaenidae*, known as the Foinland Blue.' That would do. He finished off. 'Next week I shall be writing about moorland walks and suggesting an itinerary that takes in the ever-attractive Tower Foin.'

In the morning he would drop it into the *Echo* office on his way to the inquest. 'Ever-attractive' didn't sound very good. What he really meant was that Tower Foin exercised a perennial attraction, drawing people by its beauty and its majesty, but he couldn't say all that. It would have to stand. Nothing he ever wrote came near to conveying to the reader the way the moor really was or the way he felt about it. The grandeur of the moor, its wildness, its timelessness and peace, seemed to get lost in his prose. He didn't know why because he took pains and there was no doubt of his writing talent. This particular inheritance was as striking as his physical resemblance to Tace. Perhaps the articles turned out badly because his heart wasn't really in that kind of parish pump, chatty writing. It would have been a different matter if they had let him write his own account of what he had found at the Foinmen.

He clipped the sheets together and put them into an envelope. Then he put the cover back on the typewriter and tidied up, lining up the pile of sheets of A4 bank paper and his box of carbons with the edges of the desk. Might as well put the butterfly book back in its proper place. He had more than three hundred books on his shelves now; everything that had ever been written about Vangmoor, of course, its history, geology, geography, wild life; all his old school textbooks, all the adventure stories of his boyhood. He didn't know why he kept them really, except that they helped to make up the number on the shelves. In pride of place were the Bleakland novels, *Quenild Manor*, *The Mountainside*, *Elizabeth Nevil*, *Wrenwood*, *Lady Irene*, *Last Loves*. Stephen had them in the handsome, leather-bound edition of the International Collectors' Library and also in the paperbacks that had come out to go with the television series. His study, which was in fact the second bedroom, was acquiring an important, even scholarly, appearance. On one wall was a big map of Vangmoor, on another a print of the only painting Constable had ever done of the moor, Loomlade church with Big Allen behind. His paperweight and doorstop were of ground and polished foinstone. The calendar was the one produced by the *Echo*, 'Moorland Views', turned now for April, by the purest coincidence, to a photograph of the Foinmen at sunset.

On a small round table, polished for him by Dadda, was a bust of Tace. The bust looked like bronze if you didn't examine it too closely. In fact it was papier-mâché on which someone had done a skilful paint job. Stephen still remembered the delight he had felt when, wandering through Jackley market, he had come upon the bust on a junk stall. He could have sworn, though it sounded silly, that Tace's eyes with their hooded, ironical gaze, had compelled him to approach, and Tace's mobile lips had adjured him, 'Buy me!' Only £1.50, it was almost laughable. Although the room and the whole house was full of really good stuff made or renovated by Dadda, secretly he valued nothing more than this bust. Its features, high, intellectual forehead, straight nose, long upper lip and fine-cut mouth, were so absolutely his own that he wondered others didn't remark on it.

He closed the door of his study and went across the landing to the bathroom. Lyn had had her bath and was in bed, her new cat, his birthday present, in a basket on the floor by her side.

'Just till he gets used to us.'

'Good Lord, darling, *I* don't mind.' Stephen had his bath in the mornings. He washed his hands and face and cleaned his teeth with the water pick he had bought with Dadda's Christmas money. The time was after eleven and he was tired but he could never sleep without reading for a few minutes at least. Currently he was rereading Tace's autobiography of which the author had completed only Book One, dying in the midst of describing his thirtieth year. He read for a quarter of an hour and Lyn read, and then Lyn put her book face downwards on the floor by the cat's basket. Stephen put a leather marker with an engraving of Tower Foin on it in his book and switched out the bedlamp.

'Good night, darling.'

'Good night, Stephen,' said Lyn. 'Sleep well.'

A pathologist called Dr Paul Fleisch described how Marianne Price had died. He used a lot of abstruse terms like 'cricoid' but what it amounted to was that she had been strangled. The murderer had done it with his bare hands. Before this evidence Stephen had had to give his. He was the first witness at the inquest. Once he had begun he didn't feel nervous, he spoke slowly and levelly, and once his part was over he began to enjoy the rest of the proceedings.

Ian Stringer, sitting with the dead girl's parents, he recognized at once. At school he had been an ace rugby player and had become a big burly man. The inquest was adjourned and Stringer came up to Stephen outside the court.

'I don't know if you remember me. Byss Comprehensive. I think I was a year behind you.'

Stephen nodded and took Stringer's outstretched hand.

'It's only — well, I thought I'd ask you — how she looked when — I mean they say some people who die like that, they look sort of, their faces . . .'

'Good Lord, no, there was nothing like that. She looked as if she was asleep.'

Stringer didn't believe him but he was grateful for the kindness. Together they walked along the High Street towards the Market Place where they parted,

Stephen for Whalbys', Stringer to return to Cartwright-Cageby's where he was a foreman fitter. Dadda was out, doing something to a very ancient, very special ceiling in Jackley Manor with Tudor roses carved on its beams. Stephen worked on the armchairs till lunchtime. After he had had a sandwich in the Market Burger House, he loaded the van with small stuff to be returned and went out delivering. There was an early nineteenth-century firescreen to go back to a house in Trinity Street. Next to Trinity Church where Dadda and Mother had been married was the old people's home called Sunningdale. Stephen parked the van and delivered the screen. The matron of Sunningdale was an easy-going woman who let visitors come pretty well when they pleased, this entailing no great inconvenience as few did please.

Helena Naulls was in the day room with the dozen or so other old women and the two old men. In the Three Towns, as elsewhere, the men died and the women lived on and on. A big colour television set was on and one or two were looking at it, at a programme designed for seven-year-olds, but most were just sitting. One woman was knitting, an old man was reading the *Daily Mirror*. Mrs Naulls was among those who just sat.

Seeing her there, Stephen had to remind himself — for nothing in her bearing hinted at it and no vestige of handsome looks remained — that she had once been the mistress of Alfred Osborn Tace. She was a scrawny flabby woman who had once been stout. Her face had become big and vacant, the eyes sluggishly furtive, the mouth vague. Her hair, snow white and abundant, had been lopped off in a ragged uneven way by the home's hairdresser. Today — such muddles often happened — she was wearing a cardigan of matted grey wool belonging to a much smaller and slighter inmate, a long brown skirt, brown stockings that wrinkled round her still-narrow ankles, and blue check carpet slippers.

Once she had been pretty and lively with a twenty-three-inch waist. She had been second housemaid at Chesney Hall and Arthur Naulls had been under-gardener. They had had several children, of all of whom but the eldest Arthur was the father. Mrs Naulls was in Sunningdale because her son Stanley was a Hilderbridge councillor and had pulled strings. Otherwise there wouldn't have been a chance for someone with such a large family, almost any of whom could have taken her in. The only one, in fact, who had offered had been Lyn. Stephen had vetoed that, though, before she had made her offer to anyone but him, and now he tended to tell people they couldn't have his grand-mother because it wouldn't be fair on his wife. He had been brought up to call Mrs Naulls 'Nanna' but had had more luck with her than with Dadda when he wanted to change this mode of address.

'How are you, Grandmother?' he said. He had brought her a box of fruit jellies, the only passion she still had. She took them in unsteady hands stained with grave marks, and peered with suspicion at the manu-facturer's name. 'How have you been getting on?'

'Just the same.'

'Anybody been to see you?'

Mrs Naulls shook her head. 'Nobody ever comes to see me.' She took the cellophane wrapping off the box. 'Not a soul.'

'Oh, Mrs Naulls, what an untruth!' said the old woman in the next chair. She was the one who had been knitting. 'Your son Leslie was here only yester-day.'

'Haven't got a son called Leslie, have I, Stanley?' said Mrs Naulls, dropping cellophane on the floor.

'Leonard. And I'm Stephen.'

'Nurse'll be after you,' said the knitter. 'You're what they call a litter bug.'

Mrs Naulls ate a crimson jelly and then a green one. She didn't offer the box. A bovine contentment came into her face as she chewed. Stephen had never been able to talk to her about her relationship with the great novelist. He had been over twenty before he had even found out about it but he hadn't been old enough to dare ask his grandmother how it had been and how she had felt and what they had talked about. Now when he might dare it was too late. But still he searched for ways to bring the conversation round to Tace.

'I expect you've been watching those "Bleakland" programmes, haven't you, Grandmother?'

'Pardon?' she said, her mouth full.

'On the television, Saturday nights.'

A woman who had been looking at the screen turned to him and said, 'I saw one, round at my daughter's. It was lovely. Lovely dresses.'

'Why can't you see it here?'

'They get us to bed,' said the knitter. 'Eight they start getting us to bed.'

'That's a pity,' Stephen persisted. 'You'd have liked to watch that, Grandmother.'

'How's Rosemary, Keith?' said Mrs Naulls.

'If you mean Lyn, she's fine. And I'm Stephen.'

He looked at her hopelessly. She had come to this, to a limp white heap who had forgotten the names of her nearest and dearest. Once he had tried to extract so much from her, and not just details of the Tace affair. She was the key to a past he needed to understand. Dadda's temper, that he had inherited along with Dadda's darkness and Dadda's height, had got the better of him and he had attacked her, physically attacked her. But that was more than half his lifetime ago. He got up.

'Time I was on my way.'

Mrs Naulls said lucidly, as if veils had suddenly, when it was too late, fallen from her mind and her speech, 'It was good of you to come, dear. Thank you for the jellies.'

The knitter waved. Stephen was sure his grand-mother had fallen asleep before he was even out of the room. It had begun to rain. Soon it was raining hard enough, Stephen noted dismally, to keep him off the moor for the evening. He felt as he had done when a small boy and rain or some other calamity of nature had kept him from a picnic, resentful and somewhat indignant.

It was the end of the week before Lyn took the cat bas-ket back. There were ten birthday cards on the mantel-piece, but they had been there two days and she took them down. Two of them made her feel, not old ex-actly, but as if life was passing her by. They were the one from Joanne that said, 'You've reached a quarter century' and the one from Stephen, 'My dearest wife'. She was uneasy about going to the pet shop. In her im-agination she saw Nick Frazer as a young version of his uncle, a young wolf instead of an old one. But if she didn't take it back he would only come along and ask for it. She was surprised he hadn't already. Peach was sitting on the window sill, watching the raindrops run down the outside of the glass and trying to catch them with his paw. He behaved as if they were insects. Lyn stroked him and reminded him she would be back at lunchtime.

Nick Frazer was locking up the shop when she came along at one. She had remembered him quite differently from what he really was. He looked at her with a preoccupied air before he recognized her, perhaps because she had put up her hair rather severely — deliberately — into a tight knot on the back of her head. The pleasant, serious face, the steady brown eyes, disconcerted her. Was this the wolf who was going to make double-edged remarks, even a pass, at her? He took the basket, thanked her quietly, locked the shop door again. She was so surprised by the warmth of his smile, by his being able to smile so frankly, so like a friend, that when he said he was going to lunch at the Blue Lagoon and would she come too, she said yes, all right, without thinking.

They walked along by the river. The rain had almost stopped. The Blue Lagoon was the old Red Lion renamed, no one knew why, on the corner of Bankside and Trinity Street. She had already had second thoughts.

'I ought to get back to Peach.' She had told him what the cat was called.

He smiled again. 'The great beauty of keeping cats is they don't tie you.'

She sat at a table while he went to get their lager and ploughman's lunches. Lyn took off her gloves. She saw that her left hand was bare. In washing her hands after breakfast she had taken off her wedding ring and must have left it on the side of the basin. It was the kind of ring you had to take off to wash, a kind of chased inlay of platinum and gold that Stephen had had specially made on Dadda's advice. She was always taking it off and forgetting it. Kevin's brother, who fancied himself as an amateur psychologist, said you didn't really forget things like that and it meant Lyn must unconsciously want not to wear it — *ergo*, not to be married.

Nick brought their drinks and food on a tray.

'And how is Peach?'

'Quite happy, I think. He's not shaking any more.'

'But you are,' Nick said.

It was true. Her hands were trembling, she could hardly hold the glass. She managed to laugh, held her hands for a minute in her lap. 'It's a nervous thing I have.'

He made no comment on that. It was then that she noticed how gravely and interestedly he was looking at her, had looked at her ever since they met outside the shop. It was as if he was very concerned with her as a person. But when he spoke it was not of her but of Peach, how to feed him, what sort of supplements he should have, that although he had had his routine immunizations, he must have a booster at a year old and also an injection against a new sort of feline virus.

'How is it you know so much when you only took the shop over last week?'

'Well — ' Again that warm, frank smile. 'I'm a vet.'

'Are you really?' A hangover from Lyn's childhood — a mother who cleaned at Chesney Hall, a father at Cartwright-Cageby's — was to feel respect that had once amounted to awe for the professional man. But good sense asserted itself. 'Why aren't you being one then?'

'I've only just qualified.' He added almost apologetically, 'It takes a long time. I've got a job waiting for me in London, but I can't start till August when the man retires. Hence Hilderbridge and Uncle Jim.'

'And are you living over the shop?'

'I think Uncle rather hoped I'd live in the two rooms at the back but they smell a bit too powerfully of monkey and parrot so I've moved up into his flat. It's nice, you must come and see it.'

This was a remark that three days before she would

have thought of as wolfish. Now it seemed merely friendly. But she didn't answer it. She was afraid he would ask her about herself and to forestall this she asked him to tell her about his training and what he hoped for in the future. He talked. They ate their bread and cheese. Lyn's hands had stopped shaking.

'That's enough about me,' he said. 'Tell me about you.'

I am twenty-five, I am married, I was married in church and have lived with my husband four years, so I must be married, I have no children and never shall have, but I am waiting, waiting, for what I don't know . . . 'Nothing to tell,' she said. And there was nothing, nothing she *could* tell. Mr Bale would come back in two or three weeks and she need never see Nick Frazer again. 'I really must go now.'

While they were in the pub, in a corner far from a window, the rain had come on heavily, the kind of rain that will soak you to the skin in two minutes. Nick stopped her inside the door.

'Will you wait for me? I'll be very quick.'

He came back, and he had been very quick, with an umbrella from which, as he plunged in through the swing door, he was tearing the plastic wrapping.

'You bought it specially!'

'I had to have an umbrella to walk you home.'

'But I live in Chesney,' she said. 'I'm going on the bus.'

'To walk you to your bus stop then.'

It was something she hadn't looked for and she was almost dismayed. Under the umbrella they had to walk very close together and after a while he took her hand and hooked it through his arm. It was precisely the action of Joseph Usher in *The Mountainside*, and Isabella Thornhill had slapped his face for it before rushing off, unprotected, into the downpour. Lyn felt the blood come up into her face. She held Nick's arm and felt him warm and somehow tough against her side. He talked about the town, how he had never before been to this part of the country, how one day soon he must try to get out on the moor. There was an opening for her here. My husband, who is in fact the grandson of Alfred Osborn Tace, is really quite an authority on Vangmoor . . . She didn't take it. She would have found it hard to speak, anyway. It was taking all her concentration to breathe normally, not to begin shaking again, with their arms linked and their bodies so close.

The bus saved her. As they turned up River Street it was coming down the hill and there wouldn't be another for an hour.

'There won't be another for an hour!' she cried.

'Would that be so terrible?'

'Oh, yes, yes, it would. Thank you for lunch, thank you very much. Goodbye!'

He stood on the pavement, smiling in perplexity, making swirls in the air with the umbrella. Her cheeks burned and she turned away from the window. The bus pulled away, through the rain, up towards the moor.

A full week had gone by and it was Saturday again before Stephen went out on the moor. There was not a soul to be seen, though it was a weekend and the sun was shining after many days of rain. The week before last, when it had been colder, he had seen parties of hikers, a fisherman coming from the Hilder, cyclists on the Loomlade road, campers with tent and calor gas stove and blankets on their backs. This morning Vangmoor was deserted. It was impossible to avoid the conclusion that the murder had emptied it.

At first he disliked this thought. It meant that the moor had in the past few days become known not as somewhere unique and beautiful but as the place where a young girl had been killed. Then, as he crossed the Loomlade road and entered the Vale of Allen, his feelings underwent a change. The moor seemed more his own when it was unpeopled, so that his childhood fantasy might have become real and he be the lord of this wild country.

Big Allen, the highest peak of the foinland, which was so often veiled in mist or appeared as a blurred blue shape, this morning showed every crevice and crag on its slopes, every wind-bent bilberry, every clump of ling. The air was as clear as the air only is after prolonged rain. The crinkle-crankle path that traversed the hillside was a bright brown hairpin, woven between the green and purplish and silvery heather. Now, in the dales beyond he could see the remains of the old mine workings. No lead had been mined on Vangmoor for a hundred years, but the engine houses and the housing for water wheels, once deemed so hideous, now in ruin had a beauty of their own. He climbed the lower slopes of Big Allen and stood, looking westwards. From here the Foinmen were hidden by the bulk of Ringer's Foin with the rock on its top like a bell. In order to see them he would have had to climb a couple of hundred feet more. But the Hilder revealed itself, running down like a tinsel thread, crossed at one point by stepping stones, at another by the massive stone pillars that once had supported an aqueduct bringing water to the buildings of the Goughdale Mine. The waters of the river were broken and scintillating, splashing in bright sparks where it bounded over rocks on its way to the town. And Hilderbridge lay in the sunshine, its slate roofs all turned to planes of silver, its spires sharp needles, as if a silversmith had made it and dropped it in the valley between the meadows and the moor.

Beneath where he stood, under the western slopes of the foin and the wastes of Goughdale, was a network of subterranean chambers and passages and galleries. The last of the mines had been closed around the time of Tace's birth and the entrances to the shafts had been closed or blocked by rockfalls. Stephen walked down and back to Loomlade. An hour later he was in Chesney, having seen no animate thing but two bumble bees and a rook. The gatehouse lodge to Chesney Hall that the police had taken over also looked deserted today. David Southworth, who owned the hall and who was the nephew of Tace's widow, had done up the lodge as a home for his wife's mother but since her death it had stood empty. Stephen went up the path and looked in the window. He hadn't been in the lodge since Helena Naulls had left it on the death of her husband. The old wallpapers, nasturtiums in the living room, stripes and posies and true lovers' knots in the hall, were gone and the walls painted white. There seemed to be no dark corners left, no little cupboards and half-hidden shelves through which a boy could hunt for evidence of his lost mother.

A man was sitting at a desk, typing, another stood by a filing cabinet. Both had their backs to him. Stephen moved away before they could become aware of his head blocking out some of their light. He walked home through the quiet and at this hour deserted village.

The fanbelt on the car broke, making Lyn late for work. Stephen tied it up but the string broke and he had to drive the car into Hilderbridge very slowly and carefully so as not to overheat the engine. Mr Gillman had had to attend to his own patients. He said to Lyn, 'The young chap from Bale's was in here asking for you. Asking for "Miss" Whalby actually, but I put him right on that one.'

Lyn took off her coat and came back to where her desk and typewriter and appointments book were. Two women had come in and she asked them to wait, giving them magazines to look at. She felt disproportionately upset. It was ridiculous to be upset at all, since she had herself intended to tell Nick she was married as soon as she saw him, or to make sure he saw her left hand on which today she had taken care to wear her wedding ring. She was imagining him shocked by what Mr Gillman said, leaving without a word, returning to the pet shop and alone there ever since, brooding on his disappointment and her treachery. But why should he have reacted like that? How did she know it had been like that? She could hardly ask Mr Gillman. Nick might have laughed when Mr Gillman told him — 'I didn't know she was married' or even, 'Married, is she? Just my luck.' Come to that, he might have been relieved. He might have thought he had said too much on Friday, buying the umbrella specially and walking arm in arm with her, and be afraid she would think he had meant more than he had. Why couldn't she believe that and stop thinking about it?

'Mr Gillman's ready for you now,' she said to the older of the women, and helped her gently into the consulting room.

Of course it couldn't be that Nick had been relieved. In calling at Gillman's at all, he must have been coming to ask her to go out with him. The idea burst into her mind, a sudden radiant solution, that she could rush along to the pet shop at lunchtime and apologize, ask him to forgive her and make everything all right. Just as swiftly, she saw that this was absurd. How could she apologize to a man for being married to someone else? And even supposing she did, what then? Could she unmarry herself? Make Stephen vanish? And for what? To go to the cinema with Nick Frazer?

She *could* unmarry herself. She could have done that any time these past four years. It would only have taken a word and the simple, undeniable proof. She had often thought of it and each time she did Stephen's face came before her eyes, as clear as some mystic's vision, the most vulnerable face she had ever seen, the face of a brave child.

* * *

It was cloudy for most of the day of 30 April but the sky cleared in the late afternoon and by five the sun shone out boldly. At about half past six Stephen set out to take the crinkle-crankle path up the fell, the way he had brought the policemen three weeks before. Never, since he was a child, had he missed coming up to the Foinmen on Beltane.

There was little enough to see, of course. On 29 April and 1 May the setting sun's rays were scarcely differently placed, but an ancient tradition attached to the eve of May Day. The rays, just as the red orb of the sun sank beneath the slope of Ringer's Foin, touched the very centre of the Altar. Long ago, thousands of years ago perhaps, a rune had been carved in the centre of the broad flat stone, and the faint marks which still remained indicated that the rune had been in the shape the shadows of the Foinmen made at sunset. No doubt some very holy ceremony had once taken place there on Beltane. Stephen liked to stand and watch, to imagine the druidical forms as they must have been, going about their ritual, and to wait in silence and stillness for the sun to perform his precise function.

It had not always been possible for him to observe the phenomenon on his own. Others often came to watch too. Once there had even been a party of tourists, disturbing the peace with their groans and giggles as they struggled up the steep path from their coach. On sunless Beltanes he had invariably found himself alone there, but never on such a glorious evening as this. Nevertheless, he had met no one, could see no one on the whole spread of Foinmen's Plain. In the past days people had begun cautiously to return to the moor, but not this evening and not here.

It was much warmer than on that last visit and warmer than last year. There was scarcely a breath of wind. The stones threw long, flaring shadows that suggested the shape of some ancient harp, only lengthening imperceptibly as the sun's angle grew more oblique. Great towering clouds were massing behind Big Allen but to the west the sky was as clear as the inside of a mother-of-pearl-lined shell, of a pale, tender, pin-stained azure. A flock of birds flew homewards very high over Ringer's Foin. Thin streaks of cirrus lay parallel to the horizon, and between them the sun's orb had become a well-defined sphere of a rich rose-crimson. It was five to eight.

Stephen had no feelings of aversion or horror because Marianne Price had lain dead over there. He felt as he always did on the moor, and especially on this spot and on Big Allen, peaceful, without care, without self almost, at one with nature and the past, and as if nothing that happened down there could hurt or vex him any more.

The rays crept across the slab with its skin of yellowish lichen. The granite was gradually being dyed carmine by the progress of the dying sun. And now, as Stephen looked at his watch, the tide of red colour crept to touch that central point where the rune was. For a moment the rune gleamed in a pool of red light. The shadows of the stones stretched to their maximum length, while the sun seemed to rest on the horizon. It was poised there, a rosy ball, and then it began to dip below the rim of the land. Down in Chesney St Michael-in-the-Moor tolled the hour — six, seven, eight, and on the last note, the red light glimmered and failed, the harp-like shadows fled and the Altar became once more a sheet of half-buried stone. For another year the sacred meeting of the rune and the sunset was over.

With the departure of the sun a breeze came, making ripples in the turf and bending the ling to the ground.

Stephen made his way down and crossed the Hilder-bridge road a little south of Chesney. The road bisected Vangmoor, and north of the village the Loomlade road crossed it, thus dividing the region roughly into four quarters. This south-eastern quarter was to Stephen's mind the least beautiful, but it was some weeks since he had been there and he liked to keep the whole of the moor under surveillance. It consisted mainly of a large area of more or less flat heathland that was in places marshy and out of which rose the only hill to be found here, the broad, low Knamber Foin that looked from a distance no more than a heap of stones. Away in the distance, beyond the foin, the land became fertile and fields began, enclosed by dry stone walls.

Stephen went first to Knamber Hole where they had found Marianne Price's bicycle. Not a trace of the search or the find remained — or not as far as he could see. Dusk was fast approaching. All colour had gone from the landscape, leaving the ground a kind of shimmering, bright grey on which every bush and stunted tree appeared as a black silhouette. The sky was pallid and clear between the encroaching tides of cloud. You could not have called it grey, it was of some colour that had never been given a name, and it glowed as if the moon and stars were behind the skin of it, waiting to break through. But whatever lit it was not the moon, for this Stephen now saw slowly rising out of clusters of cloud on the rim of the moor, a reddish, mottled orb like the ghost of that sun. It seemed bigger than the sun and it sailed with a peculiar swiftness up into the heavens, growing paler and brighter as it did so until it lit up the plain with a dull, yellow light. He was glad of the moon, for he had been walking away from the road and the quarry for a long time and had reached the rising, stony ground at the foot of the foin.

At this point he decided to turn back, for even now it would be eleven before he was home and it was seldom he stayed out as late as that. Lyn would worry. To the north and west, in the right angle the roads made, lay a tree-dotted plain called the Banks of Knamber. It was covered with birch trees, thousands of them, small and frail, none of them much taller than a man. There was gorse as well and of course the omnipresent bilberries. It took Stephen about half an hour to reach the banks and he began to head across them towards Chesney.

In the dull moonlight, which seemed to paint the landscape with phosphorescence rather than illuminate it, the region resembled a pale sky scattered all over with puffs of black cloud. And from time to time the moon dulled even further as thin wracks of cloud and then denser masses passed across its face. Once it disappeared altogether, and although a fair degree of brightness remained in the sky, the land became very dark and in this pathless place it was not easy for Stephen to find his way.

It was when the pale flood of light returned that Stephen saw the man. He was quite a long way off, not far in from the road, and he was standing quite still as if waiting for someone or watching. There was no reason why this man shouldn't be out on the moor on a fine spring night, except that hardly anyone but Stephen ever was. What was more remarkable was that he was not walking but standing still. The figure remained absolutely still among the little birch trees and right in the path Stephen had mapped out for himself to take. He walked on steadily. Although nothing could be seen of him but a silhouette Stephen was sure the man was looking at him, staring insolently at this approaching form across the intervening, pallid, tundra-like land. Stephen perceived that he had no torch, or that if he had one he wasn't bothering to use it, which meant he must know the moor well, as well perhaps as Stephen himself did. He felt a mounting resentment. Although he could see no more than the man's black outline, he sensed it was a rival he was moving towards, one who saw himself as having rights in the moor, even rights of possession over it.

Stephen had no clear idea, no idea at all really, as to what he would do when he and the man encountered each other. Now no more than a hundred yards separated them. He wasn't afraid, though the man was evidently waiting for him, not moving at all. To defy the man, to show him, he began to run this last lap. The man went on waiting, almost as if he were teasing Stephen, and when at last he did move, it was suddenly and with a strange dancing skip. It seemed to Stephen that he was skipping among the trees.

The moon went in. At one moment the Banks of Knamber were bathed in pale light, at the next a gush of cloud had obscured the spotty yellow orb of the moon. As it vanished, absorbed in the veils of blackness, Stephen stumbled over a twisted root and fell headlong.

He wasn't hurt. But when he picked himself up he was shivering in the darkness. Where the man was, gone or waiting for him behind the next tree, he had no idea. It was now impossible to see more than a few yards. He knew roughly where he was, or he knew in theory, and he stumbled slowly along in a westerly direction, sometimes holding onto the trunk of a birch tree. Once he thought he heard a movement among the trees to the left of him, as of footfalls rustling the grass. He stood still and listened but the sound came no more. Then, it seemed hours later, when he sensed or smelt or somehow divined that he was almost at the road, there came, as likely as not out of his own imagination, the delicate sound of an indrawn breath.

It was midnight when he came home to Tace Way. Lyn was in bed but not asleep. She came down to him and made him a hot drink and felt his forehead which was burning hot and covered in drops of sweat.

In the past Stephen had sometimes been like this after being out late on the moor, feverish next day and light-headed. Lyn left him in bed and took the car to work, promising to be back early to give him his lunch. It was to salve her conscience, she thought, and make up for her obsessional preoccupation with Nick Frazer.

Although she hadn't seen him again, he was always in her thoughts. In her mind she talked to him, telling him about her life, day-to-day things, carrying on with him a long intimate dialogue. It was in vain that she told herself he was a stranger, a man who had probably by now forgotten her. This revolving of him in her mind led invariably to the same end, the same fear, that he would go away from Hilderbridge without her seeing him and then she would never see him again.

When her morning's work was finished she thought, as she thought every day, that she would walk along the Mootwalk to Bale's and at last set her mind at rest. But she didn't do this. She drove home. She was afraid Nick might treat her with coldness and pretend he had forgotten who she was.

Stephen was still in bed but sitting up and there were books on Vangmoor all over the quilt. Lyn put a cloth on a tray and laid it and on an impulse picked a small blue iris and put it in a vase to go on the tray as well. Stephen's dark blue eyes were very bright and there was a flush on his cheekbones. Otherwise he seemed much better and he ate his lunch like a hungry school-boy.

'I say, Lyn, did I ever tell you how I actually got into one of the old mines when I was a kid?'

She shook her head. Vangmoor bored her. Sometimes she even found it oppressive, living in the middle of it. Their bedroom window, by a lucky chance for Stephen, had the best view of the moor of any house in Tace Way. The curtains were drawn back as far as they would go, and whenever she looked up the green-brown panorama confronted her and the pale bowl of sky. She made an effort. 'Aren't they very dangerous?'

'Kids don't care about that. We'd heard there was a way into the Goughdale Mine somewhere on the slopes of Big Allen. Actually it's mentioned in one of the Bleakland books, though I hadn't read them then. I was about twelve. I went looking for it with my cousin Peter.'

'Peter Naulls?'

Stephen nodded. 'Uncle Leonard's son. We started looking for the hole in the long summer holidays. We were jolly methodical, I can tell you. Each day we covered a set area and we marked the bit we'd covered with sticks. But it took us weeks and weeks to find it.' He hesitated. He had begun his account, intending to tell Lyn the whole of it, but now that he had reached the point of disclosing the site of the hole into the mine and of describing it and what happened there, he felt uneasy. Dadda he had told, though even to him he had given only a vague location, but he hadn't said a word to his grandmother and he was sure Peter wouldn't have told Uncle Leonard and Auntie Midge. Why divulge the secret now? 'We found it,' he said and lied, 'but we didn't go in or anything. Too scared for *that*.'

'Oh, well,' she said.

'It was pretty enterprising of us to have found it, wasn't it? Dadda thought so. He said what a waste of bloody time and then he gave me a five-pound note.'

'How exactly like Dadda.' She straightened his pillows. She took away the tray. There was no point in asking him if he would like the curtains drawn. He would come down soon anyway and say he was all right and going out on the moor again. Perhaps she could write to Nick and explain things. Explain what? Even if she were to write she knew she would never post the letter.

'You were wrong about another one being killed in a couple of weeks, Mum,' Joanne said on a Sunday afternoon. 'It's been more like six.'

'Listen to who's counting,' said Kevin. 'Thank God there hasn't is what you ought to say.'

'Well, I do. I do say that. I only meant it doesn't look like there's going to be another.'

'Early days,' said Mrs Newman. 'It could just be he hasn't been able to catch anyone.'

Joanne shrieked. She was big now and the child vigorous. The women had been amused — though the men, especially Dadda, embarrassed — when its movements, or so Joanne averred, had bounced a plate off her lap. Stephen told them how that morning he had seen a girl out on the moor alone.

'Some folks want their heads examined,' said Mr Newman. 'I just hope you two girls have got more sense than ever to set a foot out there.'

Dadda, voyaging day by day farther out on his black sea of depression, made his one contribution to the talk. 'That's right, keep your feet under your own table.'

Joanne got to her feet ponderously. Her belly swayed, her ankles were like those of a woman with

Ruth Rendell

dropsy. 'I go climbing hills every day, of course. Like a mountain goat, aren't I, Kev?'

There was laughter at that, shamefaced from Mr Newman. Joanne fetched more biscuits, her current craving. Stephen hadn't much to say. The first thing he had thought of when he awoke that morning was that it was his mother's birthday, 25 May, and he had been thinking about it ever since, as he always did on that day. Somewhere, on the other side of the world, she must be celebrating it. She and her husband and Barnabas and Barbara . . .

'You never told me about that old Mr Bale, Lyn,' said Mrs Newman. 'You never told me he'd had a heart attack coming round from the anaesthetic. I had to hear it from Kevin's mum.'

'How could I tell you when I didn't know?'

'Well, I'd have thought you'd know that, working next door but four or five or whatever it is. And there's no need to colour up like that, it isn't as if it matters.'

'Do you mean he's dead?' said Lyn.

'No, of course he isn't dead. I'd have said if he'd been dead but Kevin's mum said he was on the danger list.'

The conversation, in which neither Stephen nor Dadda took part, then turned upon whether 'danger list' was merely a figurative term or if hospitals actually maintained such ominous catalogues. Stephen wondered if Dadda also remembered what day it was. Probably, for he forgot nothing, his memory was prodigious. But it was impossible to tell what went on behind that massive, tortured brow, perpetually corrugated as if in a continual wince and recoil from life.

It was a family gathering, though one very different from what was now taking place in Tace Way, that had first alerted Stephen to the true facts of his descent.

48

5

Arthur and Helena Naulls had had their Golden
Wedding party in November about the time of Stephen's own twenty-first birthday. Before that he hadn't
known Helena's wedding date. Who but a genealogist
knew his grandmother's wedding date? But he had always known his mother's birthday and at primary
school he had been allowed to make her a birthday
card. He could still remember it, a picture of a house
and a tree and a sun with rays like a starfish. Three
weeks later she had gone off with a long-distance lorry
driver.

Her birthday was 25 May and her parents had been
married in November, though not perhaps the previous
November. They had been married for fifty years, but
was his mother forty-nine or only forty-eight? There
was no one he could ask. The idea of asking Dadda!

What he did was to go to Holy Trinity Church and look at the parish records where he found that his parents' wedding date was also May — the 27th. Birth dates are not given on marriage certificates, only ages, and his mother's was there as twenty-five, which meant she must have been born in 1926 and have been twenty-seven when he was born. Stephen was almost sure this wasn't so, that she had been twenty-eight when he was born and thirty-four when she ran away. Perhaps there had been a muddle because her birthday and her wedding date were so close together.

He puzzled over the dates on the backs of photographs, most of which seemed to have been taken in May, and he tried to get from his aunts the precise age gap between his parents and between his mother and Uncle Stanley. Their answers were always, 'A couple of years' or 'Oh, three or four years.'

The true facts came out simply and when he wasn't even looking for them. Looking for his own birth certificate for his own marriage, he found his mother's too — in a desk in the house in King Street. The Holy Trinity marriage entry was wrong. Brenda had been born in May 1925 and therefore conceived during the previous August when Helena was still second housemaid at Chesney Hall.

The other clarification followed swiftly from a photograph of Tace he saw in a newspaper review. It was a few weeks after his marriage and Stephen had been feeling unsure of himself, unsure of life itself. The discovery fortified him. When he looked at the picture of Tace he might have been looking into a mirror.

Of course it had to be! He had always felt he couldn't be the descendant of Naullses. The Whalby connection was bearable, for they were good honest craftsmen, respected for their skills. But to be a Naulls, formed out of the same genes as Uncle Stanley, mouthing platitudes in the council chamber, or weedy, weak-eyed Uncle Leonard, that was intolerable. It was also false. His mother wasn't the daughter of Arthur Naulls but born of a summertime passion between a pretty servant and one of the greatest novelists of the twentieth century.

Tace was married, so there was naturally no question of his marrying Helena. But he hadn't deserted her, he had arranged a suitable marriage with his under-gardener, had given the couple the lodge to live in and had had the child named after one of his sweetest heroines, Brenda Nevil of *Wrenwood*.

Stephen never much cared to think about sex. In the past, when his thoughts had turned to it as a young boy's thoughts will, his body hadn't followed his mind. All he had been able to envisage was his mother, so slight and fair, being mounted first by Dadda and then by the lorry driver. So it wasn't the sexual aspect of Helena's affair that interested him but its romantic side. He imagined Helena coming to some trysting place on a summer night, to the Banks of Knamber perhaps, or like Lady Irene and Alastair Thornhill, to the ghost of a road, the Reeve's Way, as it threaded through the Vale of Allen, and Tace meeting her there in the twilight. Love children, he had read, were more beautiful, more charming and more favoured by destiny than those born in wedlock. His mother was and must still be such a one. For the loss of her he had compensated as best he could, first with the imaginary friend he called Rip, then with the moor itself, but in May he thought of her still and with a curious longing.

It wasn't for many weeks after coming to Chesney that Peach ventured out. His favourite places to be were the chestnut leaf table and the top of the mahogany tallboy under the landing window on which he lay for hours, staring at the peaks and plateaux of the moor.

He grew large and plump and round-cheeked, but he was without kittenish ways as if his sad experience had robbed him prematurely of his youth, yet when he sat on Lyn's lap in the evenings he gave himself up to a drowsy and contented purring. His first excursion from the house took him no farther than the garden. Next time he was off and away. When two hours had passed and he hadn't returned, Lyn imagined him finding his way back to Bale's and by this act leading her there in search of him. She imagined herself reunited with Nick through the cat's agency, as lovers might be in some fairy story.

But Peach didn't go to Bale's or to his former home in Hilderbridge. He came back in the evening, bringing Lyn a fieldmouse. Her mother had come over to tell her Joanne had been kept in hospital with high blood pressure and threatened eclampsia. She had gone to St Ebba's antenatal clinic and they had kept her there. When Mrs Newman saw the mouse, though it was dead, she jumped on a kitchen chair and squealed. Peach took back his gift, which he had laid at Lyn's feet, and sat with it in his mouth, making cross twittering growls.

Stephen wrote for 'Voice of Vangmoor': 'Those who declare our moorland puts up a poor showing when it comes to wildlife, should contemplate some of the offerings of my ginger tomcat: fieldmice, a shrew and even a water vole.' Author's licence, he told himself, though he had hesitated over the water vole. 'Wild flowers too are to be found in abundance. Not only is the bilberry putting forth its globular pinkish-green blooms and the uva-ursi prolific with blossom this spring, but a few orchids may be spotted. I myself was lucky enough last week to see a fine sample of the Lesser Twayblade and another of the Small White Orchid, rare occurrences as far south as this and in these times. Readers of our great Vangmoor novelist, Alfred Osborn Tace (or viewers, as one must say these days!) will be familiar with the scene in *Wrenwood* in which Brenda Nevil hunts for specimens of this orchid for her bridal bouquet.'

It was true that he had found the orchid. A little cluster of it was growing among the damp rock ledges between Big Allen and Mottle Foin near where the Hilder ran down. Stephen came upon the flowers by chance after he had left the path and struck out across the rough marshy ground.

The sky was the way he liked it best and thought best suited to the terrain it overcast, piled with cloud in pillars and columns and towers and ramparts, so that in places the vapour seemed not insubstantial but composed of solid masonry. The surface of the moor itself glowed with the flowerbuds on the grasses and the tiny recumbent plants and there was a feel in the air of new springing life. The orchids, fresh and perfect against the damp stone, growing between cushions of bright green moss, had creamy flowers, fragrant and triple-lobed. Stephen had hardly been able to believe his eyes.

Tace, describing the orchid in his novel, had also told where it was to be found, and within a few years every tuber and plant of *leuchorchis albida* had been stripped from the moor. Here, by the Hilder, was far west of the site of the plants mentioned in *Wrenwood*. Stephen resolved to be wiser than his grandfather and, while telling his readers of his discovery, not to disclose its whereabouts.

He didn't even tell Lyn. She liked flowers and planted flowers in their garden but he often felt she didn't really care about the moor. When she asked him if he would come with her to see Joanne he put forward the excuse of having his article to write, so Lyn went with Kevin.

'I reckon you're very wise not going in for this lark,' Joanne said, shifting the mound of her body uncomfortably under the bedclothes. 'If you get like weakening, just remember me. D'you know, they could keep me in here right up until the baby's born.'

'They won't do that,' Lyn said. 'They haven't got the beds.'

'She's brought it on herself with overeating,' said Kevin.

For once Joanne didn't round on him. She sighed. 'It's all fluid, they say. The baby isn't even very big. I'm like one of those water beds, stick a needle in me and I'd go down to nothing. Pity they can't.'

Lyn left the two of them together. St Ebba's, the maternity hospital, was a good way farther down North River Street from Hilderbridge General, but there had been no room left in St Ebba's car park and she had used the car park of the rambling, foinstone, turreted building that had once been the Three Towns workhouse. It was nearly eight o'clock of a sunny evening, still light, as light as afternoon, but cool as early June often is. The trees in the grounds were in full, fresh leaf, and behind them the sun declined towards the moorland horizon, its rays making a brilliant silver-gold glare through the tracery. Lyn took one of the gravel paths into the grounds of the general hospital, walking towards the sun that dazzled her eyes so that she screwed them up against it. Her hair was loose today and she wore a blue and white striped cotton dress with her mother's birthday gift cardigan. She had several pairs of sunglasses, perks of Gillman's, but she had forgotten to bring a pair with her.

She saw the man, not very tall, thin, wearing jeans and a tee-shirt, coming along the path towards her, towards the main gate into North River Street, but the sun blinded her and she didn't know him. He saw her and stopped. She closed her eyes and passed her hand over them and looked again. When she saw it was Nick Frazer something very curious happened. She behaved as she had never thought it would be possible for her to behave. She didn't think. It was a reflex, the result of those weeks of thinking and longing and wondering. She ran to him and into his arms. He put out his arms and caught her and held her, and they stood there on the gravel path in the grounds of Hilderbridge General Hospital, embraced as if they had long been lovers and had known each other with profound emotion and physical joy and had been parted only to meet again now, by chance, so felicitously.

'I've thought about you every day, all the time,' he said.

'Oh, I know, I know,' she said.

'I knew exactly why you didn't come and I thought you knew why I didn't come to you. But it was a deadlock, no way of breaking out of it. I even hoped that damned cat would find his way back so that I'd have an excuse to ring you.'

'I had a sort of fantasy he'd go to Mrs Africa's and I'd go there after him and so would you and we'd meet.'

'Did you? I had a feeling like that too. How mad we've been, Lyn. Lyn, Lyn, that's the first time I've said your name. Except to myself, I've said it a hundred times to myself.'

She said in a level voice, though her hands were shaking, like puppets jerked on strings, 'I've been visiting my sister. My brother-in-law's with her now but visiting ends at eight and I have to take him home. I brought him so I have to take him back.'

'Let him take your car and you stay with me,' Nick said.

'I can't do that.' They stood under a cedar tree. Nick took her in his arms and kissed her but, when his lips parted and she could taste his mouth, she drew back. There were movements in her body that frightened her. She said, and her voice wasn't steady any more, 'I have to take Kevin home now. Should we — should we see each other tomorrow?'

'Lunch at the Blue Lagoon?'

She nodded.

'I don't want to let you go, but d'you know, I feel so ridiculously happy. I am awake, aren't I? I haven't succumbed to weariness at Uncle Jim's bedside and fallen asleep? Of course I haven't, I don't dream, never have. It's early closing tomorrow — we can have all the afternoon together.'

She smiled at him. Then she walked away quickly along the path to the car park. Kevin was waiting by the car, leaning his arms on its roof, bored, smoking a cigarette.

'What d'you think of her, then?'

Lyn blinked at him. He seemed curiously unreal. 'I'm sorry?' she said.

'Jo. I said what d'you think of her?'

'She seems okay. How would *I* know?'

He got into the car beside her, gangling, long-legged, with big hands and feet. She realized for the first time fully consciously that she was ill at ease with, even afraid of, very tall men. Nick and she, they were proportioned to each other, they seemed to belong to the same tribe.

'Okay if we pick up Trev?'

Kevin's twin worked in some factory or mill in North Hilderbridge where he did the maximum overtime. He was waiting on the Jackley Road outside a pub called the Ostrich, Kevin's double in every particular until he had grown a moustache.

'Where's old Steve got to, Lyn?'

'Where d'you think?' said Kevin. 'I tell her she's a moor widow.'

'Yeah, but what's he escaping from, Lyn? What's with him he can't adjust to reality?'

'The moor's real enough, I should think.' She didn't want to discuss Stephen.

'It's either an acute case of claustrophobia or his super ego could be compelling him to confront agoraphobia.'

'Why don't you apply for a grant and go and do a psychology degree at the tech?' said Lyn.

Trevor began to explain why not, about the pointlessness of formal education in an area where knowledge depended so much upon intuition, and also about how much he earned with his overtime at Batsby Ball Bearings. She didn't listen. She thought of Nick and then of Stephen. But what difference could this make to Stephen? She was depriving him of nothing, taking from him nothing he wanted or could possess.

A flock of sheep were in Goughdale, cropping the turf, dark-wooled, long-horned sheep of the breed called Big Allen Black. The outward signs of the disused mine workings beneath, the old windlass, the boundary stones, the ruined coes, rose out of the plain and showed black against the setting sun.

Would he, seventeen years afterwards, be able to rediscover the mouth of the hole that led down into the

Goughdale Mine? He thought he could remember roughly where it was: on the side of Big Allen facing him, the northern face, almost at the foot and a little to the right of centre. Somewhere among the crags of limestone that made a broad shelf along part of the foin's lowest slopes.

The hole was referred to by Tace as 'Apsley Sough', though 'sough' in these parts meant a drain or channel. He had sited it far from where it really was, half a mile down from where it was; he had obviously never seen it. And it couldn't have been a sough or drain, for there could have been no reason to drain water *into* a mine. Joseph Usher, Tace's hero, had hidden himself in a chamber of the mine but had been driven out by hunger and thirst and, having given himself up, been taken away to trial and execution. Stephen made his way across the dale towards the mountain by a path that ran to the west of the ruined engine house. It was growing cool, even cold, with the departure of the sun. The sheep lifted their heads and looked at him as he passed by but they made no sound.

The weather had been hot that August when he was twelve. Peter Naulls and he, searching for the hole into the mine, had got as suntanned as if they had been on the kind of holiday they never had, on the beaches of Spain or Italy. Peter had, literally, stumbled on the mouth of the hole. Running in some ritual or phase of a game — for they didn't spend every minute of each day crawling and peering and prodding the ground — he had caught his foot in a root and fallen headlong. He had found himself looking into the infinitely complex growth of stem and grass and leaf and tendril and fine twig that covered the moor in a thick springy upholstery, but also beyond this, through and beside this, into clear darkness. Under his face, half overlaid by a crag shaped like a mushroom growth on a tree trunk, entirely obscured until his eyes were close up to it by the thick vegetation, was the open fissure which for thirty days they had searched for in vain. He had sprung to his feet and thrown out his arms and cried, for he had just been doing Archimedes' Principle at school, 'Eureka!'

Where was Peter now? The uncles and aunts presumably knew but Stephen himself hadn't heard a word of him since he went away to college in London when he was eighteen. That departure to university of a man far less intelligent than himself had been a blow to Stephen. And Dadda's comment — he occasionally deigned to recognize the existence of the Naulls clan — had done nothing to mitigate his sad resentment. 'Bloody degree won't get the lad a living in Naulls's shop.' Peter hadn't been expected to work in the men's outfitters, never had and never would.

But even in their search, strictly speaking, it had been Peter who had succeeded and not he. Peter, though fortuitously, had found Apsley Sough. It had been he who, with truth, had cried out, 'I have found it!'

Next day they had gone back with ropes and a book on rock-climbing from the library to teach themselves about knots. Dadda would have locked Stephen up if he had known what was going on. Uncle Leonard and Auntie Midge, more appropriately to their characters, would have had nervous breakdowns.

The hole was not a vertical shaft. If it had been they might not have dared penetrate it very far. It had been bored or dug or had occurred naturally at an incline of about thirty degrees, so that all the way down into the mine, holding onto the rope, they had had purchase for their feet, had almost been able to *walk down*, though describing it thus made a dull and orthodox act of what had been the great adventure of their boyhood.

After a long descent the shaft widened a little, and the light of their torches showed them the interior of the mine, the southern end of the tunnellings. They dropped down into a chamber, the roof of which must have been seven or eight feet high, and where the air seemed quite fresh. It was cold, though, by contrast with the heat outside, and there was a cold, damp, metallic smell. They lit the candles they had brought and made their way along a passage which led out of the chamber, gazing wordlessly — he couldn't remember that they had spoken at all while in there — at the arched limestone walls, at the tunnels that from time to time branched from this central artery, once into a wide gallery whose egress had been blocked by a fall of stone. And then the flames of their candles had gone out. They had noticed no difference in the quality of the atmosphere but the flames of their candles had gone out.

They had said nothing. They had stood in the dark until Peter had put his torch on, and then they had turned back, glad though, relieved, when they could light a match again. Stephen had gone out first, scrambling up the shaft, putting all his weight this time on the rope and wondering what would happen, whether they would ever be found alive, if the rope came unfastened from the spur of rock to which they had tied it. But not really frightened, buoyed up always by a child's invincible courage, the courage that comes from a sense of immortality.

When he came out into the bright white daylight he had a shock. There was another boy there, standing by the mouth of the hole, looking down, looking at the twitching rope. Adults in those circumstances would have spoken to each other, but not children. Stephen didn't know who the boy was or what he was doing on Big Allen and he didn't speak to him. Nor did the boy address him or Peter. He stood a little apart from them, kicking at the scree, and then he walked off across Goughdale between the crumbling towers. Stephen could remember how hot it had been, the sky a dazzling white-blue, the heat making the air wave and shiver above the dry yellowed turf.

Dusk now brought a stillness and its own grey translucent light. He walked along the ridge of rock, trying to picture once more the place where Peter had run and fallen. At one point he knelt down and parted the heather with his hands, so sure was he that he had found it, but there was nothing but the scree and the tiny plants which grew amongst it. It had become too dark to search any more and it was cold. He shivered a little as he set off for home.

6

They had meant to go out to lunch, or Nick had. He said to come upstairs to the flat only to fetch his jacket, and then they would go and eat and talk and maybe sit by the river. It was the first really warm day of summer. Lyn went first up the stairs and into the set of big, shabby rooms with arched windows that seemed full of sky.

She turned to Nick as he came in. He looked like a thin, young boy, much younger than he really was, his brown hair like a monk's without the tonsure. His skin was brown and his eyes a light clear hazel. One of his hands was on the door, the other extended to her. She looked at his fine, thin hands, the turned wrists where there were fair hairs on the brown skin, and put her face up to his.

He kissed her. He smoothed her hair back and held it

and kissed her, tenderly, then harder, and this time when his mouth opened into hers she didn't pull away. Her heart had been beating fast and her hands were shaking, but as he kissed her and his body pressed close against hers, the length of his body hard against hers, those signs of fear gradually ceased and she grew weak and curiously fluid in his arms. He put his hands on her breasts and she made a little soft sound.

The sun on the river threw reflections across the bedroom ceiling, down the wall. The ripple reflections moved in a continuous, tiny fluttering. They danced over Lyn's body as she undressed, over lean, brown Nick, waiting for her. Her arms felt languorous, her flesh soft and relaxed as if she had just awakened from sleep. He felt with his hands the smooth, sleepy flesh and she took his mouth on hers, himself into her.

With pain. She twisted her face away and kept herself from crying out. Her body went as taut as a bowstring, and when she opened her eyes and looked into his face she saw there awestricken astonishment. He lay still inside her. And then, for his sake, she did what she had read should be done: raised her legs and arched her back and held him embraced and reached her mouth to his, and began to enjoy what she did. To enjoy as much as she was going to for this time, she knew that, and she smiled and held him and kissed him when she felt the convulsion and heard his breath released. The quivering net of light from the river seemed now to have set the whole room trembling. Down in the Mootwalk a woman laughed and from the water a swan gave its harsh, grating cry.

Nick, holding her, said quietly, 'That was the first time for you.'

'Yes.'

'I don't understand.'

'I've never understood,' she said, 'but there it is. Doctors are only of use if a — a person wants to be cured.' She was very near to crying. She sat up and wrapped her arms round her knees, her hair falling round her like a cloak. He said nothing. She thought that if he said the wrong thing now everything would be over for her and him. And she was so used to the wrong things being said, to her tactless family, a mother and sister who shouted where angels feared to whisper, to Stephen and his inept words. If Nick made the mildest joke about virginity, about his luck, about impotence, about needing to eat after their exertions, she would dress and run away and it would all be over. She turned to him in despair and the tears were running down her face.

He took no notice of them. His eyes were half-closed and he was smiling a little.

'Go to sleep with me for a while,' he said, and he took her gently into his arms. He didn't say he loved her but, 'I think we're going to love each other, Lyn.'

From the pulled and sagging pockets of his jacket, his Sunday-go-to-meetings suit, his only suit, Dadda produced a cairngorm and silver ring for Lyn and a pearl-handled Stilton knife for Stephen. Though they might have forgotten that the following day would be the sixth anniversary of their engagement, he with his prodigious memory had not.

'It was me brought you together,' he said as they thanked him. 'But for me I don't reckon you'd ever have set eyes on each other.'

It was true. He had more or less arranged their marriage, Lyn sometimes thought. Her first job on leaving school had been at Whalbys'. She had been a clerk-receptionist-phone-answerer-tea-maker and she had got the job through her uncle Bob who was as near to being a friend of Thomas Whalby's as it was possible to be. He had never employed a girl before or since and now it seemed to Lyn that Dadda had hand-picked her for Stephen without the knowledge of either of them. Young, innocent, they had been malleable in those hands which were so practised in making something valuable out of raw or damaged material.

Dadda, having scrutinized his previous gift, the chestnut leaf table, for white rings, cigarette burns or dust in the carving, shambled about the room examining the legs of furniture. Although he didn't say so, Lyn knew he was looking for the marks of Peach's claws. Peach, who often sat on the chestnut leaf table, marking it no more than if he had been a fluffy cushion or a nightdress-case cat, watched gravely from the basket in which he was wise enough to sit when at home on Sundays. Lyn put the ring on and said it was a perfect fit.

'Ah, I had the size of your pretty fingers by heart,' said Dadda who was adept at making one feel a heel.

Trevor Simpson came in later and Lyn's uncle Bob as well as the rest of them. There were hardly enough chairs to go round. Dadda withdrew into a corner, drawing up his spider legs. Uncle Bob said he could remember, from when they were boys, Tom had never been keen on cats.

'A mild form of ailurophobia,' said Trevor.

'Look, lad,' said Dadda, 'I don't have nothing mild. I don't have nothing bloody *mild*.'

Joanne, vast, out of hospital the day before, sat eating chocolate biscuits.

'If you go on like that,' said Kevin, 'you'll be back in there before the week's out.'

'It's not food, it's fluid. If I've told you once I've told you five thousand times, it's all fluid.'

'Chocolate's poison to horses, did you know that? It's got some substance in it, theo-something. Racehorses have been known to die of eating chocolate.'

'You mean me and racehorses have got something in common?'

'There was a woman lived in Hall cottages when you girls were little,' said Mrs Newman, 'used to feed her family on cat food. Out of tins, I mean. She used to give them Pedigree Chum too, but it was mostly cat food. She liked the fishiness.'

'No thanks, Lyn,' said her father, 'I won't have another sandwich.'

'And she had this baby and it had a birthmark like a cat's face on its stomach.'

'Ours'll have a Mars bar.'

'I've no doubt it's true,' said Trevor. 'Could be a rare form of imprinting, could even be stigmata.'

Peach jumped up onto Lyn's lap. He lay there, purring. His pale golden, ringed tail hung down and sometimes the tip of it twitched. Dadda was the first to leave. He hadn't come in the van. Bob Newman offered him a lift but he wouldn't accept it, he said he would get the bus. Joanne and her mother lingered, gossiping, by their adjoining gates as if they wouldn't see each other again for half a year. Lyn washed the dishes. She got out the mower to cut the back lawn.

'I say, darling,' Stephen said, 'I think I'll go out for a bit, blow the cobwebs away.'

'Would you like me to come with you?'

His eyes became opaque. She could see he didn't want her. 'That wouldn't be much fun for you. You have a rest, put your feet up.'

Was she still trying to retrieve something? Still hoping for something from him? 'I'm twenty-five,' she said, with the edge to her voice that was the nearest she got to temper.

'Sorry. Shouldn't have said that. I only meant you look tired. Why don't you go out somewhere? Take the car.'

'Perhaps I will.' She seemed to hear Nick's voice saying, We are going to love each other.

'All right if I'm not back till late, then?' Stephen said, eager for her approval.

'Of course it's all right, of course.'

He set off jauntily, whistling. Golden eyes looked at him from among the leaves of the yellow maple tree where Peach sat cleverly camouflaged. Stephen walked along the Jackley road, past the crossroads and up to the Vale of Allen. It had been a white day, white blank sky, white thin sun, warmish and dull. The sky was white and still, unmarked by cloud or blue.

A car was parked by the roadside, on the left hand side and facing north. Stephen thought it a curious place to leave one's car, blocking, or partly blocking, the northbound roadway, while taking it a farther ten yards on would have enabled its driver to pull in onto the bridlepath that traversed the Vale as far as the Reeve's Way. The car was a small yellow Volkswagen. Stephen couldn't see a sign of its owner. The land here was dotted about with gorse bushes and he half-expected a dog to come bounding out from among them. But apart from the gentle, almost mesmeric, hum of the bees, all was silent and still.

He climbed up on to the Reeve's Way and followed it northwards into Goughdale. The owner of the car was nowhere to be seen, nowhere in all these wide plains that lay about him, though the car was still there, a bright yellow dot on the distant road. The causeway commanded a view of all this region of the moor, but once he had jumped down and was in the shallow bowl of Goughdale, he could see nothing except the remains of surface workings and the louring slopes of Big Allen.

It took him nearly two hours to find the hole into the mine. His memory had played him false. He thought he could remember that he and Peter had fastened their rope to a spur or spike of rock and accordingly it was for such a feature that he searched. But the limestone took no such jagged form in the area where he knew the sough must be located, it was smooth and curved. He found instead the only possible protuberance to which they could safely have anchored their rope. This was in the slope of the mountainside above the shelf and below the scree on which Peter had slipped. He crawled along the shelf, peering, feeling with his hands. And there it was — a long way from where he remembered it, quite differently sited, but there beyond a doubt, a cleft into the foot of the mountain under a pendulous lip of stone.

He lay down and looked in. There was nothing more interesting to be seen than if this had been the entrance to a rabbit warren, nothing but a tunnel that led down into darkness. It smelt of earth. He got to his feet again and walked back across Goughdale, pausing at each ruin of a mine building to check if any more entrances to the underground workings remained unblocked. The George Crane Mine, the Duke of Kelsey's, the Goughdale. He had looked before, of course, he and Peter had looked, and years later he had once more investigated the rough hillocky ground, but then and now he found nothing. The mines were dangerous, the mines were not to be left open as an invitation to any foolhardy visitor. He had found, and rediscovered, what was almost certainly the only inlet remaining accessible to that network of subterranean passages, galleries and chambers, that other world beneath the moor.

The sun had set and dusk was closing in. Stephen would have preferred to walk back across the Vale of Allen and Foinmen's Plain but he had no torch and to-night there would only be a thin, new moon. So he made for the Jackley road from which nearly all the traffic had now disappeared.

He was surprised to see the yellow car still there. It had been parked on that spot for at least three hours, probably much longer, for whoever had parked it had very likely done so before the evening traffic build-up. People who wanted to get rid of old cars sometimes dumped them on the moor, the kind of behaviour that maddened Stephen. But this car wasn't of that sort. From its registration number it was only three years old, and it looked well-kept, the front tyres were new. He looked through the windscreen and then through the driver's window. A knitted sweater of cream wool hung across the back of the passenger seat and there was a striped silk scarf, cream, red and black, on the dashboard shelf. The driver's window was partly open. He tried the driver's door. It wasn't locked. Once he had opened the door, though, there seemed nothing to do but close it again.

The owner must be somewhere about. It could only be someone who had gone for a marathon walk or a sol-itary picnicker who had lain down and fallen asleep. But as he passed the crossroads and came to that part of the road that wound down into Chesney he couldn't help recalling the man he had seen skipping among the trees. He looked long and searchingly at the Banks of Knamber that tonight were as they had been then be-fore the moon rose, grey and pale as a sky dotted with tiny black clouds. But tonight there was no one among the trees.

In the morning he picked up the van in Hilderbridge and drove to Jackley the long way round through Byss, having a newly upholstered chaise longue to deliver before he made the Jackley collection. His last call would be in Trinity Road, Hilderbridge, so he stopped at a confectioners and bought a box of fruit jellies. It was a day of white sky, ground mist, chilly, an expectant day, waiting for the sun to come through.

The soft, thin mist gave to the foins a mysterious air. Their peaks seemed to float above the ground. Stephen drove south by the main road and as he came through Goughdale it occurred to him that the yellow Volkswagen might still be there. It was. He saw the spot of bright buttercup colour as he rounded the last curve before the crossroads. But the car was no longer the only vehicle parked there. It had gathered to itself, in the still white mist, on the verge of the Vale of Allen, half a dozen more cars and a large van. Stephen slowed down. Two of the cars were police cars, marked Police and with blue lamps. A man in a raincoat was standing by the rear of the Volkswagen while another was squatting down, peering underneath it.

Stephen pulled in on the opposite side of the road. He got down from the cab. He could see now that there was a driver in each of the police cars. He went across the road. Immediately the standing man called out to him, 'Nothing for you to bother about, sir, thank you very much. This is a police matter.'

It was Detective Sergeant Troth. He appeared to recognize Stephen as quickly as Stephen recognized him, but the dark wedge face registered this only in a tightening of the mouth and a jerk of the chin. It was the other man, who rose now from his squatting position to be identified as Inspector Manciple, who spoke to him.

'Good morning. It's Mr Whalby, isn't it?'

Stephen nodded. 'There hasn't been another — any trouble, has there?'

Troth said gruffly, 'What d'you mean, trouble?'

'To be frank with you,' said Manciple, 'there's a young woman missing from Jackley. A married woman. This is her car.'

'And you think . . . ?'

'We don't think anything,' said Troth in his flat Three Towns accent. His face, Stephen noticed, was badly marked with acne as if he were still in his teens, though he was years older than that. 'Not yet we don't,' he said. 'We don't jump to conclusions.'

'In the normal course of things we'd not treat such a disappearance seriously.' Manciple sounded as if he were apologizing for the other man's rudeness. He had a conciliatory air and he looked uneasy when Troth turned his back. 'Only after what you found back in April, things aren't normal. There's a couple of search parties organized. I daresay you can make out one of them up across the Vale there.'

Stephen got back into the van and drove down into Hilderbridge. At Sunningdale the same collection of old people, arranged in much the same order, was watching television in the day room. On the screen a woman with bright blonde hair and red-rimmed glasses was teaching her audience how to make profiteroles. One of the old men was reading the *Daily Mirror*, the knitter was knitting, Helena Naulls was asleep, her mouth open and her dentures slipped out of alignment. She was wearing a pink cotton dress which evidently belonged, not to her, but to the fattest resident, a mountain of a woman who was also asleep, whom Stephen had never seen other than asleep in all his visits.

Mrs Naulls awoke as easily as she slept. The knitter pushed her shoulder and she sat up and opened her eyes. Stephen kissed her.

'How's tricks then, Grandmother?'

'Just the same,' said Mrs Naulls. 'Have you brought me my jellies?'

'What do you think?' He put the box on her lap. 'Whoa there, go easy!' She grunted as her fingers scrabbled with the cellophane wrapping. 'I reckon I'll have one myself, I'm feeling a bit peckish, and what about this lady?'

'Go on,' said the knitter, 'it's a shame to tease her.'

'Leonard was always a tease,' said Mrs Naulls, putting a purple jelly into her mouth. 'His dad tried to knock it out of him but it never made no difference.'

'Knock one devil out and another in, I always say,' said the knitter.

'How's Midge getting on, Peter?'

'If you mean Lyn, she's okay, and I'm Stephen.' He lowered his voice. 'It looks as if there's been another murder on the moor.'

'Pardon?' said Mrs Naulls, her mouth full.

'We're most of us a bit hard of hearing in here, dear,' said the knitter.

'Another murder on the moor,' Stephen repeated more loudly.

The old man put his paper down. The fat woman opened her eyes and closed them again. Helena Naulls hesitated between a red jelly and a yellow one and finally chose the yellow.

Round-eyed, the knitter said, 'It turns you cold all over to think of it. Was it another young girl, dear?'

'It looks like it.' Stephen jumped up. 'Actually, I'm

off to join the search party. They're looking for the body now.' In that moment he had made up his mind. It was what, half-consciously, he had been longing to do since he had got out of the van and talked to Manciple. He'd go back and explain to Dadda. Anyway, Dadda owed him a day off for working the Spring Holiday Monday to get those Chippendale chair seats done. 'They'll need someone like me, someone who knows the moor inside out.'

'Mr Tace,' said Mrs Naulls, smiling reminiscently, 'he was a one for the moor. He *did* love it. He was a lovely man, one in a million. Bye-bye, Stephen. Mind you give my love to Lyn.'

The sun had appeared as a brighter white puddle in the white sky and the mist had begun to move. There was no sign of the search party. Stephen always kept an anorak and a pair of walking boots in the car. He parked in Loomlade and took the path that ran between Loomlade Foin and Big Allen, the direction in which Manciple had surely indicated the party was veering. It was near here that he had found the little white orchid. He came up to the Hilder at the point where the aqueduct pillars crossed it.

He could see the river winding away from its source in the springs of Pierce Foin. The land was marshy here, tussocky with reeds, the black peat showing through the heather. Distant Goughdale seemed deserted. He crossed the river by the stepping stones, wondering if they had yet searched the mine ruins. Mottle Foin, the only foin on which trees grew, little stunted pines making a black dappling on its surface, was the highest hill on the moor after Big Allen and now its rocky hump hid the Hilder's northerly curves, Pierce Foin and all of Lustley Dale. Stephen had another couple of miles to walk before the view was open to him again and he saw the men in the distance, deployed out across the ground on the river's right bank.

There must have been forty or fifty of them. One man had done that, one man had had the power to call them all out here on to the moor, away from their homes, their jobs. He had killed one girl and now, because another was missing, they had come as if he had called them, as if they were his slaves. Stephen went back across the river again, clambering over the boulders. Two or three of the men looked round, no one waved. A burly figure, tall and heavy, came towards him. It was Ian Stringer.

'No luck yet?' called Stephen.

'Luck, d'you call it?'

'Oh Lord, you know what I mean. I just thought I'd come up and lend a hand. I'm by way of being a bit of an expert on the moor, you know.'

Stringer shrugged. His blue shirt, open at the neck and showing a mat of black hair, was wet with sweat in the armpits and down the back. 'You see that chap in the green? The little dark chap? That's her husband, that's Roger Morgan. We're hoping, there's just a chance, she left her car to pick wild flowers. She was fond of wild flowers, he says, and — well, she could have got lost or passed out or something.'

'In that case she wouldn't be all the way over here, would she?'

'There's a couple of policemen with us.' Stringer pointed them out. 'They're sort of directing operations.'

Stephen had rather expected he would do that. But he joined the party as they tramped off towards Lustley Dale.

'What was she dressed in?' he asked the husband.

'I can't be absolutely sure.' He had a middle-class,

educated voice. 'A red shirt, I think. Jeans.' His face was grey with fatigue.

'We've been out looking for her since five,' said another man.

'She'd gone to see her parents in Hilderbridge and I was with mine in Jackley.' Morgan managed a wry grin. 'We didn't get on with our in-laws.'

Stringer said, low-voiced, as Morgan moved out of earshot, 'We started at the Foinmen.'

'Of course you would. Good Lord, yes.'

'We've been at it — ' He looked at the watch on his sinewy wrist with its furring of black hair ' — like nine hours. There's two other parties, one doing the southeast and one the Pertsey side.'

By mid-afternoon they were on the lower slopes of Lustley Foin. Stephen wasn't hungry. He felt invigorated, exhilarated by the search. It wasn't often that he had a whole day out on the moor. As he clambered over the rocks, parting the scrub and the brambles to peer into crevices, he heard a droning throb overhead and looked up to see a helicopter. It was circling slowly and very low down, almost touching, it seemed at one point, the summit of Big Allen.

Stringer cocked a thumb in Morgan's direction. 'That copter belongs to some mate of his father-in-law. Useful if she's out in the open.'

A bramble whipped and clawed Stephen across the neck. He put his hand up to it and saw the blood streaked on his fingers. There was no point in climbing the foin, she wouldn't be up there. They spread across the opening to the valley that was called Jackley Plain, and there Roger Morgan could go no further. He didn't quite collapse. He sat down on a stone and put his head in his hands. Of all the members of the party he was the one from whom the most endurance was called, but of all the members of the party he was perhaps the only one unused to sustained walking or manual labour, and he was also the smallest. Stephen felt a flicker of contempt for him.

'Sorry,' Morgan said gruffly. 'I'm dead beat. I've had no sleep since the night before last.' He looked at Stephen with recognition. 'You're one of the Whalbys, aren't you? You and your father came to our place to cover a settee.'

Stephen didn't much like to be reminded of this in public. 'Oh, yes. Jackley. St Edmund's Avenue.'

Morgan nodded. 'Better get on, I suppose.'

'I should sit there a bit longer,' one of the policemen said. 'Then we'll get you down to the road. We've got our vehicles at quarter mile intervals all the way from Hilderbridge to Jackley.'

Stephen started off again and the others began to follow him. He wasn't going to be left behind, nursing Morgan. Overhead the helicopter circled once more, making a black locust-shaped shadow on the sunlit turf of the plain.

They stood admiring each other.

'You're lovely,' said Nick.

'So are you.'

'I did make you happy, didn't I?'

'You know you did. Couldn't you tell?' She reddened, for she wasn't yet used to this kind of talk. 'I never knew it would be like that.'

'I get a strange feeling when you talk that way. It's a strange situation, isn't it? It makes you more mine than if there'd been others or if your marriage had been real.'

She nodded. 'And you more mine.'

'Stay with me, Lyn. I don't mean all night, I know you can't, but stay with me for the evening.'

'No.' She began to put her clothes on, blue denim jeans, white tee-shirt, shoulders thin and straight with bones like white shell. 'It's seven now. I ought to have been home two hours ago.'

Nick said, but very gently to take the sting out of the words, 'You're not his mother.'

'I'll never be anyone else's.' She hunted in the bed for the ribbon that had come off her hair while they were making love.

Nick combed her hair and tied the ribbon himself, badly, too loosely. She had to do it again. He dressed and went downstairs with her. Where Peach's pen had been in the window was a cage with a snake in it, curled up on straw. In the shop, in the dimness, she threw herself into Nick's arms and kissed him. The snake's skin trembled at the movement in the air.

She got the 7.15 bus, feeling as anxious as a mother who isn't home in time for when her little boy comes back from school. People on the bus were talking about the number of police cars on the road and someone said another girl was missing.

When she rushed into the house in Tace Way Stephen wasn't even there. It looked as if no one had been there since she left in the afternoon to go to Nick. Peach alone was in the house, having let himself in through the cat flap Stephen had fixed into the lower panel of the back door. He was sitting on one of the kitchen counters, paws folded, tail tucked up, gazing with stately patience at the larder door. Lyn fed him. She made herself a cup of tea, cut bread for toast, beat up eggs with grated cheese in a pan. At nine she put the television on for the news.

The first item was the discovery of Ann Morgan's

body. She had been found at two that afternoon by a party searching the Pertsey and north-west region of Vangmoor. The body was in a stone hut, formerly the powder magazine of the long-disused Duke of Kelsey's mine. She had been strangled and her long fair hair shorn off at the scalp. Lyn switched off the set as Stephen came in at the back door.

7

Fingerprints were taken of all the men over sixteen and under sixty in the Three Towns. Then a man in a white coat took blood samples from their thumbs. Troth was ticking off names on a list. He gave Stephen the same pinched stare as that which he levelled at Lyn's father and Trevor Simpson, as if he had never seen him before.

Stephen hadn't been in the gatehouse lodge for years. As a child he had lived there half the time, for after his mother had left the obvious person to look after him had been Mrs Naulls, however much, and by then however much more, Dadda loathed all the Naulls family. He had been at school a year but they took him away and sent him to Chesney Primary so that Helena could fetch him and take him home with her until Dadda came at six to pick him up in the van.

It had been Naulls policy to close up on him whenever he spoke of his mother. Helena didn't quite close up. She teased. If Uncle Leonard was a tease, you could tell where he got it from.

'She's on the moon, there!' Helena would say in answer to his question, or, 'Maybe she's at the North Pole with the polar bears.'

While Helena went down to the shop and Arthur Naulls dozed in the old shiny armchair that smelt unaccountably of wet dog, Stephen hunted for letters, a photograph, an address. He found nothing, he never did find anything. Helena showed him what she thought it was good for him to see, pictures of Brenda as a young girl, a lock of her fair wavy hair, twisted into a circle and tied with a piece of thin red ribbon.

'Where is she, Nanna?'

'Curiosity killed the cat,' said Helena.

Stephen had his fingerprints done and a sample taken of his blood. It was all very impersonal, a routine test for all the men. There were green baize notice boards and maps studded with pins hung up where the nasturtium paper had been, though faintly Stephen thought he could smell the old smell, that mixture of boiled greens and beeswax and unwashed woollen cloth. He came out into the sunshine and the scent of new-mown grass.

Lyn had gone to work an hour before on the bus, Stephen having escorted her to the stop and waited with her. No woman wanted to be alone on the moor or in the moorland villages, even in broad daylight. He saw the police car waiting outside his house a hundred yards before he got there himself. Manciple was sitting inside it with another, younger, man and the driver. He got out as Stephen approached.

The faintly hangdog, embarrassed air was stronger

than ever this morning. Always red-faced, Manciple looked as if he was blushing for shame. He said in his awkward, apologetic way, 'We'd like you to come down to the station, Mr Whalby. Have a chat.'

'A chat about what?'

'About the situation up here. Miss Price. Mrs Morgan. Just routine inquiries on an informal basis, Mr Whalby.'

He had no choice but to get into the car and go with them. He sat in the back with the other man. Manciple, in the passenger seat, remarked that it was a fine day, going to be warm. Apart from that, no one said a word all the way down to Hilderbridge.

They showed him into a different room this time, small, bare, on the ground floor. There was a metal table in it and three bentwood chairs, two benches, a calendar on one wall and on the opposite one a street plan in a frame. He waited in there alone for half an hour. Once, towards the end of the half-hour, he opened the door and looked out for a sign of anyone. It gave him a strange feeling to see a uniformed policeman sitting just outside the door like a warder in a film about prison.

Chief Superintendent Malm came in briskly and full of apologies like a conscientious chairman late for a board meeting. Apologies, not explanations. He had just sat down opposite Stephen on the other side of the table when Manciple came in and took the third of the bentwood chairs. The room was already growing very warm, for the large, metal-framed window, its panes still grimed with winter and spring dirt, received the full force of the sun. Malm had a grey suit on, Manciple a cheap-looking, thin sports jacket.

Stephen hadn't really believed that stuff about an informal chat, but Malm started lightly enough, asking him at what time he had gone out on the moor on Sunday, why he had gone and when he had got home. His tone was polite and pleasant, but it held a note of wonder as if Stephen's excursions were a highly unusual leisure-time activity. It was only then that Stephen understood they suspected him. They hadn't got him here to inquire about someone else, but because they suspected *him*. When Marianne Price had been killed he had told the family gathering jokingly that he was the police's number one suspect. Now it was true.

'I wasn't even in that part of the moor. I was walking in Goughdale.'

'Where might that be?'

Manciple knew, Stephen could tell that, but he didn't say. Stephen explained. Malm asked him about the mines. Did he know the location of the Duke of Kelsey's mine and the old powder house? Stephen said he knew every feature of the moor, the soughs, the flues, the now-blocked horse levels. Manciple stared at him with blue eyes that made a harsh, ugly contrast to the crimson of his skin, the pale copper hair.

'You knew Mrs Ann Morgan,' Malm said.

'I'd seen her once, months ago.'

'Not according to Mr Morgan. According to Mr Morgan, you'd been to the house once in February and you went back again when he wasn't there at the end of March.'

He made it sound as if Stephen had gone there because he knew the husband would be absent. Stephen didn't say anything. He shrugged his shoulders. The sun on his back was making him sweat but he didn't think it would have been better on the other side of the table where Malm and Manciple got the sun in their eyes. Manciple left then and Troth came in with a man carrying a tray with three cups of coffee on it and a plate of biscuits. Troth said something in an undertone to Malm and they both went out, leaving Stephen alone with the coffee. In their absence he took his jacket off, hung it over the back of the chair, and rolled up his shirtsleeves.

Troth came back, looked at Stephen's arms as if he had done something disgusting, exposed himself perhaps, and opened the window. Malm sat down.

'Mrs Morgan had a Volkswagen,' he said. 'A small yellow Volkswagen which she left parked on the Jackley road. Did you see that car while you were out?'

'Yes.'

'And touched it. Your fingerprints were on the driver's door.'

Malm nodded to Troth and Troth pounced on him with a question. How had he got Ann Morgan to stop? Had he waved her down or had she recognized him? Stephen knew they suspected him but he was still shocked to be accused as directly and as insolently as that.

'I didn't even see her. I didn't get her to stop.'

'She got out of that car for someone she knew.'

'She stopped and you spoke to her and then you opened the car door for her,' said Malm.

'The car was empty when I opened the door,' said Stephen.

'Go around opening car doors, do you, when the fancy takes you?'

They went over and over that for a long time. The room grew stifling hot, in spite of the open window. Sweat was running down his sides from his armpits. The same man came back with more coffee and cheese and piccalilli sandwiches. Stephen watched a shadow that was creeping across the floor as the sun began to pass overhead and he thought there was no reason why the table and chairs shouldn't be moved into this shade, but no one suggested doing it.

After they had eaten the sandwiches Malm said he expected Stephen would like to stretch his legs. Stephen took that to mean he would like to go to the lavatory and it did, but Malm and Troth also took him outside and showed him a car, a Volkswagen of the same model as the yellow one, though this one was green, and got him to demonstrate how he had opened Ann Morgan's car door and what he had done. He was sure they didn't believe him and he felt they were humouring him towards something.

Back in the room with the table and the bentwood chairs Malm started on Marianne Price. It was a coincidence that Stephen had been associated with both girls' deaths, had found Marianne's body and then had found Ann Morgan's car. Stephen said it wasn't odd when you considered how often he was out walking on the moor.

'Maybe too often,' Malm said.

Stephen had never been able to deal with innuendo and he couldn't now. He sat dumbly under that one while Troth went away and a man he had never seen before came in, a thin, quiet man who stared at him. Malm asked him why he had lost a day's work to join the search party. What concern was it of his? Had he expected to find Ann Morgan's body?

'It was because I know the moor,' he said. 'I thought I'd be more useful than people who'd never set foot outside Hilderbridge.' Inside him, deep down, was a small voice that whispered, because it's mine, because I need to know what goes on there, I need to control it, that's why.

'Did you often have your lunch at the Market Burger House?'

'I've been there once or twice.'

'So you knew Marianne Price worked there?'

'For the Lord's sake! Everybody knows she worked there.'

The other man said softly, lightly, 'What did you do with their hair?'

Stephen jumped up and pushed his chair back and it fell over with a clatter. 'If this is going on I want my lawyer!'

'Have you got one?' Malm said dryly, but even he seemed to think the other man had gone too far, and before any more was said Manciple was back and they were reverting to the car and the time Stephen went out and the time he got back.

He knew he gave identical accounts each time he retold what he had done on Sunday evening. When he had told them four times they seemed to give up trying to extract a confession from him. Three cups of tea were brought in and a plate of shortcake biscuits. The room was in full shade now but it was still hot and stuffy. For the fifth time Stephen recounted how he had seen the car with its window half-open and seen the scarf and the sweater, and had opened the door and closed it again.

Manciple asked him how he had come to get a scratch on the side of his neck.

'Brambles when I was out with the search party,' Stephen said, and he turned his head and pulled down his shirt collar so that they could see.

'Or a woman's fingernail,' said Malm.

Stephen shrugged wearily. It was too ridiculous. They said no more about the scratch but talked about the car again. At five they told him that was enough for today and he could go home, they wouldn't keep him any longer. If he didn't mind waiting five minutes they would take him home by car. Stephen said angrily that he did mind, he wouldn't wait, he would walk home.

'I'd keep off the moor, though, if I were you,' said Malm. 'If you insist on walking seven or eight miles when we're perfectly willing to take you, you stick to the road. And give the moor a wide-berth for a bit, right?'

Standing by the desk, talking to the duty officer, was the girl from the *Three Towns Echo* who had interviewed Stephen in April. She looked very different, prettier, in her summer dress and pale blue cardigan. A chiffon scarf, blue, green and white, was tied round her head and knotted at the nape of her neck. She came up to him as he went towards the swing doors.

'Is it you who've been all day helping police with their inquiries?'

Stephen attempted a light laugh. 'Lord, yes, I suppose so.'

'I've phoned it over to the PA.'

'What might the PA be in plain language?'

She looked incredulous. 'The Press Association. I thought everyone knew that. It'll be in all the nationals, there's been a man helping police with their inquiries into the moors murders.'

'Not my name, though?'

She shook her head. They walked out into the street together. It was warm and sunny, the sky cloudless. 'They have to be careful of libel,' she said. 'You might sue them.'

'I certainly should!'

'Would you mind telling me what they've been asking you?'

It was wonderful to be out in the fresh air again, the sunshine. It had felt like prison in there, or as if he could only be let out of that stuffy room into prison. Remembering jargon he had read somewhere, he said joyfully, 'I'll give you an exclusive story!'

They had walked into Market Square. The Market Burger House was the obvious place to go for a cup of something and a biscuit, but Stephen felt he had had enough cups of something and enough biscuits to last him a lifetime. The Kelsey Arms was just opening. Feeling extremely daring, Stephen held the saloon bar door open for her.

There were two customers in there already, a man and a woman, no one else. Stephen fetched himself and the girl two halves of lager. She told him her name was Harriet Crozier. It pleased him that she remembered he was an expert on Vangmoor and that she seemed to have forgotten the trade by which he earned his living. She referred to him as a nature writer. On an impulse, a little breathlessly, he told her whose grandson he was.

'Can I use that?'

'Oh Lord, it might be better to say "descendant".' He was thinking of Uncle Stanley making a fuss. Uncle Stanley read the *Three Towns Echo* very thoroughly. There was often something in it about himself. 'Say "descendant", and you could say some of his — well, his talent's been passed on to me, something like that.' Stephen began telling her about the two occasions on which he had spoken to Ann Morgan, though he left out the bit about covering the settee, how social conscience had led him to join the search party.

Harriet took it all down in what she called speedwriting but which looked to Stephen like ordinary words with the vowels left out. She had drunk her lager very quickly, and suddenly, announcing that she was terribly hot, she couldn't stand that thing on her head any longer, she couldn't stand it whatever the risk, she pulled off her scarf.

Her hair was as long, as golden and nearly as thick as Lyn's. It fell down over her shoulders and she pushed it back away from her face. She laughed at his look of consternation. It wasn't Lyn's face at all but sharp and knowing, the nose sprinkled with freckles, the eyes a cat's green.

'I can't tie my head up for the rest of my life,' she said.

She was holding her empty glass. Stephen didn't want to have to buy her another drink. He had begun to feel uneasy, taking a woman into a pub, buying a drink for her, being seen with her perhaps. It had never happened to him before and he felt it wasn't quite a fair way to behave to Lyn.

'Time I was on my way.'

She seemed surprised. 'Let me buy you one.'

'No, no, of course not,' he said. 'I've a long walk ahead of me.'

In spite of what he had just said he might have shirked it if the 6.15 bus hadn't just gone. He set off but it was wearisome to have to stick to the road. What did Malm's parting shot mean? That he was forbidden the moor? For how long? And what possible right had the police to lay such injunctions on an innocent man? Stephen had the impotent, resentful, revengeful feeling about that which a lover has when warned by more powerful authority off a girl. And he shared that lover's certainty that if he obeyed his life wouldn't be worth living. There was no time, since the departure of his mother, when the moor had not been to him a refuge, a domain, and in some curious way, a closer friend than any human being. It brought him a hollow, slightly sick, sensation to think of being estranged from it.

He must keep to the road. To the left of him now were the Foinmen, to the right the Banks of Knamber,

but he must not go among the standing stones nor the
birch trees, it was as if an invisible wall had been
erected between them and him. And this had been
brought about by the murderer of those girls, this man
who had usurped Vangmoor and made himself a
greater master of it than he.

It was a beautiful evening, the air soft and hushed,
the distant hills floating in a bluish haze. But Stephen
kept his eyes on the white road ahead as if he were a
blinkered horse or as if there were rows of houses, identical and dull-facaded, on either side of him. At the
stop nearest to Knamber Hole he waited and caught the
7.15 bus.

8

Next day the CID sent for him again.

This time it was like a psychotherapy session, or what Stephen imagined such a session would be, only with three psychiatrists and one patient-victim. Manciple wasn't there. Instead of him there was a chief inspector called Hook. Hook did most of the talking. It was easy to see he had been called in because he was used to this kind of thing, to asking the right kind of cutting-through-to-the-bone questions and perhaps to breaking men. Only you couldn't break and confess when you had done nothing.

Hook wanted Stephen's life described to him. He wanted Stephen to say exactly what he did on one typical day. What was there so special about the moor that he was so attached to it? Was it a fact that he was accustomed to ten- or even twenty-mile walks? How long had he been married? Why had he no children?

'I don't see what that's got to do with it.'

'You're not ashamed to tell us, are you? There's nothing to be ashamed of. Some would say there are too many people in this world without you adding to them.'

'Let's say that's the answer, then.'

Hook said he understood, he had been told, that Stephen was a grandson of Tace the Vangmoor novelist. How had that come about since Tace had apparently been childless? Oh, through an *illegitimate* child? He was by way of being an illegitimate grandson of Tace's?

Coffee and biscuits arrived at ten. It was a misty morning and to Stephen's relief the sun was sluggish in appearing. The room was cool and smelt of some sort of antiseptic that had been used in the water when the floor was washed. Troth had a pustule on his chin which worried him. He didn't scratch it but constantly brought his fingers close to it, tenderly palpating the greasy, pitted skin around it. Hook was a tall man who might have been good-looking but for his bulbous, shapeless, pugilist's nose. He drank in a curious way, holding his coffee cup in both hands. In the middle of a series of questions he broke off and said to Stephen *à propos*, it seemed, of nothing that had gone before, his eyes fixed and narrowed, his forefinger pointing across the table, 'We're looking for a psychopath — would you agree to that? Would you agree that a man who kills the way this one does, for no more motive than that a girl's young and has got long blonde hair, a man who's driven by some impulse to kill in this way, he would be a psychopath?'

'I suppose so.'

'A man who is apparently a conformist, young and physically very strong, a man who needs routine because any other kind of existence he can't handle. A man who has a fantasy life, maybe delusions of grandeur, a man with a morbid interest in death. I'm describing a certain type of psychopath. Aren't I also describing you, Whalby?'

Stephen said nothing. What could he say?

'So we have a blueprint and here we have a man who fits that blueprint — or so it seems to me. Don't you think any detached observer would see it like that? Our man knows Vangmoor. He knows it so well he can find his way about it in the dark. He's so strong and he knows the moor so well he can carry a dead body miles across it by night.'

'I haven't a morbid interest in death.' Stephen tried a dismissive laugh and felt he had succeeded. 'What was I supposed to do when I found Marianne Price's body? Not tell you? Go home as if nothing had happened?'

'We'll ask the questions, Whalby,' said Malm.

Stephen had never seen Troth smile or even look pleasant, but now as he sat a little apart from the others, sat with a certain air of deference to the others, his hand moving slightly in the vicinity of that red spot with its yellow blob, there was something in his face that Stephen recognized as amusement. It wasn't a smile, it wasn't even a lifting of those tight, bunched facial muscles, but rather a light in his eyes. Troth was amused, vastly entertained, by the spectacle of a defenceless person being insulted.

True to his word, Malm launched into a spate of questions. This time they were all concerned with the geography of the moor and Manciple, who knew it better than they, had to be called in to assist. It seemed to Stephen that he had already, dozens of times, described the walks he took and the climbs he did, but they wanted it all again. Then the door opened and a man came in. Stephen didn't even look up, he was so sure it must be their lunch sandwiches arriving, but there was no tray and no sandwiches, only another one of those whispered messages of the kind, no doubt, that yesterday had made him into a psychopath and a murderer. Malm, Hook and Manciple all left the room. Stephen was left alone with Troth.

Troth behaved exactly as if he wasn't there. He did something Stephen felt no man would do in the company of another unless he felt that other to be less than the dust. There was no mirror in the room but the street plan was framed and glazed. Troth got up. Achieving a passable reflection of his face in the glass, he squeezed the spot on his chin between his two forefingers. He gave a low grunt of pain and blood spurted, a tiny bead of it plummeting onto the frame.

Stephen sat and waited. Troth made him feel acutely uncomfortable by getting behind him and standing there, presumably to look out of the window. He resolved that whatever happened, if they kept him there for hours, if they kept him there all day, he wouldn't speak to Troth. He stretched his legs and shifted in the chair. His whole body felt tense. They couldn't do anything to him, could they? They must be bluffing. They couldn't actually charge an innocent man.

It seemed like many hours but in fact it was just over twenty minutes before Hook came back. He

came back alone. Troth was sitting at the table
again, wiping his chin on a dirty, bloodstained handkerchief.

'Right, Mr Whalby, you can go. Thank you for
your cooperation.'

'You mean you've finished for today?'

Hook looked anything but pleased. He looked dismayed, defeated. 'I mean we've finished.'

'Why? What's happened? You mean that's all
you've got to say after putting me through the third
degree for the best part of two days?'

'We put you through no third degree.'

'At least you can tell me why I'm to be let off the
hook now.'

Troth laughed. It must have been at Stephen's un-
conscious pun. His laugh was like a schoolboy's crow
and when he had uttered it he left the room. Hook
muttered something about new evidence but Stephen
didn't bother to listen to him, he felt too angry and
indignant. If he had encountered Troth then, out in
the corridor, he would have hit him as hard as he
could and damn the consequences! Troth, however,
was nowhere to be seen. It was Inspector Manciple
who came up to Stephen and said he wanted to explain about the 'small misunderstanding'.

They had just received the result of a complex analysis of the blood taken from Ann Morgan's fingernails. Stephen was suddenly conscious again of the
scratch on his neck. He actually felt it itch and tingle
as Manciple spoke. The blood belonged to group B
which was Stephen's own group and to which only 6
per cent of the population belonged. With highly so-
phisticated forensic techniques, Manciple explained,
they could now narrow down blood types much more
closely than that, and further analysis had shown

features in the blood found in the fingernails which Stephen's own didn't share.

'Pity that couldn't have been done before,' Stephen said. 'I must say I take rather a dim view of being treated like a criminal for no reason whatsoever.'

But it was over, he hadn't made a fool of himself, and now he was free. There wasn't even a threat hanging over him that they might start on him again tomorrow, for they knew now that he wasn't their man, that it couldn't be he. His relief was immeasurably greater than that he had felt the day before, walking out of here with Harriet Crozier. It was almost as if — though this was ridiculous — he *had* done it, *had* killed those girls, and was sick with joy at having escaped justice.

The sun had come through and the day was going to be hot. Sunlight and mist lay on the distant peaks of the moor and it shimmered in a golden haze. He could go there again, with his freedom the ban was lifted, he could walk there, climb, go whenever he chose.

He went into the hardware shop on the opposite side of the square to the Kelsey Arms and bought rope. It was a self-service store and in the electrical section they had on a display of campers' flashlights. Stephen chose a big one with a handle like a jug, a tubular element and a battery guaranteed to last for several hours. Because they had large-size jute sacks on cheap offer he bought two with an idea they might come in useful.

The library next for a book on old mine workings. They had one, they said, but it wasn't in stock. Would he like to order it? Stephen decided against that. It probably wasn't necessary. He had been successful enough at getting into the Goughdale mine without a book when he was twelve, so why should he need one now?

Dadda, downstairs at Whalbys', chain-smoked his little cigarettes. With exquisite delicacy and fastidiousness he was replacing the beading on the doors of a glass-fronted cabinet he had just reglazed. He was currently on an emotional peak, at the zenith of his cheerful or manic phase, and he essayed wit, something he did on an average once a year. He looked at the coil of rope and his face split into a nutcracker grin.

'Happen they'd done away with hanging in this country.'

Stephen laughed heartily. He laughed the way one does at the jokes of a man who needs to make them but hardly ever can. 'Good Lord, Dadda, I'm not for the high jump this time, I'm glad to say. They've let me go without a stain on my character.'

'I should bloody think so.' Dadda dabbed on a flick of glue, pressed in another inch or two of carved rosewood. He looked up at Stephen. 'That aunt of yours has been round asking for you.' Dadda had never addressed or referred to his in-laws by their given names. 'That one, Mrs Pettitt, they call her,' as if they called her something to which she had no right. 'She wanted to tell you your grandma's been taken into Hilderbridge General with a stroke.' He paused reflectively, wiped a spot of glue from a finger. 'Old Mother Naulls,' he said, and savagely, 'the old bitch, the old bitch!'

That policeman had more or less called him a psychopath. His euphoria past, Stephen smarted when he remembered those insults. He would have liked to take action over that, legal action, and get a public

apology out of the man, but he had an idea that that
kind of thing was privileged. In an interrogation, inside a police station, they could say what they liked
to you and get away with it. How much more might
they have said, though, if they had known he had
once made a violent attack on his grandmother!

Her life was nearly over. He supposed they had
taken her into hospital to die. How old would she be
now? Eighty or thereabouts. She had always seemed
old to him, old as the hills even in those days when he
had badgered her about his mother.

'Why won't you tell me where she is?'

'Because I won't, that's why. She's got a family of
her own, she's got a boy and a girl, and she don't
want you upsetting them all. Now then!'

'But she's married to — ' He had almost said, 'married to *us.*'

'No, she's not. She's married to Mr Evans and she's
got Barnabas and Barbara.'

'I don't believe it!'

'Don't you call me a liar, young Stephen.'

He had been 'young' Stephen then, small Stephen
who didn't come much more than up to her shoulder.
A year later he had grown six inches, and in the following year . . .

'He'll be towering above me soon,' said Arthur
Naulls, 'towering above me.'

'You can tell me her address. I could write to her.'

'You'll not get it from me, Stephen, it wouldn't be
fair. You've got to let bygones be bygones.'

She turned her back on him. He had become in
that instant an animal, without the power to reason
or reflect, and she — what had she become? He had
never quite known and he didn't know now. The
quintessence of woman perhaps. But no, he loved the

97

women in his life, Lyn, the memory of his mother. The evil inherent in women, then, in some women. He saw only a womanly shape, though, and a bush of soft womanly hair, and then even that was lost in a hot dazzling blur as he leapt on her and seized her by the neck . . .

Stephen seldom thought about it now. Nothing like that had ever happened since. The police would have made something of it, though, with their cheap, untried psychology. The interrogation must have had some kind of shock effect on him, for even the sensation of relief didn't last long and for several nights he slept badly and dreamed badly, which was something he hardly ever did. Ann Morgan's mother came on television and appealed for clues to the identity of the Vangmoor killer. Someone must know him, someone must have noticed a man, friend, lodger, neighbour, behaving oddly. She begged that person, those people, to come forward. Stephen dreamed of her. He dreamed that he and she were in the avenue of the Foinmen and she was refusing to tell the police they had been together in the Kelsey Arms at the time of her daughter's murder. Stephen made a rush at her, seized her throat and was shaking her when Lyn woke him up and said he had been shouting and thrashing in his sleep.

To go out on the moor would have been the best remedy for this. He had his rope and his powerful torch and a packet of candles, and he had planned to attempt Apsley Sough at the weekend. But the long spell of dry weather broke and on Saturday it rained all day, the driving torrential rain of midsummer. Next day the foins were shrouded in a drizzle that was more than mist and less than rain.

Stephen wrote for 'Voice of Vangmoor': 'Now that

the summer is well and truly with us, several places of interest in the "Foinland" area have been opened to the public. The historic gardens of Jackley Manor may be viewed any Sunday from now until 30 September between 2 and 5 p.m., and in response to popular demand, Mr David Southworth is for the first time opening the gardens and some of the rooms at Chesney Hall on Saturdays, also from 2 till 5. Visitors will be able to see the study in which Tace wrote the famed *Chronicles of Bleakland* and also, I understand, one of the actual pens used . . .'

'And why isn't Cinderella hastening back to her hearth this evening?' said Nick.

'Stephen's gone to see his grandmother. He'll be late home.'

'I wish you'd said. We could have gone out somewhere. The way things are, we never do anything but this.'

Lyn sat up in bed. She started to laugh. 'I don't claim to know much about these things but I understood that was something men never never said.'

His face was serious. He took one of her hands and held it in both his. 'I dwell in the suburbs of your good pleasure, don't I?'

She looked at him inquiringly. 'It comes in *Julius Caesar*,' he said. 'Portia says it to her husband, I think, to Brutus. "Dwell I but in the suburbs of your good pleasure?" That's how you make me feel. I thought I was going to be more than that to you, Lyn, I thought we could be more to each other. Here's something else you probably thought men never never said. I don't see much point in casual affairs.'

Her heart was beating hard with fear and wonder.

She was a lifetime away from laughter now. 'But when your uncle gets better you'll go away. You'll go away anyway in August.'

'And that's all there is to it? I'll court more women and you'll couch with more men?'

It wasn't at all the answer she had expected. She didn't know what she had expected. 'I won't do that,' she said. 'I didn't before. I don't see much point in casual affairs either.'

He got up. He pulled on jeans and a shirt and went out into the kitchen where she heard him starting to make coffee. When he came back he sat on the bed beside her and lifted her up in his arms and held her against him. His words surprised her.

'You'd never go out on the moor alone, would you, Lyn? Promise me you never will.'

'I promise,' she said.

Without the knitter and the old man to be stimulus and audience, Stephen didn't know how to talk to his grandmother. She was in bed for the evening visitors to the Lady Clara Stillwood Ward, and she seemed more limp and structurally collapsed than at Sunningdale. The apoplexy had pulled her face down on one side, giving a quirk to the mouth. Her skin had blanched to the matt, rubbery whiteness of a fungus. She moved one of her hands and made an inarticulate sound when she saw him.

Stephen put the box of jellies down on the white coverlet beside her. One of Mrs Naull's hands was paralysed. Though he had never loved or even liked her, though he had come to hate and fear her, then feel a deep guilt towards her, it went to Stephen's heart to see that one sound hand fumbling ineffectually with the cellophane wrapping while the other lay useless, while his grandmother's face, or the mobile part of it, contorted with piteous frustration. He unwrapped the box, fed her an orange jelly and then a green one, wiped away the coloured trickle that came out of the corner of her mouth.

'How's Midge, Leonard?' said Mrs Naulls in a new, slurred voice.

'I'm Stephen.'

There seemed to be no more to say. He gave her a red jelly and she managed to eat it without dribbling. He thought of how he had held her throat and shaken her like an animal shakes its victim animal, desiring to break its neck. She had struggled and clawed at his hands to prise off the fingers and gasped out an address to him. His hands slackened and he gave a sort of sob and she said it again, choked it out, an address in Vancouver.

He was ready with his apologies, to go on his knees to her if necessary. Dadda's temper, Dadda's violence, that had raged in him, had burned itself out with a fizzle. She had got up with surly resentment, rubbing her neck, straightening her dress and her apron. The back door opened. Arthur Naulls was coming back from what he called his 'constitutional'. She began getting their tea without a word, she never mentioned it again, never told anyone.

More than half his life ago. He felt that he disliked her no less intensely now than he had done then, yet he came regularly to see her, more regularly than her own children, so that he had a reputation in the family of being 'good' to her. Why did he come? Why would he go on coming, to sit by her and feed her with sweets, until she died? Because she was his only link with his mother and that illustrious ancestry? Did he, even now, hope for revelations or some gratuitous gift? A long-passed-over message from Canada? A tale of Tace?

'Arthur's not been in once,' said Mrs Naulls.

Stephen didn't feel he could say her husband had been dead eight years. 'He's not been too well.' That in a way was true. But she had forgotten, it seemed, the man and the grievance, and was gazing vaguely at him, clouded blue eyes, mushroom-white cheeks. He kissed her, put another jelly in her mouth, patted her shoulder. As he went she lifted her hand in the way she had done when he came. Going down the stairs, he met his aunt Joan and his aunt Kay coming up, carrying lupins from the Pettitt garden and a bottle of Lucozade.

'Stephen's always been good to his grandma,' said Mrs Pettitt.

'There was a lot about you in the paper, Stephen,' said Mrs Bracebridge. 'It was nice you putting that in about Dad working for Mr Tace.'

She must have thought 'descendant' meant 'ancestor employed by' or some such thing. The elder Naullses were all more or less illiterate. Conversely, that reminded him. 'Does anyone ever hear from Peter?'

'Peter?'

'My cousin, Peter Naulls.'

'You'll have to ask your uncle Leonard about that,' said Mrs Pettitt. She spoke in the tone of one cautioning a former associate of the Prodigal Son. 'Nobody condescends to tell us, do they, Kay?'

They went on up, whispering together, tip-toeing. They were the kind of women who behaved in hospital as if they were in church. Stephen got into his car and drove home the long way round via Byss and Loomlade. The rain had stopped and it was warm and humid, the sky feathered all over with tiny golden clouds. The evening sunlight lay like a gilding over the distant reaches of the moor. Stephen, thinking of his grandmother, remembered those letters he had written while in his teens to Mrs Brenda Evans at Tobermory Park Road, Vancouver, and to which he had received no reply. His grandmother, probably, had given him a false address. What did it matter now? He was sure he no longer cared. He had put away childish things.

9

Chesney Hall was a mid-eighteenth-century house with a central portico equal to the whole height of the building. This portico had a double tier of Corinthian columns and windows set in massive dressings of ashlar between which nestled the blue plaque: *Alfred Osborn Tace, Novelist, lived here 1883–1949.* But the public were required to enter by a side door into a garden room from which, it seemed to Stephen, they were almost furtively huddled first to the study, then to the drawing room, lastly to the library, being carefully kept away from those regions private to the Southworth family. He began to wish he hadn't come, though he had felt that now at last the opportunity was offered to him it was impossible to stay away. He recalled stories he had read of dispossessed or unrecognized heirs returning to their ancestral homes as servants or in guises nearly as humble. That was how he felt.

Southworth was there but not, as he put it to the visitors who entered somewhat cautiously among the cane furniture and potted plants, himself doing the honours. This was the province of a guest in the house, a professor of English at an American university. Southworth could be heard telling the rector of St Michael's that this friend of his was a world authority on Alfred Osborn Tace. He was a big rangy bearded man in jeans and the kind of full flowing smock worn by nineteenth-century painters. When Stephen came into the study he was holding forth, the centre of a circle of visitors, most of whom had never heard of Tace until the Bleakland series came on television. His words, learned, scholarly, uttered in the harsh accent of the Middle West, issued from out of a luxuriant brownish-greyish-fairish mass; moustache, beard, hair all meeting and intermingling to leave only a few bare centimetres about the nose and between the eyes. The expressions of his listeners were bewildered as he led them on into the drawing room.

To move around like this with the herd Stephen felt an injury to himself as Tace's grandson. He resented the professor, his learning, his enthusiasm, his seeming indifference to his audience as individual people. Yet he was once or twice on the point of going up to the man, and if it were possible to interrupt his flow of talk, of declaring himself as Tace's descendant. But the professor, he was sure, would only ask which university he had been to, a question to which he was always sensitive.

Lyn walked about, admiring furnishings, pictures, first editions, but Stephen could only feel more and more aggrieved. It was especially humiliating to have

to take his turn in a queue before he could look at the
photographs in their silver frames, Tace with his parents, Tace up at Oxford, Tace with his wife. The drawing room was spacious, the ceiling high, the walls
panelled in white and apple green, and set about were
those chairs Dadda claimed Whalbys' had refurbished.
Over the marble fireplace was John's portrait of the
novelist, in a glass-fronted cabinet his favourite reading
matter, Gibbon, Fielding, Defoe.

It made Stephen's heart swell, it was almost painful,
to think that all this might have been his, that if the law
in the 1920s had been what it was today, very probably
would have been his. Only the other day he had read in
the *Echo* about a man who had died without making a
will, yet his illegitimate daughter, whose mother at the
time of her birth even had a husband living, had nevertheless been allowed to inherit all her father's property.

Thinking of this, he looked up from a rather bitter
scrutiny of Tace with Lady Ottoline Morrell photo-
graphed at Garsington, to meet the eyes of a member of
the *Echo*'s staff. Harriet Crozier was standing by the
grand piano, taking notes on a small pocket pad. She
was differently dressed today, wearing blue jeans and a
white blouse, but once more her hair was hidden, tied
up in the same blue, green and white patterned scarf.

'I'm trying to get some impressions for a sort of atmosphere story,' Harriet said. 'Something to tie in with the
TV series.' Pointing to the photograph of Mrs Tace, she
asked rather naïvely, 'Was that your grandmother?'

'Good Lord, no.' Stephen gave her a mysterious
smile. 'Mine is a bar sinister connection, I'm afraid.'
She obviously didn't understand. 'The wrong side of
the blanket,' he explained.

She looked confused. He would have said more but
for Mrs Newman and Joanne coming up to them. He

scarcely recognized Lyn's sister. The ballooning shape was the same, enveloped in a tent of flowered cotton, but a crop and short tight curls transformed Joanne's face.

'Kev said better safe than sorry.'

When she understood Harriet Crozier let out a nervous shriek of laughter. 'Maybe you should have it dyed black as well. D'you mind if I write a story about it? I mean about Three Towns girls cutting off their hair and dyeing it. I'm a reporter. It'd make a great story.'

Joanne was huffy at first but presently relented. They all went back to Tace Way. Lyn made tea while Harriet interviewed Joanne and got what she called 'quotes' from Mrs Newman.

'What about you?' she said to Lyn. 'Are you going to defy him and keep your hair long?'

Lyn said quietly, 'Are *you*?'

'I cover mine up. I don't go about looking like Alice in Wonderland.'

Although it was hours yet before it would be dark, although the sun was still high in the sky, Stephen walked with Harriet as far as the bus stop. The last of the visitors to the Hall had gone and the professor could be seen walking back towards the house from the road.

'He's just had a biography of your grandfather published. I expect you know all about that, though. *Muse of Fire, A Life of Alfred Osborn Tace* by Irving J. Schuyler.'

Stephen hadn't heard of it but he wasn't going to say so. 'I haven't read it yet.'

'They sent us a copy at the *Echo*.' Harriet gave another of her shrill nervous laughs. 'I don't know who they thought was going to review *that*. D'you want to read it? I'll drop it in to you sometime when we've done with it.'

For a moment he had thought she was going to ask him to review the book. She didn't and he was affronted.

He said distantly, 'I expect I shall get a copy sent to me.'

Was it his imagination that she seemed disappointed? It occurred to him that she liked him, liked him in a way he had never really 'liked' a member of the opposite sex. As Kevin or perhaps Ian Stringer might have put it, she 'fancied' him. He recoiled from her with a feeling that was part distaste and part fear.

The bus came before they had waited five minutes. He saw it bear her away with relief. It had been an unpleasant day, fraught with humiliation, with intensely irritating, troubled moments. But when he looked back over the past weeks it seemed to him that all his life recently had been like that, the even tenor of his way disturbed, even his marriage, once so smooth and serene, in some indefinable way changed. He could put a date to it, he could fix the point at which this change had begun. It was on the day in April that he had found the body of Marianne Price.

A white gauze of mist, that might have been heat haze or might later turn to rain, hung over Vangmoor next morning. Stephen had got up and come out very early before Lyn was awake. He wore a sweater, an anorak and carried his rucksack in which were the rope, the big new torch, two candles, a saucer and a box of matches. He had also brought with him two bread rolls filled with sliced Gouda cheese. Taking provisions with him onto the moor was something he liked to do, something he and Peter had done daily when they had been searching for Apsley Sough. Stephen sat down and ate his breakfast. He leaned against one of the upright stones, shaped rather like gravestones, of which there were several in the dale and which had once denoted the ownership of or title to a vein of lead ore. This one was engraved with a K for the Duke of Kelsey.

Between where he was and the shelf of rock that skirted Big Allen, a flat circle of stone paving like the rim of a round pond was embedded in the turf, was now indeed partly overgrown by the turf and heather, and in its grassy centre the dark-wooled sheep were grazing. Peter and he had often wondered what this circle was, had thought it ancient, as old perhaps as the Foinmen themselves. Stephen now knew that it was centuries younger than that, a crushing circle on the rim of which a horse had walked round and round, pulling the heavy stones that crushed the lead ore out of the lighter rock. He began to walk towards the foin, not exactly reluctantly, but feeling pinpricks of trepidation now that the time had come to enter the mine again.

Two derelict coes, mine buildings erected over climbing shafts and in which the miner had kept his tools, lay to the right of him. One of these was a ruin, no more than a heap of stones, but the other, though nearly roofless, still stood. Stephen had been inside the coes before to check how thoroughly the old shafts had been filled in and blocked. He dropped his rucksack on the ground inside the stone hut that was known as the George Crane Coe, and set off with the rope slung over one shoulder, the candles in his pockets, and carrying the torch.

This time he found the entrance to Apsley Sough without difficulty. He anchored the rope to the protruding lip of rock just as he and Peter had done seventeen years before. But this time he found himself to be less single-minded than he had been then. As far as he could remember, in those days he and Peter had thought of nothing but of getting into the mine, of nothing but the adventure ahead. Now he was hesitating, feeling the warmth of the sun on his face as it permeated the mist, even gazing across the dale to what he had sometimes written of as the finest view on Vangmoor, the prospect of Blathe Foin with Tower Foin rising stark behind it, gazing as if he might never see it again, as if the earth he proposed to enter might swallow him up for ever.

With the rope and his supply of light, though, he was quite safe. He knew that. It even seemed rather silly to have hidden his rucksack, for there was no one anywhere on the moor. He hadn't seen a soul since leaving Chesney, and then only the milkman and the boy who delivered the papers. The moor had been deserted since the second murder. Apart from man's vestiges, the remains of surface workings, it was as it must have been before man or the animals came, peaceful, bare and in the morning mist, mysteriously veiled.

He parted the bushes at the opening to the shaft and peered down. Dark, a stony, earthy smell, nothing to be seen. He took the rope in his hands and lowered himself down until his feet found a purchase in the footholes that had been cut haphazardly out of the rock wall. The shaft was about two feet six in diameter, a narrow slanting tube in the roots of the mountain.

He had gone down quite a distance before he switched the torch on. The gleam of light at the mouth became a remote spot, a point only, then, as the shaft bent slightly, disappeared altogether and Stephen was left in the dark. The torch supplied a splendid broad light, a clear radiance, though perhaps rather chill and sinister. He was surprised to find that now he was in the mine he wasn't at all afraid. He felt as excited as he had done when a child.

But one of the differences was that he was much taller, and the chamber into which the shaft led, which he remembered as eight feet high, he now saw was a good deal less than this, not much more than six, for he could only just stand upright in it. He held the torch aloft and surveyed the cavern, the 'rake' from which the vein had been stripped, leaving the bare, rough, dark limestone. Out of the chamber led the coffin level tunnel which he and Peter had followed until they met the bad air. Since then he had learnt that this kind of cutting was called 'coffin level profile' because the tunnel was tapered at the roof and sole so as just to admit the human form. The miners hadn't been as tall as he. In making his way along it, he had slightly to stoop.

After a while, though he had forgotten this, the tunnel or winze in which he was met another at an acute angle to it. He had come along one of the prongs of a fork and now continued, holding his torch up in front of him, along the winze that was that fork's handle. Inside the mine it was utterly silent. No doubt it had been so that other time, but the presence of Peter must have made it seem less so. Now he was aware of the most profound silence he had ever known. Outside on the moor, in the heart of the moor, it was quiet enough, but that silence was nothing to this. Out there the wind sighed or whistled, birds called, there was a constant, softly humming insect life, aircraft passed over. In here was the silence of the subterranean, that which is called the silence of the grave. It was not so much an absence of noise as a presence of total quiet. It was as if he had become stone deaf. He stood still for a moment, listening to the silence, living in a deafness where he could hear the thoughts turning and proceeding inside his head.

Down a passage to the left of him had been that wide

gallery whose farther end was blocked by a fall. He walked a little way into the passage. It was just the same, nothing had changed in those seventeen years, not even a particle of stone, a fragment of shale, or so it seemed to him, had been added to or had fallen from that barrier of rubble. So it would still be, all of it, in a thousand years. Though the civilized world might be destroyed and the surface of the earth distorted, though the moor became a desert, this labyrinth would remain unchanged, neither added to nor depleted, scarcely a grain of dust moved, a maze of silence.

It was not far from here that their candles had gone out. Stephen lit a candle and switched off the torch. He made his way along, holding the candle on the saucer. There was a tunnel here, a low-roofed winze, he and Peter hadn't been into. It fell away from the main artery at a slight but steady downward gradient, and after a while Stephen noticed that the pieces of shale which formed the floor were damp, were moist, were now lying in half an inch of water like pebbles over which an incoming tide creeps.

He held up the candle and looked ahead of him into a huge cavern. It was a hall in the mountain that surely must have occurred naturally, so lofty was its roof and so wide its walls. It had no floor. Or, rather, what floor it had was submerged under the lake of water, unruffled, motionless, black as pitch, that filled the cavern. Stephen switched on his torch again, and in the brighter light looked with awe at the still sheet of black water and the great vault above it. He couldn't remember that he had ever before seen standing water in which no vegetation of any kind grew. But here there was not even a wisp of green scum, not a shred of moss or thin, drifting leaf, only the gleaming water, black as flint. He must be looking, he thought, at that part of the workings he had sometimes heard referred to as the Bottomless Pit.

That meant he was in the George Crane Mine, a long way from Big Allen. Returning along the sloping passage, he relit his candle and turned left along the coffin level, but only for a few yards. The flame shrank, dwindled to a little jumping point of light, and went out. As a child he hadn't noticed the bad air. He did now. There was a curious smell, like mingled coal gas and sulphur. Perhaps the water, not for a hundred years now pumped out of the levels, was combining with some chemical to produce a gas.

He turned back the way he had come, putting the candle in his pocket and relying once more on the torch. Once again he stopped to listen to the silence, a silence which his footfalls disturbed, and as he stood he was aware suddenly that he was happy. The depression of the day before, the feeling that nothing had been right for him since the day he found Marianne Price's body, had faded away to be replaced by this deep, blissful contentment. He would have found it hard to say, even at the moment he began his descent, why he had wanted to go into the mines. For adventure? Just to see if it was the same? The answer should have been because he would be happy there, to find happiness. In the timeless, motionless subterranean silence he savoured his happiness. There came to him a curious idea that if somehow he could always stay down here he would never be unhappy or suffer or be humiliated again. The sigh he gave sounded as a roar in the silence.

He set off again, past the cavern where the rock had fallen, to where the tunnel forked. When he reached this point Stephen realized that he had no memory of which branch he had come up, the left one or the right. They looked exactly the same, winzes made in coffin level profile, narrow, with arched roofs and the sweeping marks of picks on their walls. One would lead him back to Apsley Sough and the dangling rope, the other into God knew what depths of Big Allen. And if he took the wrong one, would he realize in time to find his way back again?

At school he remembered being told the story of the labyrinth at Knossos and the Minotaur. Theseus in those passages had brought a ball of string and paid it out behind him. Stephen wished he had had the forethought to do the same, for, although there was no risk of his encountering a monster, half-man, half-bull, he had no idea which tunnel to take in order to find his way back.

Were he to lose himself and be unable to find the place where the rope was, no one would ever look for him here. He hadn't even left his rucksack by the sough which might have indicated where he was and where it was, but had deliberately hidden it under the George Crane Coe, a good quarter of a mile away. He was happy down here under the ground but he didn't want to die here. He didn't want to roam the maze of levels until he grew exhausted, his candles burnt down, his torch battery spent, and lie down here to die in the dark . . .

Moving the torch beam searchingly over the entrances to the two winzes and the tooling marks on their walls, he deliberated over which one to take, the left or the right. If he had had a coin he would have tossed it. He thought, if the matches are in my right-hand pocket I'll go to the right. His left hand, the free one, went into the pocket on that side and found there only the candle and the saucer. Stephen hesitated no longer but began to make his way down the tunnel on the right-hand side.

* * *

For a long way there was nothing to show him if he was going in the direction of Apsley Sough. The walls of the winze, because of the way they had been tooled three centuries before, had a corrugated appearance. So had the walls of the tunnel he had come along, so had all the coffin levels. He couldn't remember if the passage he had come along curved as much as this one seemed to, but that was the point, he couldn't remember. However, he could go back. Very soon the tunnel, if it was the right tunnel, should enter the wider, though scarcely higher, chamber through which he had come into the mine. And here it was now. Powerful as his torch was, it couldn't illuminate the passage for very far ahead, but now he could clearly see an ending of the tunnel and at the end a broader darkness.

Stephen had never felt very afraid. With so much means of light at his disposal, with a good sense of direction — though it had seemed to let him down a few moments before — it was absurd really to suppose he could get lost or be trapped in the mine. He came to the end of the tunnel, swung his torch up to eye level for a sight of the suspended rope, and saw that though he had come into a chamber it was the wrong chamber. This wasn't the cavern at the foot of Apsley Sough.

But it wasn't only this that fetched from him a gasp of astonishment. He had thought of the mine as bare, empty, unchanged, but this wasn't so. Someone had been there before him, had made of this smallish, vaulted room in the rock a — what? Bedroom? Hiding place? Sanctuary? Wonderingly he played the torch beam across the walls, the floor, into the room's furthest recesses. It was quite dry up here, without smell, the air fresh. At the far end of the chamber had been a fall, perhaps blocking exits. Between this and a great spur of limestone that jutted out from the wall, placed on the floor on a groundsheet, was an inflatable mattress, inflated, and on it a dark blue sleeping bag, zipped up and rolled. There were some clothes in a pile, a camouflage-pattern padded jacket, an aran sweater very much like one he had once owned himself, a pair of brown cord trousers and a pair in worn and dirty grey tweed. Set on an upturned wooden box were two candles, one hardly used, one a half-burnt stump, stuck in the necks of milk bottles.

These things were by no means all the chamber contained. Stephen, who had stood for some moments at the end of the passage simply staring in, now stepped across the sacks which provided a rough carpet and lit both the candles. They made an eerie flare, sending up enormous shadows of themselves on to the walls. He looked round him slowly and with wonder. Whoever lived here, camped here, had provided himself with food and drink. In a cardboard box that had once contained two dozen cans of loganberries were a packet of biscuits, two tins of corned beef, a jar of pickled onions and four cans of beer still linked together in their plastic sling. Stephen squatted down to examine it all. In another box he found a small kettle and a can opener, in a plastic carrier dried milk and teabags and pieces of cutlery.

There was one more item of furnishing in the chamber, on the farther side of the spur of rock and half concealed by it. This was another cardboard grocer's box, its lid of four flaps closed by folding the four separate pieces under and over each other. Stephen wondered if it contained pans for cooking or possibly more clothes. It intrigued him that the top of this box should have been so carefully closed while the others were left open. He lifted it but it felt very light.

There must have been strong currents of air in the chamber, for the candles constantly guttered and flared. Sometimes the light jumped and ran up to the roof. Stephen undid the flaps on the cardboard box. Inside, in a loose nest of pink tissue paper, was a mass of small, essentially feminine objects, a hairslide, an eyebrow pencil, a black and white plastic bracelet, a perfume phial, a crumpled handkerchief initialled A, a tissue with lipstick on it, a tasselled pencil. There came from these things a cashew-like, powdery scent, very strange down here under the earth.

Beneath the objects were more layers of pink paper, and under the paper lay two smooth hanks of shining hair, each a headful of hair cut off close to the scalp. One was a gleaming white-gold, the other of a darker corn colour, and each was carefully coiled in its bed like a sleeping snake.

10

So there was a Minotaur here, after all, a monster, half-man, half-animal, who inhabited this maze. The images of the candle flames and the arcs of light from them shuddered. It was as if someone had come into the chamber to move the air and the shadows. Stephen jumped, his heart racing, but there was no one there, there was nothing but the bed and the tins of food and the things in the box.

He looked at the two coils of hair. Cautiously he put out his hand and lightly touched them. Then he lifted out the paler blonde hair and held it in his hands. Was this Marianne Price's or Ann Morgan's? He had no way of knowing, just as he had no way of knowing which items in the pink tissue paper belonged to which girl except for the handkerchief with A on it. When, almost reluctantly, he had put the hair back and had closed the lid of the box again, he looked around the chamber for the knife or scissors which the man must have used, but he found nothing. It was going to be something to tell the police, all this, a gift of evidence as would rarely come their way. Stephen thought of Malm's face when he coolly informed him of what he had found and of the respect even Troth would have to accord him now.

Would the man know someone had been here? Stephen put the box back as nearly as he could remember into the position where it had been before. He switched on his torch and blew out the candles. Perhaps the man would notice a change in the height of the candles but there was nothing Stephen could do about that. In any case, it was unlikely that he came here every day or more than, say, twice a week. He didn't *live* here. It was just a camp, Stephen thought rather wistfully, a hidey-hole, an occasional refuge from the world.

He went back along the winze and took the other fork.

In a few moments it brought him to the place where the rope lay along the lower wall of the shaft. He clambered up, putting out the torch when the spot of light appeared ahead. The sun had come through and all the mist been dispersed while he was in the mine. The brilliant light blinded him and for a while he lay on the turf, shading his eyes with his hands until he became used to the sun. A sheep bleated at him as he fetched his rucksack out of the George Crane Coe. It seemed as if he had been half a day in the mine but when he looked at his watch he saw that no more than an hour had passed and it was still only ten. Dadda was coming to lunch as usual on a Sunday. He had better get back.

There wouldn't be time to go to the police before Dadda came. Once he had been to the police, he would certainly be with them all day, answering their questions, leading them down the shaft, conducting them along the winze to the secret chamber. He repeated those words 'secret chamber' under his breath, relishing them. Why hadn't he thought of making such a hiding place for himself? He envied the man for it. It would have been just the thing for him to have had such a sanctuary on the moor, *in* the moor. No rain could have kept him from it, no trippers have irritated him. He could have camped there, picnicked there, slept there, gone to ground in his own place like a fox.

It was too late. Someone else had thought of it first. He would go to the police when Dadda and the rest of them had gone, he would tell Malm or Manciple or whoever it was that he had gone down into the mine in the afternoon and then come straight to them. This discovery would probably lead the police quite quickly to the killer of the girls. There must be all kinds of clues among the clothes and food and equipment. It would be almost as good as being taken to the man's home. Stephen wondered where that home was. It was even possible that he knew the man. He and Lyn knew most people in the Three Towns either to speak to or by sight or had heard of them or knew their relatives. Of course he could be a newcomer, arrived in April just before the first death, but would a newcomer know about the mines? Perhaps, when the man had been arrested and the police had taken everything they wanted out of the mine, he, Stephen, could go quietly back and use the secret chamber for himself.

Whalbys' van was parked outside the house. Dadda had come early. While he washed and put on a clean shirt Stephen debated within himself whether to tell them about the mine and the secret chamber while they were having lunch. Or should he wait until they had all gone and then tell Lyn? He could hardly go to the police without first telling Lyn why he was going.

They sat down to roast lamb. Lyn always cooked a roast on Sundays. Both he and Dadda expected it. Stephen started to talk about the Vangmoor killer and the two dead girls as a preamble to what he had to tell them, but Dadda threw down his knife and fork and cried, 'That's no bloody talk for the dinner table!'

Afterwards he thought of whispering it to Lyn in the kitchen, but she was busy, running in and out. The Newmans came in the back door and then Joanne and Kevin with Trevor. Hesitantly, Stephen brought up the subject of lead mining to test how he would feel about talking of something that for years really, not just half a day, he had nursed secretly to himself.

'Don't talk to me about tunnels,' said Mrs Newman. 'I never could stand tunnels. When we've been in London when you girls were little I never would go in the underground, would I, Lyn? My mother was the same. She was staying with your auntie in Finchley and they got in the underground to go down to London, only it wasn't underground there if you take my meaning, that was the trouble. When they started and your auntie said it'd be underground in a minute, Mother pulled the communication cord.'

'It's a handle in tube trains,' said Joanne.

'Well, handle or whatever they call it. They stopped the train all right and Mother never did go underground but there was a real carry-on and she got fined. I don't know the ins and outs but she had to pay this fine. I hate tunnels myself.'

'Some like them,' said Trevor, 'and we all know what that means.'

'There's one here as doesn't, lad,' said Dadda, frowning grimly.

Trevor floundered then, talking about getting back to the womb and not much liking having to explain what he meant by such expressions as 'female principle' and 'a kind of opposite of the phallic' in the presence of Dadda and the Newmans. Stephen thought about going to the police and wondered if he should phone first and whether policemen of the rank of Malm or Hook were to be found on duty on a Sunday. And when everyone had gone and it was after seven, he felt it would be too late to go to the police that evening. By the time he had got there and explained to them and they had come back together and gone by car to the nearest point on the road to the mine workings, it would be starting to get dark. He would go tomorrow.

But the next morning it seemed altogether too late, his delay beyond explanation. And then he knew he wouldn't go at all, had perhaps never intended to go. The idea of telling the police became bizarre. How had he come ever to contemplate such a thing? Had he really intended to betray to men like Hook and Troth the location of the secret chamber?

At the moment, he was sure, only he and the killer of the girls were aware of the chamber's existence. It began to seem to him a precious secret which it would be something like treachery to betray, though treachery to whom he couldn't have said. And if he told the police or told anyone, even if he only told Lyn, he wouldn't be able to go there again. The mine would be closed to him for years, perhaps for ever. He imagined them, in the name of safety, shovelling concrete into the mouth of Apsley Sough, as in the past they had blocked up the openings under the coes and the old pony level down by Knamber Foin. That would be bound to happen if he told.

Stephen felt light and free once he had decided

against telling the police. What had they ever done for him that he should help them? Insulted him, called him a psychopath. When he went back to the mine he would go alone.

Lyn went into the bedroom and picked the dead shrew off the counterpane with a handful of tissues. Peach, who had accompanied her upstairs, walking beside her and chattering to her in little chirping mews to announce, perhaps, what awaited her, watched the removal of his tribute with arched back and raised tail.

'What d'you expect me to do with it?' Lyn said. 'Eat it?' She flushed the tiny velvety corpse down the lavatory. 'I should have thought a poor little mite like that would have been beneath your dignity.'

Peach stalked into Stephen's room and jumped up onto the table where the bust of Tace stood. Stephen didn't like Peach in his study. Lyn went to fetch him out but was distracted by the calendar, the *Echo*'s 'Moorland Views', the Hilder at Loomlade for the month of July. Calendars, dates, the passing of time, she had become obsessed with them. For the third or fourth time that day she counted up the number of days since 24 June. It was easier, but more unrelenting and uncompromising, to do it on a calendar. Ten days. She had made it nine this morning, doing it in her head, but it was ten. Unless, of course, she had made a mistake over 24 June and it really should have been 1 July. It wouldn't have been the first time she had made that kind of mistake, though in the past it had hardly mattered whether she made a mistake or not.

She picked Peach up. He was very soft and though his body was warm the rosy-gold fur felt cool and sleek to the touch. The rejected shrew forgotten, he began a sonorous purring. Lyn counted the days on the calendar again and made it either ten days or three, but she was sure it was ten. Her body felt unchanged, static, stilled in its rhythmic cycle and waiting. She went downstairs slowly, carrying the cat. It was a warm afternoon, the kind of sunny, cloudy, faintly breezy day that sometimes means a heatwave is coming, but Lyn tied her hair up in a scarf. She tucked in the wisps of hair that showed. There was a chicken and rice dish in the oven for Stephen and Lyn set the timer to start it cooking at five. She wouldn't leave him a note, she never did. Because of what had happened to him in his childhood, he didn't like notes left.

She walked along Tace Way and up the village street and across the green to wait outside St Michael's gates for the bus from Jackley. She thought of how it would be, coming back later in the dark, but Nick wouldn't let her come back in the dark, he would bring her in Bale's van. Out alone in Chesney she often felt a little afraid, even in broad daylight. She wondered sometimes if the man who had killed those two girls knew which girls had long blonde hair and which did not, if perhaps he had marked them out for a long time, so it made no difference whether you covered your hair or not. She wasn't quite alone now, though. In the churchyard the American professor in a broad-brimmed felt hat and blue jeans and Dr Scholl sandals was standing in front of the angel on Tace's grave. He came out into the road and raised his hat very courteously to Lyn and said good afternoon, though he didn't know her at all.

The bus came and she sat in the front. She was longing to see Nick, though she hadn't long to wait, had seen him that morning and the evening before. And yet sometimes, when she thought of Stephen, she wished she had never met him. All this was very like the way she felt about those ten days, dreading as if it were the end of the world that she might be going to have Nick's child, yet hoping it was true.

Next day the hot weather began. Every morning, very early, a mist hung over Vangmoor and then the sun came up into a sky without clouds, without even those shreds of cirrus that over the moorland nearly always flecked the expanse of blue. It was very hot in Goughdale and the Vale of Allen and each day was a little hotter than the last until there was a short break of coolness and cloud but not of rain before the heatwave came back with a renewed fierceness.

Stephen went out on to the moor every evening. Once he was sure he was going to keep the secret of the mine to himself, his feelings for the man who had found and furnished the underground chamber began to undergo a change. It was as if he had done the man a particular favour in not betraying him, and this seemed to bring them closer together. They were joined now in a common bond. Stephen no longer felt fear of the man, he no longer felt abhorrence. He even imagined their meeting and himself being invited into the chamber as a fit associate of its denizen.

When, after a week or so, he went back again he examined everything carefully to see if any changes might indicate a return during his own absence. The candles looked exactly as they had done after he had blown them out on that last visit. This time he had brought a ruler with him and he measured them, in centimetres to achieve greater accuracy. One was 18.5 centimetres long, the other only 6. The bed and bedding seemed unchanged. Nothing had been removed from the boxes or added to their contents and the pile of clothes was just as he had seen it before. The hair lay coiled and as if sleeping in its burial place.

That evening he remained for a long time on the slopes of Big Allen, crouched down among the heather, watching for someone to come. What exactly he would do when the figure appeared, climbed up the ledge and lowered itself into the mouth of the shaft, Stephen didn't know. And he need not have speculated, for no one came that night or the next, though he remained out on the hillside, waiting, until long after the sun had gone. He had to find his way home in the dark.

Perhaps it was due to the suspense of waiting or perhaps to sunburn, for he had been out in the dale since noon and his face and arms were fiery, that he fell into another of those fevers of his. He woke up in the night in a sweat that soaked his thin pyjamas and crying, 'The master of the moor! The master of the moor!'

There was no abatement of the heatwave. On a Wednesday afternoon, an early closing day, Lyn and Nick drove up on to Vangmoor for Nick to see it. He wanted to see the Foinmen and the Hilder and Bow Dale. They sat on the turf in the deep dark shade the standing stones made and looked over to Big Allen and down across Foinmen's Plain to the roofs of Hilderbridge glittering in the sun, and they saw that as far as they could see, as far as they had been able to see in all their drive and climb up here, they were the only people on the moor. A universal fear had brought them solitude.

'I haven't been up here for years,' Lyn said, 'and I expect it'll be years before I come again. There's something chills me about it even on a day like this.'

'It's beautiful.'

'So is that snake in your shop but I wouldn't want to live with it.'

'You don't like living here?'

'It's rather hard to answer that when I've never lived anywhere else.'

She turned on her side away from him. She was sure now. It was nearly three weeks. Tomorrow she would take her specimen into St Ebba's and have the test and then she would know for certain — but she knew for certain anyway. The child would be born in February, by which time Nick would have been gone six months. She hadn't told him about the baby and she thought it might be better not to tell him, not ever. She had a plan forming in her mind for Stephen and herself and the child.

Nick touched her shoulder and turned her face towards him. He kissed her lips. 'Your hands don't shake any more.'

'No.'

'I think you're the gentlest person I've ever known,' he said.

'I think you mean I'm a weak person.'

'No, not a bit. Gentle and strong. Lyn, we're going to change things, aren't we? We're not going to go on like this, never talking of your marriage, never talking about what we're going to do when next month comes. I have to go away next month. Lyn, look at me.'

She got up and began to walk away, holding out her hand to him. Even with Nick there she was afraid of the moor now. The silence and the emptiness seemed only to conceal an unseen watcher, the avenue of monoliths eyes that gazed at her hair. And when Nick caught her up and put his arm round her, she pressed herself close against him.

'You really do hate it here, don't you?' he said. 'You must never come up on the moor without me.'

'I live on the moor,' she said, and as she said that the sun seemed to go in. It was only momentary but it made her shiver. Someone walked over my grave, she thought, but she didn't say it aloud for fear of upsetting Nick.

Like the lead miners of old, Stephen was becoming used to moving swiftly through the narrow, low-roofed winzes. He was more practical and prudent too than he had been on previous visits, bringing with him a spare torch battery in case his failed. After the heat of the hillside, the intense, glowing heat of early evening, it was cool inside the mine and there was a smell of damp and of far-off stagnant water.

A feeling of sharp alertness took hold of him as he padded along the passage. It wasn't fear, though there was a breath of fear in it. It was the sensation of adrenalin entering the bloodstream. He was prepared to see a little dim light at the end of the tunnel ahead of him, the light from the two candles. And if he did, would he retreat as quietly as he could, reascend the shaft as quickly as he could? Or would he go on towards the candlelight to meet the man squatting there with his cans of food and drink and his secret hoard? Stephen felt himself tall and strong and physically powerful enough to resist the man in any circumstances. But he didn't think he would have to resist him, be forced in some way to struggle with him. This wasn't at all the idea he had of the shadowy relationship which already seemed to exist between them.

However, no light showed at the end of the winze. Stephen shone his torch slowly round the chamber. The bed was as it had been, as far as he could remember. The flak jacket and the two pairs of jeans were still in a heap on the floor, but were they exactly as they had been before? Certain it was that the aran had gone. He looked at the candles and there too there could be no mistake. He had no need to measure them. The small stub had gone and been replaced by a new candle, the other was burnt down to the length of his thumb.

The man had been back.

He had eaten some of the biscuits out of the packet, drunk one of the cans of beer and brought in half a dozen magazines, all Sunday supplements. Stephen had a sense of satisfaction. He was excited too but mainly he felt satisfaction. Here was proof that the chamber was *used* and wasn't just an abandoned lair deserted by the creature who had formerly gone to ground in it. He packed the food and the beer cans back into the box just as he had found them. And then a daring idea came to him. Why not show the man he had been here by leaving behind some clear indication of his visit? By substituting for the candles two new ones, for instance, or by placing on the wooden crate table some object from his pocket such as his penknife. He decided against it. The inhabitant of the cavern, however brave and intrepid, would be alarmed, would suspect a trap. His thoughts would turn at once to the police. It would be stupid to make the man think he was betrayed to the police when in fact he, Stephen, had actually gone out of his way to avoid betraying him. For the time being, at any rate, he would be discreet, he would show respect for the man's privacy.

But instead of leaving the chamber, he sat down on the mattress and gave himself up to enjoyment of the silence and the peace. He ate a biscuit, just one. He switched off the torch and lit his own candle, standing it in the saucer. It was a wonderfully relaxed and comfortable place to be in, and in spite of the possibility of the man's arriving at any time, a place which felt peculiarly safe and secure. Reclining there with his eyes closed, he asked himself how long it had been since he had felt as safe and, yes, as happy as this. More than twenty years. And when he had gone back along the winze and climbed the shaft he was surprised to find how long he had been in the mine, for the sun had set and dusk had come, though the sky was still a clear flame-pink, streaked at the horizon with long bars of black cirrus.

Goughdale had a sinister appearance at this hour, more so than the Foinmen about which there was always an air of sanctity. The heaps of stones, the skeleton of the windlass, the coe, black silhouettes in the silvery-grey dale, all seemed apt for concealing shadows and flitting forms. And there was such a stillness, an immobility as profound as the silence in the mine. Nothing moved. Even the sheep had been taken away to pasture elsewhere.

There would be no moon tonight, however clear the sky, no more than a sliver of crescent. Stephen thought he had better go home by the road and he set off to walk across the dale towards the east. The sky was deepening to purple and filling with stars. It was a nuisance Lyn being at home, waiting for him, when if he had been on his own he could have camped out here, night after night until the meeting point came. He was growing out of Lyn, growing beyond her and the domestic ties that kept him in a job and in a valley. He drew in deep breaths of the summer night air. Suppose he were to look back now and see a figure on the hillside, a figure that showed up in the twilight only because of the gleam of its white aran?

He did look back. Nothing stirred on the slope of Big Allen or in the dale. And when he had come among the gorse bushes in the vale and turned round for the last time it had grown too dark to see anything at all.

11

The headlights lit up the whole bedroom and made twin rivers of light run down the walls. For a while a diesel engine throbbed, then died away, though the lights remained. Lyn, who had been lying awake, thought at once of the police. She looked at her watch and saw it was a little after five, the dawn coming. The two murders and the fact that Stephen had been questioned made her think it might be the police.

She got up and went to the window. An ambulance was parked outside the Simpsons' house and as she watched her sister came out. She wasn't carried out, she walked, holding on to Kevin's arm, laughing with the driver. Her labour must have begun, Lyn thought, and she laid her hands gently over her own flat stomach in the thin nightdress.

Stephen slept. Lyn watched the ambulance turn

round in the horseshoe at the top of Tace Way, then move off towards the village and Hilderbridge. The sun was coming up now, spreading a flush across the milky blue sky, promising another day of heat. She lay down for another hour beside Stephen, thinking about Joanne, thinking about herself. In February, sometime about the middle of February, and perhaps also at dawn, it would be she the ambulance came for, she who walked out to it on her husband's arm. That part she couldn't imagine. When she saw herself holding a man's arm it was always Nick's arm she held. After a while she got up, went downstairs to make tea and was immediately very sick.

Stephen took the news about Joanne impassively.

'Talking of hospitals, darling, I think I'll just pop in and see my grandmother after work. I've got the poor old dear on my conscience.'

'Do you want me to come with you?' Lyn asked him.

He never did want her to, she didn't know why. 'Lord, no, what a drag for you and in all this heat. She wouldn't know you anyway, darling. She mixes us all up.'

'Just as you like.'

He wanted her to be there when *he* wanted her, not otherwise. He was capable of leaving her for hours on end, days, but she must be there waiting when he got back. She had to be his rock, his haven, his mother. These things she had never completely understood about Stephen until she had known Nick.

Perhaps it would change when they had a child in the house. Stephen ought to be a good father, to be good with a child, he was in many ways so much a child himself still. It was as if some part of him, when he was a boy, had stopped growing. But which part? Not his strong tall body. Not his active brain. Unless it was that curious undefined object that was mentioned in the Bible or you heard old people talk about, the soul.

The dark night had been closing in on Dadda, slowly but inexorably, for some days now. He had come to Tace Way for lunch on Sunday but he had brought no gifts, had eaten little, had folded himself into that chair in the corner, and so deep was his wretchedness that he hadn't even narrowed his eyes or shaken his head at the sight of Peach sitting with overflowing tail and hind paws on the chestnut leaf table. While the Newmans were there he hadn't spoken and he had left early.

Depression rarely prevented him from working. Work, if not a cure, if not even an alleviation, was still all he could do, the only possible occupation for him, while the blackest period of the black time lasted. But now he had become almost inactive. An oval walnut table was before him and the wadded lint dipped into the french polish, but his fingers could scarcely form the figures of eight on the prepared surface. Stephen came upon him seated immobile, the lint in his hand, his sombre eyes staring sightlessly, a Samson idle at the mill.

For days he would be like that. Then, suddenly, a fever for work, for making up for lost time, would overtake him, and with it an explosive temper to be vented on Stephen. Afterwards, presents, lavishly bestowed, to take away his guilt. At the moment he was too far gone, Stephen thought, to reproach him for all the days he had taken off lately. He knew better than to speak to him and went on upstairs to his upholstering which had rather mounted up during the past weeks.

It was cool in Whalbys' works, almost windowless and in a corner of the square where the sun scarcely penetrated. Dadda took himself off next door in the middle of the afternoon, and Stephen, who hadn't stopped for lunch, thought he might as well go too. There was visiting at Hilderbridge General from three till five. After that he would go up on the moor and wait in the dale until dark. He would conceal himself as he had been doing for several evenings past in the George Crane Coe and wait, even if he had to wait until midnight, for the denizen of the chamber to appear. The moon was now beyond it first quarter and would offer partial light.

Half Market Square was in shadow, half in sunlight. Passing from the shadow into the light was a daunting experience, so hot and powerful was the sun. It was a screen of hot metal, dropped with a clang, that must be wrenched aside, it was a scorching breath on the skin. Stephen couldn't remember such hot weather as this, such another August, unless it was when he was a child that first summer after his mother went and Rip came. There had been a heatwave then and another five years later when he was searching for Apsley Sough with Peter Naulls, but neither could have measured up to this one.

His car had been parked in the sun and the steering wheel was too hot to touch. He had to hold it with his handkerchief. He opened all the windows, looked at the very pale blue, white-hot sky. The drought had persisted for twenty days now and there were notices up telling people not to use hoses. Stephen drove along the High Street into North River Street and turned into the hospital car park.

It wasn't until he was climbing the stairs which led to the geriatric wards that he remembered the jellies. He had forgotten to buy them and the nearest shops were half a mile away. It couldn't be helped. There was just a chance one of her other visitors had brought her jellies since last he had, though it seemed unlikely, they never did.

The old women were all up. With lolling heads, with gnarled hands clutching shawls and blankets to them — for the heat was nothing to them, their skins and veins impenetrable — they were bundled into chairs so that movement might be maintained and bed sores prevented. All the windows were wide open, the flowered curtains drawn back, and the heat shimmered in the long room as if the hospital stood on the brink of an open furnace.

Stephen saw from the doorway that his grandmother already had two visitors. His aunt Joan and presumably some friend of his aunt Joan's. He wasn't entirely sorry to see them, for alone he never knew what to say, and there was also the matter of the forgotten jellies.

As soon as she saw him Mrs Pettitt jumped to her feet. She and her companion and Helena Naulls were all sitting in chairs on this side of Helena's bed but Mrs Pettitt alone was facing him. She jumped up and there came over her face a look of shock. It was rather a violent reaction to his unexpected arrival at four in the afternoon, but Stephen wasn't much interested in Naulls behaviour, or in any human behaviour, come to that. He said, 'Hello, Auntie Joan,' and went up to kiss his grandmother.

She wasn't one of those whose heads were lolling. There was far more life in her than when he had last seen her. She was leaning forward, both hands clasping the arms of the chair, and in her eyes, as he withdrew his face, he saw a gleam of malice so sharp that it made him step backwards. It was a gleam as cruel as any he had seen there in the old days at Chesney Lodge, and it was as if the senility which had brought to her a soften-

ing and a sweetening of the personality had in a flash
fallen away.

Before kissing her he had made some sort of apology
for forgetting her jellies and now he thought that what
he saw in that flat white face and small blue eyes was
only simple anger. But from behind him there came a
whispered, almost a whimpered, 'Oh, dear, oh, dear,'
from his aunt Joan, and he turned round. The other
woman, a plump woman in her late fifties with hair
dyed cornfield gold, was giggling the way schoolgirls
do, holding a handkerchief up to her mouth.

Until then Mrs Naulls had remained silent, though
eager in her silence, very nearly trembling as she clung
to the chair and slipped forward on to the extreme edge
of it. She seemed to be trying to speak, to be struggling
to get the words out, but now she succeeded and uttered in a high cracked voice, brittle with malevolence,
a typical Naulls phrase. For years, all his life, Stephen
had known Naullses to telephone — if they had tele-
phones — and ask you if you knew who this was, or to
show you letters and ask you to guess who they were
from. Now his grandmother said to him, 'I don't suppose you know who that is.'

The fat woman stopped laughing and covered her
mouth entirely with her hand. The explaining was left
to Mrs Pettitt who plunged into the middle of things.

'You were the last person we expected to walk in at
this hour, Stephen. You could have knocked me down
with a feather. I mean, I didn't even know they were
coming till I got this cable, and then here she was, *and*
Fred *and* Barbara. Well, of course she wanted to come
in and see your nan first thing what with them all going
off on this five-countries tour Saturday which is why
they're here at all. I mean, I don't want you to think

you'd have been kept in the dark, it's just that every-thing's been like such a rush . . .'

He didn't need her added, '. . . hasn't it, Brenda?' to know who it was. She was as fat as Helena had been before the processes of age had pared her down and shrivelled her. Now that she had moved her hand away he saw her face exactly like Helena's, only a painted Helena, shaded in various beiges and touched up with scarlet and black. She wore a tight shiny jacket and skirt in some fussy, damask, transatlantic material with a frilly braid trimming, and in the armpits were spreading dark stains of sweat.

He wanted to cry, 'I don't believe it!' but a robot voice spoke for him: 'Good Lord! Good Lord!'

There was a silence that seemed endlessly to endure. The curtains swayed in the faint hot breeze. Sweat broke out in little beads on Stephen's forehead and up-per lip and prickled his skin. Brenda Evans broke the si-lence.

'Long time no see.'

From the sigh she gave it seemed Joan Pettitt had been holding her breath. 'Now, then, would you have known him, Brenda?'

'He's grown a bit.'

Helena uttered a thin shriek of laughter. Having pulled herself as far forward on her chair as she could without sending it skittering from under her, she reared herself up on to her feet and stood there, swaying, chuckling softly. It was perhaps the first time she had stood unaided for a year. She looked radiantly happy, as if she had waited all her life for this, as if she had seen Naples and now had nothing left to see. She swayed, giggling, turning her head to look from one to the other of them. And then Stephen saw what he knew he would remember all his own life, the fearsome spectacle of someone suffering an apoplectic stroke.

Her laughter ceased on a retching sound and her face contorted in a spasm. It was as if she had been struck from behind with a massive but invisible hammer. Her hands flew up and she pitched forward on to the floor with a slithering crash.

Mrs Pettitt jumped up and screamed. Brenda Evans shouted, 'Oh, my! Oh, my!' and put her hand up over her mouth. A patient shouted and a nurse came running.

Stephen walked out of the ward like a man in a dream.

That evening, within an hour of each other, Chantal Tanya Simpson was born and Helena Beatrice Naulls died. Lyn was invited across the road to drink champagne with Kevin and her parents, but she didn't go. She had come home to find Stephen in a state of shock, scarcely able to speak, although Helena was still alive then. Joan Pettitt phoned with the news that she had died and Lyn broke it to him gently. It seemed neither to relieve him nor make him worse.

He sat beside her, holding her hand so tightly that the bones ached. She had never felt his need of her so strongly. It was as if he were drawing a current out of her, recharging himself from some source of comfort in herself. For a long while he didn't speak. Then he began talking about his grandmother, about how hard her life had been and how terrible the latter part of it, how awful her death. Lyn had never heard him talk about anyone like that before. She hadn't thought he cared much for old Mrs Naulls but had visited her out of duty and in the hope of finding out more about her relationship with his grandfather. This outpouring of love and pity was strange from Stephen. And uneasily Lyn began to feel that he wasn't really talking about his grandmother at all, but that it was someone else he meant when he talked about suffering and cruelty and neglect.

He knelt down on the floor and laid his head in her lap, clasping her body in his arms. He had hardly ever before touched her so closely and intimately. Lyn sighed. She put her hand on his head and stroked his hair. Nowadays, her body and perhaps her mind too in a constant process of change, she felt less able to be Stephen's support. It ought to have been a mutual thing, for she needed his support as well. The temptation to tell him about the baby and her idea of their future was suddenly very strong, the words were waiting on her breath. She suppressed them. Stephen had gone very white and his eyes were closed. She seemed to see Nick's face, eager and smiling, the antithesis of this life in death, and as she bent over Stephen, murmuring softly to him, the tears came into her eyes and ran down her face.

Great ceremonial attended Naulls funerals and expense was never spared. Naullses were so intent on being buried or burnt with dignity and display that some of them saved up all their lives for their own funerals. Arthur Naulls, from the age of fourteen when he became gardener's boy at Chesney Hall, had put aside a penny a week into some insurance scheme to this end, though when the time came, as his son Stanley had remarked with a sneer, it hadn't amounted to nearly enough.

For his widow there were to be four black Daimlers to follow the hearse. The clans would gather first at uncle Leonard's and partake later of a doleful banquet at the Bracebridges', and in between there would be the

139

old Prayer Book funeral service at Holy Trinity as well
as a service in the chapel at Byss Crematorium. Mother
couldn't have died at a better time of the year for flowers, said Mrs Pettitt in classic Naulls style.

Leonard Naulls, the only really prosperous one, lived
in west Hilderbridge in a district called Callowford. All
the other Naullses lived round about, but Leonard's
house was the biggest and in the smartest street. Stephen got there early. He brought a sheaf of red dahlias
and carnations with him and put them with the other
flowers in the hall. His aunt Midge kissed him and told
him how good it was of him to come, he had always
been good to his grandma, and then she went back upstairs to finish adjusting her black crimplene turban.
He had already seen his uncle Leonard walking slowly
round the garden with his sister Joan and his brother-
in-law Sidney Pettitt, showing them the flowerbeds.
Showing visitors the garden, even though they were
one's own siblings, even though they could see it daily
from their own windows, was a Naulls habit, indulged
in on solemn occasions. Stephen noticed that the photograph of his cousin Peter, which last time he had been
in this house had stood on the hall table, was gone. He
pushed open the door into the living room.

This room had french windows overlooking the lawn
and the meagre herbaceous borders. Standing in front
of them, her back to Stephen, looking out at the gloomy
strolling figures, was Brenda Evans. She was alone.
Her round plump form was swathed in clinging pleated
black and she had high-heeled black patent leather
shoes on, stockings with black seams, one of which was
very crooked. She hadn't yet put her hat on. A shiny
small black straw, probably bought specially for the oc-
casion, lay on the arm of the settee beside her. Her yel-

low hair was newly done, yellow, incurved, glossy, like a chrysanthemum.

She hadn't heard him come in. Stephen stood in the doorway, looking at a woman's back, a woman standing at a window. A great many things seemed to happen to him as he stood there. Impressions passed in clear bright pictures across the screen of his mind, a pile of coins at eye level on a table, his hands round an old woman's stringy throat, thin blue air mail letters dropping into the post box on Chesney Green, letters that would never be answered.

A hot dazzling blur fell over Stephen's sight, he was blinded to everything except that curvy shape, its outlines fuzzy now, the window behind it, and because of the bright light, the green of the lawn transposed to its opposite in the spectrum, blood-red. His hands went up, the fingers bent as if to claw. He was poised for the leap at her. She heard his breath drawn in and she turned round.

'Why, Stephen! How nice.'

He put up his hand to his forehead, felt on his fingertips the drops of sweat. There was a fierce drumming in his head. To explain the gesture, his robot voice said, 'Lord, isn't it *hot*?'

'Lovely,' said Brenda Evans. 'It just suits me. On our way back from Europe you and me must have a real cosy get-together. I'm dying to meet your wife. Linda, isn't it? But Stephen, believe me, there just hasn't been a minute what with Ma taking a notion to die like that. Though in one way it couldn't have been more convenient, with me on the spot and not having to be fetched over.' Whatever she had become, she was clearly still a Naulls. 'They didn't want to have the funeral till Monday but your uncle Stanley insisted. It has to be before my sister leaves for Paris, France, he said, so of course they gave way.'

The robot said, 'Well, have a jolly good holiday.'

'We deserve it. It's twenty-two years since Fred or me set foot outside of Canada. Now, dear, tell me how's your father?'

'He's fine. Fit as a fiddle. Still at the same old trade, you know.'

'And you're his right-hand man. I bet you've made yourself indispensable, eh?'

'I don't know about that.' Stephen began to laugh. He couldn't stop once he had begun and he rocked about on the sofa, sobbing with laughter, his chest aching with it, water running out of his eyes. He could see she was staring at him but he couldn't stop. At last he got up and ran out of the room, colliding with auntie Midge and the Bracebridges coming in. Both his hands and his handkerchief were over his face and they thought he was crying.

'Stephen was always very good to his nanna,' said Mrs Bracebridge.

Afterwards they understood he was too upset to stay for the lunch. Stephen had meant to go to work in the afternoon, and when he left the crematorium he drove back by way of the market square, he even slowed briefly as he passed Whalbys', but he didn't stop. While his mother was in the town he didn't want to face Dadda in case he too had heard of her arrival. Dadda's reaction was beyond his imaginings, he didn't want to try to think about it.

He changed his clothes and went out on to the moor, keeping as best he could to the shady places, the Vale of Allen and the eastern side of the hill. The air was heavy and humid, there had been no rain for twenty-four days, but although the sky was still a pale, dazzling blue, it was hung all round the horizon with white clouds mottled with indigo.

It was far too early for Rip to come. Surely he would never come in all this heat and light. Why had he called him that? It had been quite involuntary, calling the man, the girls' killer, the denizen of the cavern, by the name of his imaginary friend. Yet it was a good name, it had the right daredevil, ruthless, fearsome sound. Rip. When he had killed Ann Morgan it had been broad daylight, though, but the moor no doubt as deserted as it now was.

Stephen took shelter from the sun inside the George Crane Coe and lay down on the dry brittle grass. The peaty soil had turned to dust and ran away through his fingers like salt. A throb of thunder made itself felt, vibrating through his body like a tiny earthquake tremor. He lay on the ground inside the broken tower, waiting for Rip to come.

Someone had bought the grey parrot and the rabbits. Apart from themselves, there was no living thing left in the shop but the snake. They were closed, the blind on the door was down. Nick sat on the edge of the counter, Lyn on the drum of corn. He was looking at her intently and she wondered if he could possibly guess or tell. But no, he was a vet, not a doctor, and she a woman, not a dog. The thought made her smile a little.

'I love you, Lyn,' he said. 'I shall come back for you. I'll come every weekend until I can make you say you'll leave him and go with me.'

So he would, she thought, for a week or two or three. But two hundred miles away and with new things around him, he wouldn't go on coming. He would forget.

'I'm not leaving until Monday. When you change your mind I'll be waiting by the phone.'

'I shan't change my mind,' she said. 'Shall we go out for a last walk or a drink or something?'

'It won't be a last walk, we're not going to talk in terms of last things. Lyn, we've only just begun to know each other.'

She got up. Though she was as thin as ever, her body felt heavy with the child. They walked out of the shop into the sultry heat. As they passed the glass cases in the window an unpleasant thing happened. The snake, which scarcely ever moved, which had always when Lyn had seen it lain stretched out or coiled, suddenly reared up the forepart of its body, hissed and lashed its head at the glass. Its tongue flickered and Lyn drew back against Nick's arm with a shudder.

12

The heavy atmosphere, charged with the threat of the coming storm, was inside the house as well as outside. Lyn felt it as soon as she woke up. She looked at the white sky of low cloud and felt the weight of the air and remembered that the evening before she had parted for the last time from Nick. Stephen was still asleep beside her. He looked very young as he slept and there was a droop to the corners of his mouth.

It was already very hot, though the sun was only a white puddle of light in a mass of cloud. She got up and had a bath, made tea and took a cup to Stephen. He sat up and took it from her with a hearty 'Thanks awfully, darling,' but he was absent and preoccupied. He seemed miles away from her on some distant thought plane. She longed to throw herself on someone's compassion, tell them everything and ask for comfort. She had never been able to confide in her mother, Joanne was in hospital, only Stephen remained. Stephen was drinking his tea and looking out on to the moor, the scorched and shrivelled grass, the dull pale sky.

She left him and went downstairs. Peach came up to her and rubbed his head and soft golden shoulder against her leg. She picked him up and walked about with him in her arms. In six months she would have the baby, at least she would have that. Loneliness would pass when she had the baby. It was just that it was impossible to imagine the week ahead, all the weeks, without Nick. Peach purred in her arms. She set him down on the window sill, stared at the still, pale, brooding sky.

How many times, she wondered, had Stephen come to her for comfort? She thought of the last time, when his grandmother had died. Would he comfort her in the same way? Somehow she didn't think so, she had never asked him or tried. The idea of the plan she had made came back to her, that she had been going to present to Stephen in cold practical terms. She was afraid she would cry as soon as she began to speak. Yet she had to tell him. Suddenly she realized she had no idea at all how he would take it.

She heard him get up and move about upstairs. She put the kettle on and set things on the table for breakfast. A small wave of nausea came gently up through her chest when she looked at the butter, the cream curds on the milk. These days she never ate breakfast. The nausea passed and when Stephen came in she was sitting at the table, drinking tea.

It was on the tip of her tongue to tell him then, but still she held back. She had realized something, that for weeks, months perhaps, Stephen hadn't spoken to her at breakfast, hadn't had a real conversation with her at any time. Unhappiness or anxiety was making her acutely sensitive. The voice in which he announced to her that he would go into his study now to write his piece for the *Echo* sounded to her like the noises made by a talking machine.

She washed the dishes. Sometimes she leant against the sink and closed her eyes. She dropped a cup and it broke into three pieces and the handle with a crash as loud to her as an explosion. If she went to the door she could just hear the irregular tapping of Stephen's typewriter. She stood in the doorway listening to it, the few seconds of tapping, the pause, the tapping again. Rehearsing what she would say to him, she went upstairs and started to make the bed. The typewriter had been quiet for a long time but now it started again. She knew she would never say any of those cool decisive things. Her hands began to shake the way they did before she had known Nick.

All was silence from the study. She almost knocked on the door, but she told herself that was her *husband* in there, not to be a fool. He was sitting at the desk, looking at what he had just written, a handsome, dark, strongly built man. She thought she had never seen a better-looking man than Stephen. He turned on her those dark blue eyes that today had a curiously empty look.

'What is it, darling?'

'I've got something to tell you.'

'Can't it wait?'

She shook her head, she was at breaking point. It would have been better to have sat down but she remained standing and she put out her hand to him. Again she said, 'I've got something to tell you.'

'Well?'

'Stephen, I'm pregnant. I'm going to have a baby.'

She was breathless and the words came out jerkily. 'I'm going to have a baby in February. The man, the father, I did love him, I loved him very much, but I shan't see him again. It's over. You and I — we could never — you know what I mean, but the baby can be ours.'

He had flushed. When Stephen flushed his face became a dark brooding crimson.

'You'd like a baby, wouldn't you?' she said. 'You'd feel it was ours, and we do love — we are fond of each other, aren't we, Stephen?'

He answered her in the machine voice, the robot voice. 'You're having me on.'

'You know I wouldn't. It's all true. I'm sorry if it's been a shock.'

'A shock . . .' he repeated. He got up and went to the window and turned his back on her. 'You really said those things? I'm not dreaming?'

'Stephen . . .' She laid her hand on his arm, though so lightly that it just brushed the sleeve of his shirt.

He flung it off violently. He turned round. What she heard then was so frightening she could have screamed. She clenched her hands. He spoke in a tone she had never heard from him before. And another voice came to her out of the past, the voice of her brother, then six, shouting at their mother when she told her son and daughter that Joanne was about to be born. Stephen used the same words, precisely the same, and he uttered them with the child's shrill rage.

'If you bring a baby into this house I'll kill it!'

She didn't scream. She controlled herself, strangling her voice. 'Stephen, listen to me . . .'

'I'll kill it, d'you hear me?' His face was nearly black with blood and the high voice shook. 'I'll kill it, I'll cut it into pieces, I'll drown it, I'll trample it to death.'

She gave a gasp of pain. He raised his right hand and

caught her a ringing blow with all his force across the side of her face and head. Lyn staggered backwards and fell. She crashed on to the floor, knocking over in her fall the round polished table on which the bust of Tace stood.

She cried out at the shaft of pain in her back and side but her first thought was for the child. With a moan she pulled herself into the crouching position and clasped her arms round her body.

Stephen, kneeling on the floor, holding the head of Tace, examining the crack which had appeared in the papier-mâché cranium, made a low murmur of distress. Lyn shuddered. She got carefully to her feet, tensed to await the result of her fall, the feel of warm blood flowing down between her legs. But there was nothing, or there was nothing yet. Her heart pounded on a racing stumbling beat.

He was still on his knees, trying to bring the sides of the crack together, throwing back his head in despair when the brittle stuff parted farther and a piece split away. For a moment it seemed as if he had forgotten her. But now his eyes turned on her again and he cried in that same shrill and childish voice, 'You broke my statue!'

She looked at him in horror, her hands up to her face. Then she ran out and shut herself in her bedroom, locking the door.

The first flash of lightning of that day showed itself in the house in Tace Way as no more than the flicker a match makes when it is lighted and immediately blown out. And the sound of it, the thunder, came many seconds afterwards, thudding distantly. The storm was still a long way off. But it discoloured the sky as a dye discolours soapsuds, an inky flow seeping into the clouds.

For a long while Stephen stayed in his room, trying to mend the head of Tace. He thought about nothing but how he had to mend the crack and insert the broken piece before the breakage became worse and perhaps beyond repair. Ideally, Dadda was the man to call on here. Stephen did the best he could with the two kinds of glue he kept in his room, a simple gum and cement for use on various kinds of non-wood surfaces. Some of the papier-mâché at the edges of the crack had already crumpled and fallen away into a pulpy dust. When he had glued the pieces together, though not at all to his satisfaction, he placed the bust on a sheet of paper on his desk to dry in a shaft of weak, sultry sunshine.

He went out of the house and up onto the moor. It was too hot and too dry to bother with walking boots and he kept on his sandals. The air felt full of electricity. It was as if nature awaited the lighting of a fuse in order to explode. The Foinmen stood up pale and gleaming, silver monoliths, against a sky that now had a dark clotted aspect. Its pallor had darkened to a purplish-grey.

With his head bowed, Stephen walked up the avenue and laid himself down on the Altar. He lay with his face, his mouth, against the dry scented turf. The thunder rolled and he heard it as if it were from boulders trundled under the earth.

There was a continuous thunder in his head also, and he thought it was because he had struck Lyn, yet done no more than strike her. Remembering the child that was inside her, the child which he saw as already six years old, strong and happy, waiting in there until the time came to escape and triumph, made him beat with his fists on the limestone slab.

Presently he sank down on his face again with the calmness of despair, his mouth pressed against the warm hairy skin of the moor. There was some comfort in that, some solace in the scent that came off the grass, the warm earth. He would have liked to lie there for ever in the warm closeness, never to go back. An urge to be always alone now overcame him, to be a recluse as Dadda was, cut off by a purposeful act of will from the torturers of the world. He longed to find the house empty when he got back, his life cleansed of her as it now was of Helena and Brenda. Never to see her again was a hope he felt physically hungry for.

The ponderous, electric-charged air seemed to grow steadily more weighty. The moor was holding its breath for the rain to come. And all around now the thunder made an irregular drumbeat on the perimeter of the moor. But Stephen continued to lie there, listening to that other, lighter but steadier, drumming inside the confines of his head. The moor was like a vast warm bed, the atmosphere a blanket. He was aware of the first drop of rain as a splash on his extended left hand.

But no downpour followed. A few more splashes fell, haphazard silver ampoules, and then it was dry again. Stephen laid his head on his folded arms and longed for sleep, but sleep wouldn't come, though he lay there for a long time, hearing the double throbbing, his own and nature's, until a crash of thunder, as loud and sharp as a series of rifle shots, burst over his head. Almost immediately it was followed by a tree of forked lightning bursting into branches against the black clouds behind Big Allen, then by another crash of thunder. It had grown dark while he lay there, as dark as twilight. He looked at his watch and saw that he had been out on the moor for three hours but it was still only 2.30 in the afternoon.

He was reluctant to go home, more reluctant than he had ever been. Suppose she were still there, to come and cling to him . . . Like those druids of old or whoever they were that had placed the Foinmen here, he found himself murmuring a prayer to the Giant that she would be gone. A splash of rain struck the great monolith and trickled down the stone. Even then he would have stayed, but for the lightning. Five years before in a storm on the moor a shepherd had been struck by lightning out in the broad expanse of Bow Dale.

The lightning was springing in flares now over the Vale of Allen. Stephen began to walk away with slow dragging steps towards the crinkle-crankle path. He was halfway down Chesney Fell when the rain began in earnest. It was as if the thunder had finally shot open the sky and released a deluge. There was nothing he could do but walk on down, hurrying now, and let the million bright rods of rain soak through his shirt and his jeans and pour down his skin. His hair streamed forward over his face and he combed it back with dripping fingers. He saw the lightning strike a rearing boulder ahead of him, strike it with a vivid flash and a crack like a bullet, and the stone seemed to shiver under the onslaught. The storm was directly over his head, a battle raging in the sky.

Down on the road he felt safer. He knew better than to take shelter under a tree, it was too late anyway to take shelter now. There was no one about, the village was deserted. The rain came down in a steady crashing cascade and in Tace Way people had put lights on inside their houses as if it were evening. The gutters streamed with gurgling rivers. There were no lights on in his own house and he took heart and hurried this last lap, past his car, down the sideway to the back door.

It wasn't quite closed. A corner of the doormat was turned up and caught between the frame and the door, preventing it from closing. His heart ran into a fast irregular beat. He kicked off his sandals and pushed open the door and went in, padding across the kitchen floor to the open doorway into the living room.

He stopped. In the false dusk he could see Lyn standing close up against the front window, her back to him, looking out at the darkness and the rain. Her fair hair, long and hanging loose and covering half her back, had a higher burnish in the weak light than in strong. It gleamed like spun metal. She hadn't heard him come in. His body galvanized, tensing as a runner's does at the starting line. He saw the window and the womanly shape against it and the woman's hair, and then the shape blurred, its outlines becoming fuzzy, miragelike. He shuddered once. A dazzlement half-blinded him and fused the past and the recent past and the present, and he took a running bound, barefooted across the room, seized Lyn by the throat, grasped her neck till his nails met round it, and dug in his fingers.

She began a choking cry his hands immediately stifled. She fell forward, first into a kind of dreadful curtsey, then to her knees, then prone, face downwards to the floor. He was pulled with her, his hands anchored to the thin stalk of her neck, until he lay upon her body as he had never done in life. He lay and held on. It seemed to him, so locked were his hands and so enduring the clutch, that when he took them away her head must come away with them. And when at last he did release his grip, his fingers were swollen and his palms marked with weals as hands are that have carried heavy baggage.

Stephen, huddled in his sodden clothes, rolled over on to his face and fell at once into a deep sleep.

13

The storm was over and rain was falling silently. The cat awakened Stephen. He awoke when Peach rubbed himself against his outflung hand. His sleep, he saw from his watch, had lasted an hour and a half and had restored him to a thinking aware being without deluding him as to what he had done. Tentatively, not looking, he reached out one finger and touched one of Lyn's fingers. It was cold.

Peach sat on the carpet between the living and the dead, washing his face. Stephen got up and went into the kitchen. The back door had been open all the time, had now blown wider open. Anyone could have come in. That made him understand what the future might hold. He filled a glass with water and drank it. He locked the back door. Then he went upstairs and took off his cold, damp and wrinkled clothes, put on a clean pair of jeans and a clean shirt, went into his study and fetched one of the cheap-offer sacks he had bought when he bought the rope and the torch. The glue on Tace's head hadn't held, and he sat there on the desk, contemplating the moor, with a hole in his skull like a shrapnel wound.

He took the sack downstairs. From the top of the bookcase Peach watched him with placid, light-filled, yellow eyes, his pendent tail swaying gently. Stephen couldn't stand that. He shut the cat in the kitchen and, keeping his eyes averted — for this time he wasn't attracted by the sight of the dead as he had been by Marianne Price — he bundled the body into the sack and fastened the top with the hemp strings attached to it.

It was five o'clock but much less dark. Lights no longer showed in any of the houses on the other side of the street. As he watched, Kevin's car came splashing down Tace Way and turned into the driveway opposite. Kevin got out from the driver's side, Mrs Newman from the other, and with coats pulled up over their heads they plunged to their front doors. Joanne and the baby hadn't yet been brought home, Stephen noted. If they had it would have been difficult, almost impossible, for him to have explained Lyn's absence.

He lifted the sack in his arms and laid it between the settee and the wall, pushing the settee back against it so that it was entirely concealed. There, for a while, it could stay while he thought what to do. The attack, the murder, had broken nothing in the room but Lyn herself, had left no signs of what had happened but an overturned stool and a displaced cushion. He picked up the stool and put the cushion back, repeating the word 'murder' to himself. Although he could scarcely quite believe it yet, he had done murder, he had done what Rip had done and they were equal. He reached behind the settee and felt through the sacking the shape and firmness of the body in order to convince himself. It was true, he must believe, he had done murder.

And having done what Rip did, why shouldn't he dispose of his victim as Rip did of his, by laying the body on some chosen spot on the moor? Why shouldn't it be the third in the slowly progressive series of murdered girls, long-haired, blonde and young?

Even though this time it was his own wife who was dead, there could be no question of the police suspecting him. This time there would be no interrogation in a little stuffy room. Hadn't Manciple told him he was exonerated from suspicion because his blood subgrouping wasn't that of the killer of Marianne Price and Ann Morgan?

Stephen sat down on the green velvet cushions under which Lyn's body lay and began to think what he would do. His car was on the driveway with its bonnet pointing towards the road. Before putting the sack in under the hatchback it would probably be safer to wait until dark. Marianne Price had lain among the Foinmen, Ann Morgan in the powder house of the Duke of Kelsey's Mine. This time should it be the George Crane Coe perhaps or Knamber Hole? It might be risky to attempt to carry a body across the broad and exposed Goughdale, and on a dark, wet, moonless night impossible.

A sudden knocking on the back door made him jump. He looked quickly round the room to check that all was well. The cat slipped past him as he went into the kitchen. Through the frosted glass he could make out the shape of Mrs Newman. Suppose he hadn't locked that door and the body had still lain where he left it while he slept!

His mother-in-law came in, untying a plastic rainhat, tipping her umbrella into the sink.

'I don't know when I've seen rain like it. And all that lightning! My auntie was a one for storms, she used to cover up all the mirrors. In the war they had one of those Morrison shelters, Morrison or Anderson, whatever they call them, and after the war was over my auntie said to her husband they'd keep it so as she could get in it in a storm. Where's Lyn?'

'Well, actually, she went charging off into Hilderbridge before it all started and I expect she thought it was too jolly wet to try and get back.'

'Why ever didn't she take the car?' Mrs Newman asked, but she didn't pursue it. 'I just popped over to say we won't come in tomorrow, Stephen. Joanne's being fetched home in the morning with Chantal, but Kevin says you and Lyn come over in the evening and I'm to say they'd love to see you. You haven't seen my little grandbaby yet, have you?'

Stephen said eagerly but without preparatory thought, 'Good Lord, I'm terribly sorry but we're going out tomorrow night.'

Well might Mrs Newman look astonished. When had they ever gone out together on a Sunday night or on any other night, come to that? He said hastily, 'To be perfectly honest with you, my uncle Stanley asked us after the funeral yesterday and in the circumstances I couldn't say no.'

He didn't much like the way she still looked mystified but there was nothing he could do about it. A fresh and very useful idea came to him. He waited impatiently while she said that some other time would have to do and began listing, actually ticking off on her fingers, all the possible times in the forthcoming week that he and the infant Chantal might be introduced to each other.

'I think I'll take the car,' he said when she paused for breath. 'I'll go down into town and see if I can't pick Lyn up. Unless I'm very much mistaken she'll be sitting in the bus shelter in North River Street, waiting for the six fifteen.' It was wonderful the way inspiration came to him when most he needed it. 'I'll do that,' he said, 'and at the same time I'll take a piece of sculpture that got broken round to my father's.' Mrs Newman wasn't surprised by anyone's listing his future, petty intentions, it was the way she talked herself. 'If anyone can repair it my father can,' said Stephen.

The rain continued to fall but it was no longer torrential. When Mrs Newman had gone he locked the back door after her, rolled out the settee and pulled the sack out from behind it. He found he could carry the sack quite easily. Lyn had weighed a few pounds less than a hundredweight.

A light came on in the Newmans' living room. They would watch him get into the car. He carried the sack out, holding it upright, the head upwards. Once, outside Byss Town Hall, he had seen a statue carried out, wrapped in sacking like that, to a waiting van. He lifted up the hatchback and laid the sack gently on the floor of the car. When he had locked the hatchback he went back into the house for the kitchen scissors and his small torch.

The rain and the heavy clouds were maintaining a permanent twilight, but it would be a long time before it was dark enough to carry a body out on to the moor without being seen. As he drove away Stephen realized he would have to stay out and stay with the car for at least four hours. He drove north out of Chesney in the direction of Jackley. The car was going to be a liability, he would have been better without the car, yet without it how could he ever have got the body out of the house?

It was a little after six now and something like nine hours since he had had anything to eat. He hadn't felt hungry but now he did. Only it was impossible to use up some of the time by eating a meal because it was unthinkable to leave the car. He went into the last garage on the road outside Jackley and bought five pounds' worth of petrol and then he turned back and drove towards Pertsey, parking the car in the shadow of Tower Foin.

Time passed very slowly. He hadn't even brought anything to read. The rain enclosed him in a dome of reeded glass. Sometimes other cars passed along the road, splashing through the pools of water, their lights gleaming palely like dull reptilian eyes. At seven he moved off again, not because he had an idea of where to go but because the water was rising up the car's wheels. With his particular cargo, it felt safer to be on the move. There was no water lying in the newly paved Jackley municipal car park, so he sat there for a further half-hour. Gradually the rain was slackening. It had become a misty drizzle, hanging in swathes of grey over the moor. Stephen drove down the Hilderbridge road, concentrating now on where to put the body when dark came.

It was a question of how to avoid the car being seen while he positioned the body the way Rip would have done and in the sort of place Rip would have chosen. If he took the car into the bridlepath in the Vale of Allen it would be seen by anyone passing along this main road. Besides, the path would have become a quagmire. He might hide the car in one of the lanes around Loomlade, but how to carry the body away from there without risking being seen? There seemed nothing for it but to attempt the Banks of Knamber with its cover of birch trees. At the crossroads he turned left into the

Thirlton road, but without even leaving the car he could see that this plan was impossible. The banks themselves, a thousand little round hillocks they said had once been burial mounds, were dry enough but the valleys between them lay under water — a thousand little hills with a thousand little lakes between.

Wherever he left the car tonight it was going to have to be on a metalled road. He drove through Thirlton and took the moorland road that ran through Bow Dale and under the lea of Knamber Foin. The road wasn't much frequented but it was in use and it would be too much to hope that no other vehicles would pass along it that evening. But Stephen had remembered a possible place to hide the car which would be safer than any bridlepath or copse.

Apart from the workings in Goughdale, the only other mine on Vangmoor, Stoney Bow Mine, had been here in Bow Dale to the east of the foin. No surface evidence remained except for the portal of the incline level which had been used to allow the access of horses and was known to local people as the 'old pony level'. The road passed over the top of it, its pediment of three stone blocks, engraved with the date 1819, forming a short length of low wall along the roadside.

Stephen got out of the car, which he had parked on the 'bridge' over the portal, and clambered down the slope. It was so high up here that most of the water had flowed away, not into the level, which was blocked some ten feet inside the tunnel by a concrete barrier, but down the drainage sough that fell away into the dale. The ground was wet but not waterlogged. He saw at once, though, that he couldn't bring the car down here without leaving the grossest evidence of tyre marks imprinted in the mud.

No other cars had passed. He had kept one eye on the

road all the time he had been down there. Now as he climbed out again he surveyed the whole length of empty road winding away on either side of the 'bridge', the thin twisty white road like a piece of string that contorts itself as it falls. There were no cars in sight and not a figure. It would be a long while yet before dark, but what difference would darkness make if there was no one to see? He couldn't put the car into the old pony level but what was to stop him putting the body there?

Only the risk of a car passing and the driver seeing his car there and later on remembering. The portal under the road was exactly the sort of place Rip himself would have selected if he instead of Stephen had committed this third murder. The Foinmen, the powder house, the old pony level, they seemed a logical, a balanced, sequence. But if a car came by? He could do it in a moment. He could see so far from where he stood, he could see if a car was coming five minutes off. There was nothing in either direction, only the low-hanging cloud, the drawn-out dusk in which the white string of road, curling and twisting more on the left than on the right, glimmered with a greater clarity than in sunshine. He could see if a car was coming five minutes off but he could do the deed in less time than that.

He was nervous, though, lifting up the hatch and lugging out the sack. The road was still empty. He walked on the grass, on the bent-over tussocks of long grass, to avoid leaving footprints, but he plunged down the slope for all that, taking long strides, holding the body in the sack slung over his shoulder, and when he was a few feet out from the stone-coped arch, he threw it with all his strength into the tunnel opening. There was no time now to take it out of the sack or perform that other task which must be done. He scrambled up the bank, expecting all the time to see the car he had missed, the car that had been hiding round a bend in the white road, the car that had been one minute and not more than five off, hurtle over the 'bridge' ahead of him.

But there was nothing. The road was still empty and the gleam on it was fading as the dusk deepened. He encountered his first car ten minutes later as he was driving into Thirlton, and the owner of it who was talking to the person in the passenger seat hadn't particularly noticed him, he was sure of that. There was some sort of meeting or social event going on in Thirlton village hall. Its car park was crowded with cars and so was the road outside it. Stephen left his among them and set off to walk the four or five miles back to the old pony level, keeping to the moorland paths and avoiding the road.

It was the region of Vangmoor least familiar to him. But he took the long, low, rubble-crowned crest of Knamber Foin as his landmark. There was no moon, but no matter how dense the sky and how dark it grew, the irregular, tumbled shape of the foin never quite became invisible, but was always a deeper blackness against the dark. And as deep a silence prevailed. For all that distance he saw only two cars, saw them by their lights that threw up arcs into the indigo air.

When he reached the portal to the pony level, coming up to it from below out of Bow Dale, he put on his torch. It gave a poor thin light. He had grown used to the other one and had forgotten how inadequate the small one was. But he didn't need much light, not really. The scissors were in his other pocket.

He knelt down on the shale splinters, the small flat stones, that formed the floor of the tunnel, untied the mouth of the sack and pulled the sack down off the body. It lay face-downwards, the hair which cloaked it colourless and dully lustrous in the weak little beam of light.

A car passed over the 'bridge'. Stephen froze. He switched off the torch and knelt there in the pitch darkness. But the car wasn't going to stop or even slacken speed. When Stephen thought about the geography of the place, the way the road passed right over where he was as a road might over a railway tunnel, he knew he or his little spot of light couldn't possibly have been seen. For all that, it was unnerving.

After a little while he put on the torch again. He took the scissors out of his pocket and clipped off all the hair close to the scalp. Another car passed along the road above his head and he felt the roof of the tunnel rumble. He twisted the single thick hank of hair into a skein, laid it in the bottom of the sack and rolled the sack up around it.

14

The morning was dull and grey, the air still. Before leaving the house Stephen phoned Dadda, intending to tell him not to come for lunch as Lyn wasn't well. But Dadda himself had entered that phase of his depression which was a kind of dark night of the soul. He picked up the phone but he didn't speak. Stephen only knew the phone had been answered because the ringing stopped. Then he heard breathing and catches of breath.

'Dadda? Stephen.'

The voice when it came sounded infinitely remote and small. 'You needn't expect me, I shan't be coming.'

'Right. Well, you know best, Dadda.'

'Aye. I know I'd be bloody better off dead.'

Peach was sitting on the kitchen counter, staring at the fridge. Stephen remembered he hadn't fed him the night before. He opened a can of cat food and Peach, though never quite abandoning a calm stateliness, fell upon it. The cat would have to go, Stephen thought. The kindest thing would be to have it destroyed, better than finding it yet another home. He'd see about it to-morrow.

He took the hair out of the sack and put it into the pocket of his zipper jacket. Then it occurred to him that if by some mischance the house and his clothes were to be searched, it would look bad for him to have a stray blonde hair found inside his jacket pocket. He wrapped the hair in a length of plastic clinging film and put it in his rucksack with the sack, the rope and the torch. Kevin was getting his car out to go down to St Ebba's and fetch Joanne and the baby home. Stephen waited until he had gone and then he too left Tace Way.

The moor, as if its thirst had been quenched, lay calm and sleepy under the low, still mass of cloud. The roads were dry now and the surface of the moor appeared so, except that sometimes where Stephen trod a puddle of water would well up around his boot. He met a fisherman coming away from the Hilder with his tackle and an umbrella. Along the Reeve's Way two boys were walking with an Alsatian. People were easing their way back onto Vangmoor, but today or to-morrow when Lyn's body was found it would be cleared again and this time surely for good. That would be the final scouring that must make it over exclusively to Rip and himself.

Big Allen was veiled in whitish cloud like a sheet of frayed net that hung part of the way down its slopes. In the dale the stillness was such as to make Stephen feel that the whole bleak landscape with its ruined coes, paved circle and skeletal windlass was waiting with held breath for something to happen. For drama, for tragedy, for some violent act. A gust of wind would have blown away that impression in a moment, but there was no wind and the air hung with suspended moisture.

By now he thought he could have descended Apsley Sough without the rope but he used it for safety's sake. It was cold in the shaft and the walls felt clammy. When he reached the bottom he made his way not directly to Rip's Cavern but along the winze that must lead under the George Crane Coe. It seemed to him that, since the rain of the night before, there was more water underfoot than formerly, so that the feeling he had had of walking on the seashore was heightened. The shale lay in at least an inch of water, and as he came towards the place where the subterranean lake was, water was trickling steadily down the walls of the passage.

But he didn't go to look again at the lake. He went into the chamber where egress had been blocked by a fall and there, under the heap of fallen rubble, he buried the sack. He found he was breathing rather shortly and rapidly and when he tried to light one of the candles the pinpoint flame guttered and went out. Something in the atmosphere, something no doubt brought about by the rain, was depleting the oxygen in the mine.

The air was pure enough back the way he had come. This time the candle flame burned steadily. At the fork he took the right-hand winze and here the only sign that the atmosphere above ground and the weather had changed was a strengthening of the metallic smell, the smell perhaps of vestiges of lead. Stephen paused on the threshold of Rip's Cavern, moving the candle in a slow surveying circle.

What he saw made him blow it out and shine his

torch. There were new candles in the bottles and a third candle in a brass candlestick. An unopened bottle of cider stood there also and a tankard, and between them was a box of Swan Vestas with a spent match on top of it. But what most excited Stephen, almost making him gasp aloud, was that the sleeping bag on the mattress lay half unzipped and on the pillow in a worn white cotton pillowslip was the impress of where a head had rested. Rip had passed the previous night here.

Stephen went farther into the chamber. The biscuits and the corned beef had been eaten, all the beer had been drunk. Never before had Stephen been so conscious of the recent presence of Rip in the chamber. It was as if he had left only minutes before he arrived, perhaps even while he was at the other end of the mine, burying the sack, or that they had passed each other, ghostlike, unhearing, unperceiving, one taking the passage out to the sough, the other padding along the winze to the newly vacated chamber. Stephen trembled with excitement. He had to sit on the floor, on the carpet of sacks, and breathe deeply to calm himself.

After a little while he undid the flaps on the top of the secret box. It occurred to him that he should have brought some small possession of Lyn's, a hair fastener or a brooch or even that cairngorm ring Dadda had given her, to put with the mementoes of Marianne Price and Ann Morgan. The most important thing, though, he had remembered. Carefully he unwrapped the long smooth skein of hair. In colour it came somewhere between the shades of the other two, being darker than the dazzling white-blonde Stephen liked to think of as Marianne's and fairer than Ann Morgan's deep corn gold. He put the hair he had brought beside the others and tried to imagine Rip's feelings when next he opened the box and saw it for himself. Astonishment, wonder, amusement — it might even make him laugh. Somehow Stephen didn't think he would feel fear.

He closed the flaps on top of the box. He considered performing some other act to show Rip he had been there. But what other act was necessary? What disturbance could he make or message could he leave that wouldn't slightly undo the subtlety of what he had already done?

Back along the coffin-shaped winze he made his way, along the left-hand fork and into the egress chamber, half-expecting all the time to meet Rip returning. He emerged with a feeling of letdown into the close white air, remembering that first time all those years ago and the stranger boy's freckled face looking down at him. And this sense of disappointment and growing fear remained with him, darkening his mind. It intensified as he plodded homewards across the spongy, sodden peat. It was as if he had used up all his resources in the strategic placing of Lyn's body and the depositing in Rip's Cavern of her hair, and now a kind of reckoning had come. The time had arrived to think instead of act and he began to see that he hadn't thought well.

For Rip, of course, there had never been need of thought. He had only to kill, cut off the girl's hair and hide in the mine until it was safe to resume whatever daily life it was that he led. But Stephen had murdered his own wife. It was his own wife that was missing and, as the successor to Ian Stringer and Roger Morgan, he should have been the first to search for her.

He tried to imagine himself not her murderer but the husband only of a woman missing on Vangmoor. She would have been missing by now for something like twenty-four hours. He had told her mother on the previous evening he was going to meet her in Hilderbridge. When she wasn't there, when he hadn't been able to find her, wouldn't he naturally have told someone? If not the police at that juncture, wouldn't he have told her parents?

None of this had struck Stephen before. He felt a little sick and his skin prickled. It was after one when he got back to Chesney. Surely a man living in a village on Vangmoor, where two girls with long fair hair had been murdered in the past three months, would suspect the same might have happened to his wife, a girl with long fair hair, if she didn't come home all night? The natural thing would have been to have conferred with her parents last night, to have got in touch with the police last night, to have organized a search party last night. He had been too busy last night to think of any of that. If he went to the police now the first thing they would ask was, hadn't he been worried when she didn't come home? Why hadn't he reported her disappearance on the previous evening? Knowing the danger as he did, he who had found the body of the first victim, he who had been so exhaustively questioned by the police, why had he done nothing until lunchtime the next day?

As he came along Tace Way he saw ahead of him a crowd of people in the Simpsons' front garden. It was too late to turn back and wait somewhere until they had gone in. Mrs Newman was waving at him. He went on, the question pounding in his head: what was he going to say when they asked where Lyn was? What was he going to say?

'There you are then, Stephen. Wherever's Lyn got to?'

'Isn't she in?' he said, stammering a little.

'She hasn't been in all the morning. I said to Joanne, you give her a ring and get her to come over and see Chantal and Joanne did but she didn't get any reply or anything, did you, Joanne? So I went over, thinking the phone might be on the blink or whatever you call it, but the whole place locked up and not a sign of her.'

His sister-in-law was sitting in a wicker chair that had evidently been brought out into the garden for that purpose, holding in her arms the small, red-faced child, its face wet and gleaming in patches with saliva or tears or both. It had large dark blue eyes in red wrinkled sockets and a little wispy reddish hair. Kevin was talking to a couple of neighbours and his brother to another pair from the far end of Tace Way, but it seemed to Stephen that as Joanne spoke they all fell silent and turned to look at him.

'I've just never known Lyn be out on a Sunday morning. What's got into her? I mean, it has to be deliberate. I come home with my baby and she's not even in and then Mum says you're going out this evening.'

Stephen didn't answer. Joanne looked at him and her lip quivered.

'Is it jealousy? Is that what it is? She only came in once to the hospital, and she does work in town, she was *there*. What does she expect, that I wasn't to have a baby because she hasn't got one?'

'Joanne,' said her father.

'Now come on, love,' said Kevin. 'Lyn'll come over the minute she gets back, won't she, Steve?'

Two of the neighbours discreetly escaped. Joanne burst into noisy tears and this made the baby start crying. She jumped up and rushed into the house.

'Typical post-partum neurosis,' said Trevor.

Mrs Newman looked at Stephen with her head on one side. 'Where is Lyn, anyway?'

'I don't know.'

'Well, when she gets back mind you get her to pop across the road. If Joanne's going to get in a paddy like that it's bound to upset the milk, it always does. There was a woman lived in one of those houses round the back of the church when my three were little . . .'

But what had happened to this woman Stephen never knew, for he turned away abruptly and without a word and crossed the road and entered his own house by the front door. To leave them like that was a stupid thing to do in the circumstances, he knew that, but it might have been worse if he had stood there any longer. He had already begun to tremble and he seemed to have no voice. At the kitchen sink he drank a glass of cold water and did some more deep breathing. When Lyn didn't appear in the course of the afternoon either Mrs Newman or Joanne would certainly come here. They would want to know where Lyn was. He had no idea what he would say to them.

Because he and Lyn had seldom drunk alcohol they usually had a plentiful supply in the cupboard Dadda had made them. Stephen found a nearly full bottle of whisky and poured himself a generous measure. Again he hadn't eaten, he wasn't used to whisky, and it rushed immediately in a pounding tide to his head. He sat down on the green velvet settee.

Why hadn't he gone to the police last night? Obviously he couldn't go now, yet any time now Lyn's body would be found. When it had been found and identified the Newmans and the Simpsons and those neighbours would remember how he had stood trembling and tongue-tied when they asked where Lyn was. Mrs Newman would remember how he had said on the previous evening that he was going into Hilderbridge to pick Lyn up at the bus stop. They would remember seeing him carry out to the car something in a sack, something far too large to be the broken bust of Tace.

He put his head into his hands. But it was panic he was beginning to feel rather than despair. He was convulsed with terror so that he leapt up and began walking feverishly about the house. He drank some more whisky. Every hour that went by made it more strange and suspicious that he hadn't reported Lyn's disappearance, and every hour that went by increased the likelihood of her body being found.

Certainly he had given her parents and her sister the impression that she had spent last night at home in her own bed. If he hadn't actually told that lie he had acted it. He had allowed them to make the assumption. They would remember that when Malm and Manciple and Troth came asking. Made unsteady by the whisky he had been drinking, Stephen staggered into the study and fell into the chair at his desk. Broken-headed Tace gazed at him with sad irony, with a cynical gleam in his eye that came perhaps from his battered appearance and the way a watery sun gleamed in on his features.

Last night he had been too busy aping Rip, following in Rip's footsteps, using Rip as his cover and his guide, to think of that most important step — to announce Lyn as missing. Even if he hadn't done so till he returned from putting her body in the old pony level, even if he had waited until eleven at night, he would have been safe, would have exonerated himself. And what help would it be to him now that his blood belonged to a different subgroup from that of the murderer of Marianne Price and Ann Morgan? Malm would assume the obvious truth, Hook would see it at once, that he had killed his wife and arranged things to make it look as if the killer of the other girls was responsible.

Stephen was shivering with fear now. He had always believed himself to be brave and strong but that belief now shook and foundered. In his fear he whimpered out loud that he had no one to turn to, no one who would help him. For twenty years and more Dadda had been useless. He remembered with bitter hatred his dead grandmother and that fat fair woman now jaunting round Europe in a tourist bus.

It was Lyn on whom for love and comfort he had always cast himself, and Lyn he had murdered. He fell on his knees and buried his head in the seat of the chair as if in her lap.

15

In acute fear of what it might tell him, Stephen
brought himself to switch the television on for the news
at 5.45. He had only to listen to the headlines to know
that Lyn's body hadn't yet been found. Few people
would venture out onto the moor today, he thought,
standing at the window and looking out as she had
stood and looked out. The rain had begun again, it was
very dark for early on an August evening. He heard
some more news on another channel at seven. Still
nothing.

There was a chance, of course, a probability even,
that if he didn't report Lyn as missing her body
wouldn't be found for weeks. One would have to go
right down into the gully if not into the tunnel itself to
see it. However, during those weeks he was going to
have to account to her family for her absence. During

the afternoon, after he had pulled himself together enough to go downstairs and have some more whisky, he had lain on the bed and fallen intermittently into a drunken doze. The back door he had locked, another departure from normal behaviour. From his bedroom he had heard Mrs Newman rattle the door handle. A few minutes later she or Joanne rang the front doorbell. The phone had rung twice. But he had answered none of these summonses, though knowing that in failing to do so he was only plunging himself deeper and deeper into this morass of his own creating.

His head ached. In spite of that, he didn't dare stay in after having told his mother-in-law that he and Lyn were going to his uncle Stanley's. He forced himself to put on a clean shirt and a jacket for the benefit of those watching on the opposite side of Tace Way, though there was no way of showing them Lyn. In the hall, just about to leave, he heard a click and then a faint clatter from the back door and he jumped, almost crying out. It was only Peach, letting himself in through the cat flap, leaving small, dainty, wet footprints across the tiles. Stephen got into the car and drove away, very conscious of being alone and of being seen to be alone.

When he started off he had no idea where to go, but once he was driving through the village he felt an urge that was nearly irresistible to take the road that led past Knamber Foin and over the old pony level. It would be madness to do that. Later, anyone who had driven along that road would be questioned as to what cars they had seen. He felt pulled towards the place, though, teased by a nervous desire to see if the body were still there, to push it deeper into the tunnel, to cover it, even to remove it, take it away and deposit it elsewhere.

He got as far as Thirlton, parking where he had done on the previous night, near the village hall. *He would not go on*. With all his strength he would resist this compulsion. He would sit here in the car for an hour, two hours. Two hours would be enough for this supposed social call, surely. For just that length of time he would stay here, stick it out and wait, and then he would go back and take the phone off the hook and lock the back door and bolt the front door.

With the engine off, it was cold in the car like winter. The rainswept moor rolled away to the right of him, blending without visible demarcation into the rolling grey sky. He thought of running away. He could lock up the house, take the car and go away somewhere. There was money in his bank account, about five hundred pounds. If he made up his mind now he could even take the body with him, retrieve it tonight, drive south . . .

Anything to escape the questioning and probing of Lyn's family. He had never thought much about it before, but now he realized how much he hated Lyn's family, indistinguishable from Naullses, Naullses all. A race of creatures set on this earth to frustrate and torment him. What was he going to say next time they asked him where she was? He couldn't run away, he could never leave this place. He could no more imagine life without the moor than he could without one of his limbs or his eyes.

The ceaseless rain drove him to despair. It streamed down the windows of the car, having a claustrophobic effect, something he had never felt down in the mine, in Rip's Cavern. Suppose Lyn's mother phoned uncle Stanley? She might, she was capable of it. They had known each other all their lives, Lyn's father and Stanley Naulls had been at school together. What was he going to say when he got back and Mrs Newman came over and asked where Lyn was?

I don't know. I haven't seen her since yesterday morning. I don't know where she's gone. She never came back from Hilderbridge. Stephen turned all these hopeless responses over in his mind, and out of the mêlée of them came one that wasn't hopeless. It came to him gently and clearly and seemed to hang trembling, waiting for him to seize it.

He did so and repeated the words to himself: I don't know where she is, she's left me.

Something had stopped him thinking about the events of yesterday morning, something which that idiot Trevor would no doubt have called an emotional block. He had blanked them out of his memory without apparent will or effort. But now he forced himself to remember what Lyn had said to him that had led to his striking her and her breaking the bust of Tace. Not what had led to his killing her, that had been something different, something beyond analysis. He had struck Lyn because she had been unfaithful to him. Therefore there must be some other man.

Stephen hadn't given this a thought until now. That she had somehow cheated him, that she was going to have a child and bring it into his home, these things had been enough. But now, warily, he turned his mind to that shadowy figure, Lyn's lover. He didn't know much about this sort of thing, it had never interested him. He had supposed it would never concern him. But he had been unable to escape noticing that marriages broke up, men left their homes with other women, women theirs with other men. Why shouldn't he say that this was what Lyn had done? Why not tell her mother that

Lyn had left him in order to go and live with this other man?

Indeed, if he hadn't intervened it might have been true. The man must exist. When Lyn's body was found it would be assumed that she had left Tace Way on Saturday morning to join him in, say, Hilderbridge and, having missed her bus, had accepted a lift . . .

Stephen started the car and put on the windscreen wipers. The clear arcs they made in the streaming glass showed him the sun setting in red streaks through splits in the cloud. He would go back home, no one would expect him to stay out visiting when his wife had just left him. Reversing, starting back, he began to rehearse the words he would use.

It was a relief to be in the house again. He put on the lights and left the curtains open and awaited the arrival of Mrs Newman. Peach came over to him, hoping perhaps to sit on his lap as he had so often sat on Lyn's. Stephen pushed him away lightly with his toe. There was a book lying on the chestnut leaf table which made that inaccessible too, so Peach sat in an armchair, looking offended and uneasy. He was waiting for Lyn, Stephen thought, but it hardly mattered, his days were numbered, his hours even.

It was only nine o'clock. He switched on the television and found a channel with some news on it. There was nothing about Vangmoor murders, Lyn's body hadn't been found. Stephen began to wonder why Mrs Newman didn't come. She could see he was back, she must want to see Lyn as much as ever, must even by now be growing anxious about her. He thought of going across the road and volunteering the information about Lyn's leaving him, but on reflection it seemed an unwise move. It seemed to him not quite in his own character.

Instead he went into his study and tried to finish the article he had been writing for this week's 'Voice of Vangmoor'. He had unlocked the back door but even so he left the study door open so that he wouldn't miss the sound of a knock or ring. After a while he went across the passage and looked across the street from his bedroom window. The Simpsons' bedroom lights were on and the lights elsewhere in the house had all gone off. The curtains were drawn across the Newmans' living-room window but through them he could see the light still on and the bluish glow of the television screen.

Back in the study he found it hard to concentrate. Why had they made three or four attempts to get hold of Lyn during the afternoon and then, in the evening, abruptly stopped? Suppose they suspected him of killing her and were keeping quiet over there, lying low, because they had told the police of their suspicions?

That was impossible. Why should they suspect him? It was more likely that they were simply offended. But their silence, their non-appearance, he began to find more disquieting than answering any questions of theirs could have been. At twenty past ten the downstairs lights in the Newmans' house went out and the landing and bedroom lights came on. Stephen was staring out with the light on behind him, when suddenly Mrs Newman's face appeared between her parted bedroom curtains. They looked at each other, their eyes meeting. Then Mrs Newman blanked out her window by jerking the curtains together, but Stephen had had a distinct impression, from the brief glimpse he had of her face, that she was very angry and aggrieved and that she had looked at him as at someone particularly blameworthy.

He couldn't sleep. As he lay down in the dark his body began to jump and there were stars and floaters before his eyes. He thought how terrible it would be if he were to fall asleep and be awakened by a thundering on the front door, if he were to creep out of bed with pounding heart and see the police car outside, its lights blazing, Manciple and Troth at the gate. He couldn't sleep but he was uneasy about turning his bedlamp on. Just as he could see Newman and Simpson lights from his side of the road so they could see his from theirs. He wanted to lie lower than they, to lie so low, if only that were possible, as utterly to be swallowed up in the earth and hidden.

But in the small hours he couldn't stand it any longer. He got up and walked about the house, made himself tea, tried to read, tried even to complete his piece for the *Echo*. 'After such a deluge as we have seen in these past days, a considerable greening of the moor may be expected to take place . . .' The paint on Tace was dry, he looked as good as new. It had stopped raining and as the dawn came the sky was brindled in many shades of grey.

Stephen went back to bed then, but he lay sleepless and at eight he got up again. This was going to be another of those days he took off work. He felt ill and worn. If Mrs Newman didn't come across the road in the next half-hour he would go to her. Had he ever before done that of his own volition? Probably not, but these were exceptional circumstances. His wife had left him. Have you heard from Lyn? We've split up, she's left me, gone off with some man she says she's in love with. Did that sound right? A frightening thought came to him. If Lyn really were alive, if she really had left him, wouldn't she have told her mother? Wouldn't she have got in touch with her?

The cat made him jump by coming in through the flap with all the bursting suddenness of a circus animal leaping through a paper hoop. A dog would have made it plain he was looking for Lyn, would have run into corners, poked under furniture, sniffed at doors. Peach walked sedately through the rooms with tail erect, hardly moving his round handsome head, hardly vibrating a whisker. He made a graceful leap on to the window sill to watch for Lyn to come from inside or out. Wouldn't Mrs Newman wonder that Lyn had gone and not taken Peach with her?

It got to nine and no one had come. Stephen tried to phone Dadda to say he was ill, he had a virus infection, but Dadda didn't answer. He saw Kevin go off to work, he saw Mr Newman go. At 9.15 Joanne came out of her front door, pushing a high-sprung shining white pram which she put on the front lawn. Stephen put on his walking boots and his zipper jacket. As he came out of his house Mrs Newman came out of hers and hesitated on the step, looking towards him. What happened next made his heart lurch. She shrugged her shoulders, slowly turned her back and went indoors again.

Stephen forced himself to continue down to the gate, to close the gate after him, to walk along Tace Way and into the village. There was a roaring in his head that seemed to get in the way of coherent thought. And his legs felt flaccid, boneless. Once or twice even he found himself stumbling on the smooth dry road. Again, though, difficult as walking was, awkward as that most familiar and satisfying of all his activities had become, he found himself being drawn a great distance, being compelled to that part of the moor where Lyn's body was. His awkward stumbling walk was leading him in the direction of Bow Dale and Knamber Foin.

After the crossroads he moved in among the birch trees. He refused to lift his eyes to the ridged, boulder-strewn summit of the foin or the grey-green sweep of the dale beyond it. It was here that he had seen Rip, for the first and only time, seen him dancing to entice him. Stephen felt that Rip would know what to do, if only he were here, if only he would come out into the open and join with him and be his friend. Act normally, Stephen thought, was what Rip would surely say, for that must be what he himself did when he had done his murders and after spending a night in the mine, returned to his blameless and respectable life as a citizen of the Three Towns. Act as if you knew nothing. In your case, act as if your wife had really left you and gone away you don't know where.

Stephen wandered among the trees whose leaves, no matter how still the day, were always faintly and delicately tremulous. He leaned against one of them, resting himself, supporting his arms on its thready thin branches, for it was too damp to sit down. The pale trembling leaves and his own pale face were reflected in the pools of water which lay everywhere between the tree roots and the hussocks of grass. So far, perhaps, he had acted normally. For someone like him it would *be* normal not to go crying to his wife's relatives, to lie to them even, to wait until they asked him directly before confessing she had left him for another man. Fear began to trickle off him like sweat. He felt cooler, cleaner, freer. Being on the moor always made him feel better. Last night, hadn't the atmosphere of the moor at Thirlton positively saved him from losing his mind? He hung against the tree, closing his eyes, resting there, inhaling the clean green scent of the leaves and grass with raindrops on them.

And the rain began again as he came out of the Banks of Knamber and began to walk back. A gentle warm rain it was, dropping out of the thousands upon thousands of tiny white clouds that streamed across the sky like galaxies. He walked slowly, lifting his face to the rain. No one would suspect him, even though he had been Lyn's husband, for this murder was so obviously another of Rip's murders, the victim lying as before within the confines of one of the landmarks of the moor, her death the result of strangling, her long fair hair cut off close. And he couldn't be Rip, his blood was wrong. Alike though they were, with the same love of the moor, of solitude, of adventure, strong tall men of power and endurance, yet there was this tiny difference of blood between them. Brothers they might be, but not quite twins. Their blood was slightly differently constituted, and that would save him.

Now, he thought, he could sleep. He could eat something and lie down on the bed and sleep peacefully and innocently. Tomorrow when he was rested and fit again he would go back to work. Perhaps Lyn's body would never be found, perhaps as time went by there would be nothing left of it but the bones and these would gradually crumble and dissolve until they became one with the stony surface of the moor . . .

The pavements of Tace Way were covered with a gleaming skin of rain and water dripped in heavier drops than the rain from neat little front garden trees. Outside Mrs Newman's house was parked a van with Bale's Pet Shop on its side. That reminded Stephen about having Peach destroyed, something which would now have to wait until tomorrow, but which would be a very natural act on the part of a deserted husband. Hadn't he read somewhere, whether as fact or fiction he didn't know, that Elizabeth Barrett's father had destroyed, or wanted to have destroyed, her spaniel when she ran away with Robert Browning? Act normally. The normal thing would be to rid oneself of the runaway woman's pet.

He went into the house and into the kitchen but he felt too exhausted to eat. Mrs Newman would come across the road soon, now she had seen he was back. He locked the back door and took off the phone receiver, took off his boots and jacket and went upstairs. Still wearing his jeans and shirt, he lay down on the bed and pulled the covers over him. For a moment or two he lay there, listening to the gentle patter of the rain, and then he slid into sleep.

A sound from downstairs awoke him, he didn't know how long afterwards. It was still raining lightly. The sound had been one of the interior doors closing, and now he could hear footsteps. Had he, after all, forgotten to lock the back door?

Surely Mrs Newman wouldn't come upstairs after him, but these footsteps were mounting the stairs. Stephen sat up as the bedroom door came open. He jumped off the bed and backed against the wall with a cry of terror.

Lyn had come into the room and was looking at him.

16

His nerves must be very bad, she thought. He looked as
if he had seen a ghost. She stood about a yard in from
the door and spoke to him gently.

'I'm sorry if I startled you, Stephen. I've come back
for my things and for Peach.'

He didn't speak. He stood against the wall, his hands
flat against it as if he were only prevented from further
retreat by that solid mass.

'I saw the car, I knew you couldn't be at work, but I
thought you must be out on the moor. I wouldn't have
come in like that if I'd known you were here.'

Still he didn't answer. She began to feel afraid of him
again. For a while she had succeeded in conquering this
new fear of Stephen. Because she couldn't let herself
feel afraid of *Stephen*, poor frightened Stephen, she
had stopped Nick coming with her to Tace Way, but

now the fear was coming back. She forced herself to take a few steps forward and to speak steadily.

'It wasn't right of me to run away like that while you were out on Saturday. It was because I got in a panic.' She didn't mention his having hit her but her hand went up involuntarily to her bruised left eye. 'Being away these two days,' she said, 'I think it's made me understand — you'll be glad to be rid of me, won't you, Stephen? You don't need a — a mother any more.'

He moved away from the wall and she flinched a little. But he wasn't coming near her. He sat or half fell onto the bed and turned away his face. She was sure then that he wasn't going to speak to her. The cupboard where her clothes were was on his side of the bed, but she went up to it and slid back the doors. She took out an armful of clothes almost haphazardly, the skin on her back tingling with apprehension. Again she drove herself. She turned and held out her hand to him, though she knew better than to touch him.

'Won't you speak to me? We may not see each other again. Stephen?'

He jumped up and climbed away from her over the bed. It would have been funny if it hadn't been so horrible. He scrambled across the bed on all fours, dropped on to the floor, ran across the passage and into his study. She heard the key turn in the lock.

Nick had made her promise not to lift the suitcases herself. She had laughed at him but she had promised. She had survived Stephen's violence and the baby had survived and she was going with Nick to London. Except that it would have upset Stephen she would have sung out loud as she carried the armfuls of clothes downstairs and packed them in the cases.

Her mother came across the road. 'I knew something was up when he said you were going to his uncle Stanley's. I said to your dad, Stanley Naulls wouldn't have folks round, he might have to give them something to eat and drink.'

Lyn smiled. 'I kept phoning you but you don't hear the phone when you're out in the garden. I knew you'd start wondering, it was a relief when I got hold of you in the afternoon.'

Mrs Newman carried the cases out and put them in the back of the van. 'I can't help feeling a bit weepy, Lyn. We've never had a divorce in our family. It's a shame you ever married him, he was never a real husband to you. When you three were little there was a man like him lived in one of those pair of cottages on the Thirlton road . . .'

'Mum,' Lyn said, 'don't send Stephen to Coventry, will you? Don't not speak to him or anything.'

Joanne was in the garden, standing by the baby's pram. Lyn went up to her and they embraced clumsily because it was the first time for years that they had kissed each other.

'I'll miss you. I'll be so dead bored I'll die.'

'I'm not going to Australia,' said Lyn. 'I'm not going to the other end of the world.'

'Might as well be. Oh, I do envy you, you are lucky.'

'I know,' said Lyn, 'I know I am.'

She picked Peach out of the yellow maple tree and gathered him into her arms and put him on the passenger seat of the van. He sat erect, staring out. Lyn turned the van round, waved to her mother and her sister. She saw her mother wave, burst into tears and rush into the house, but she hesitated, slowing only for a moment before driving on and out of Tace Way. And soon the moor unfolded on either side of her, Chesney Fell and Foinmen's Plain to the right, to the left the quivering copses on the Banks of Knamber. She would never need to see it again except as an occasional visitor. Once when she was first married, walking along the Reeve's Way with Stephen, she had found lying on the turf a skin shed by an adder. Now it seemed to her that the silvery-grey moor was her own snakeskin that she was sloughing off, peeling it off behind her, as she went on to new ways and new things.

The skin that was the moor wrinkled and shrivelled and rolled away and Lyn drove down into north Hilderbridge, down North River Street, over the bridge to the Mootwalk and Nick and the southbound train.

The shock of it prostrated Stephen. He lay face downwards on the floor in his study. He listened to Lyn's footsteps moving about the house, to her voice and her mother's, a distant wordless sound like the twittering of birds, to the front door closing. By that time he knew it had been Lyn, was Lyn, not a ghost or some frightful emanation from his own fear or guilt. He knew by then that it was Lyn who had walked into the bedroom and therefore that he hadn't killed Lyn on Saturday afternoon.

He got up and went across the passage and into his bedroom and looked out of the window. Bale's van had gone. The baby's pram stood on the Simpsons' lawn but both women had gone in. It had stopped raining and a pale sun was shining through the layers of cloud. He could remember so clearly the events of Saturday afternoon. He had come home and seen Lyn standing at the window, standing there in her blue jeans and white tee-shirt, her hair cloaking her shoulders, and without motive, without even particularly wanting to do it, with nothing but a desire too urgent to resist, he had sprung at her and killed her. Yet just now he had seen her and heard her speak.

Was he going mad? Was it that his mind hadn't been able to stand the battering it had lately received? The death of Helena, the defection of Lyn, the reappearance of — his mother. Had it all driven him mad so that he believed he had done things he hadn't done? Perhaps the events were no longer so clearly memorable. He could recall his fingers digging so hard into Lyn's neck that it seemed he must behead her, but quite lost were the details of his drive to the pony level and the times and sequences of the steps he had taken after the killing. Half an hour ago he would have sworn he had hidden her body but now the remembrance had grown vague, confused, like a dream at morning. He could remember nothing clearly of that killing but the feel of her neck in his hands. Yet even that must be a false memory, a dream . . .

Hook had told him he had fantasies and therefore must be a psychopath. At any rate now there would be no fresh confrontation with Hook. He hadn't killed Lyn. He hadn't cut off her hair, folded it into a sack, buried the sack in the mine. He hadn't put the hair with that of Marianne Price and Ann Morgan into the box in Rip's Cavern. Part of the shock of seeing Lyn had been the sight of her veil of pale bright hair.

He didn't know whether to be relieved or sorry. For a while he had been Rip's equal. The whole thing, he supposed, had been no more than a sort of wish-fulfilment. He had wanted to be on a level with Rip, so fooled himself he could do, had done, what he did. Stephen gave a dry mirthless laugh. He must recover from it now, take up the reins of life again, never never let his emotions get such a hold over him again.

He went down to the kitchen, made himself scrambled eggs, a mug of coffee, cut off two hunks of bread. Perhaps it was because he had been starving himself that he had had these delusions. When he had eaten he felt so much better, clearer-headed, calmer, that he could look back on his imaginings and laugh at himself. He actually did laugh aloud. There, alone in the house, he laughed so uproariously as he went back up the stairs that he got a stitch in his side.

In the study he tore up the sheet of paper on which he had attempted those first puny sentences of an article the night before. A fresh sheet went into the typewriter. Now Helena was dead he need never see a Naulls again. This would show them, this would be something more pungent than the ending of the drought, than an account of a thunderstorm. It was a chance for him that Tace's birthday happened to fall this week, a peg to hang his article on.

'The present writer's maternal grandfather, Alfred Osborn Tace, would have been ninety-eight years old this week had he lived. His sole descendant will be honouring the great man's birth date as he always does, as he always did himself, by private celebrations of the beauty of his beloved Vangmoor, in short, by going out on the moor for a picnic on one of our fine August days . . .'

Stephen said a good deal more about his relationship with Tace and invented two Tace anecdotes as told him by his grandmother when he was a child. He didn't quite dare say he remembered Tace or even that he had been told of being dandled on his knee, since Tace had died three years before he was born. When the article was finished he thought it the best thing he had ever done. He put it in an envelope, addressed it to the *Echo*, and went off down to the post box on the green to post it.

From St Michael's churchyard one obtained the best view in the village of Knamber Foin. Stephen leaned over the lychgate and gazed across the intervening land. Had he truly suffered so much agony and fear sitting in the car at Thirlton, driving down the long bleak road to the 'bridge' over the portal, lying sleepless and tortured in his bed, or had that too been a dream? He stared, perplexed, across the moor. The wind was getting up. A breeze blew out of the west, ruffling, then smoothing, the birch foliage in the Banks of Knamber as if an invisible hairbrush had passed over it. Why shouldn't he take the car and drive to the pony level now? It might be that Saturday wasn't a dream while this morning was. The dead Lyn might lie over there, the dream Lyn have appeared to him . . .

He told himself not to be a fool and he chuckled out loud at the very thought of having such ideas. Back at home again, he walked about the house, thinking of changes he would make now Lyn was gone and the place all his. Tomorrow he would have to shop for food, replenish the fridge, cancel half the milk, remember to buy bread. For a while he amused himself tidying the kitchen, rearranging things, putting Peach's food dish and all the tins of cat food into the dustbin.

The repeat showing of Saturday's episode of *Elizabeth Nevil* began at 7.30. Stephen switched on the television as they were playing the by now familiar, even famous, introductory music. The first episode started with Joseph Usher's finding Apsley Sough while walking his Irish wolfhounds in Goughdale. The joke was that the scriptwriter and the director had no more known where the mineshaft was than Tace had. Stephen laughed aloud at the sight of the actor playing Usher peering down a hole a few feet away from the George Crane Coe. A rabbit warren, that's all that was. And when they showed the inside of the mine it was obviously something rigged up in the studio and not at all like the real thing. Stephen wondered if Rip was also watching and laughing. After that they didn't show any more of the moor, but only interiors and the 'lovely dresses' Helena's fellow-inmates of Sunningdale had talked about.

He lost interest because the scriptwriter hadn't stuck very closely to Tace's text. He kept thinking of the body in the pony level, the body that wasn't there, that had never been there. Yet he had only to close his eyes to see it lying there, face downwards and with its shorn head, the light of his small torch playing faintly on it. He had knelt down and cut off the hair and coiled it into a skein and rolled it up in the sack. Then, on the following morning, he had taken it out of the sack and put it in the pocket of his zipper jacket, only to think immediately that this was an unwise move in case any hairs adhered to the lining of the pocket. Surely he had done those things, surely he had done them yesterday morning, had wrapped the skein of hair in clinging film, put it into his rucksack with the rope and the torch while he waited for Kevin to depart and the coast to be clear.

He turned off the television and went to the hall cupboard. His zipper jacket was hanging there. He brought it to the living room window but the daylight wasn't strong enough to see much by. Under the central light he turned the pocket inside out. A single blonde hair clung to the slightly magnetic nylon lining.

Stephen pulled the hair off and dropped it onto the carpet. He put on the zipper jacket and went out and got into the car. There he sat for a moment or two, breathing deeply, for his heart was racing and his hands were unsteady. He had to concentrate on keeping his hands from trembling as he drove out of Tace Way and down into the village.

The sun had set and the moor lay in a bluish twilight,

not yet dark enough for any but the most prudent motorist to have his lights on. There was hardly any traffic. He only passed one car on his way to Thirlton. A wind was blowing, sweeping the grass and heather of Thirlton Plain with that brushing effect, bending the few, already wind-twisted, trees along the roadside. The sky was heavy with bands of grey cloud, between which, all over the west, the remains of the sunset lay in blood-red streaks.

Now that he was approaching the spot he had been yearning to revisit ever since he had left it on Saturday, he had that curious choking feeling of one's heart in one's mouth. That hair could have got into his pocket in other ways. From proximity with some garment of Lyn's in the cupboard, from when Lyn had last washed the jacket. An aversion to going near the pony level seemed to take him by the throat. Yet he couldn't make himself drive more slowly, his foot on the accelerator refused to obey him. He was compelled steadily on, out of Thirlton village, over the first hump of the moor, out onto the empty road that wound into Bow Dale. And then, as the road curved round the base of Knamber Foin, the point where the dale opened its whole prospect, he slammed on the brakes and brought the car to a juddering stop. He stopped as dead and as shockingly as if something had burst out from among the boulders and had dashed across the road a yard in front of him.

Down at the 'bridge' the road was ablaze with car lights. The lights threw a brilliant white radiance, still and constant, up into the dark blue air. It was like seeing the site of some frightful, multiple accident, from afar off on a motorway, for amid the white light blue police car lights rippled on and off, on and off, and yellow lights winked in a slow regular rhythm.

Stephen's body broke out in a flood of sweat. He

could see a crowd of people moving about, black silhouettes in the dusk, illuminated into men when they moved into the encompassment of the lights. He sat still, sweating. The engine had stalled. Down there the blue lights on the roof of a police car rippled, on and off, as pretty, as diverting, as a shop-window display. The yellow lights winked. But Lyn was alive, he had heard her speak, seen her in the living flesh and the living golden hair!

To drive down there and find out . . . ? It was impossible. He doubted if he were physically capable of it. He drew in a deep breath and at the second attempt managed to start the car. The steering wheel was wet with sweat from his hands. Once he had turned round and had his back to the brightness and the activity down there in the valley, he put his own lights on. Then he drove back slowly, tensing his body, hunched over the wheel. A police car with its lamp flashing passed him in Thirlton village.

There was news on the television at ten. He had half an hour to wait and he paced up and down. Suppose there was nothing on the news, nothing tonight, tomorrow, ever? Suppose he had hallucinated what he had seen in Bow Dale just as he had hallucinated killing Lyn? He got on to his knees on the carpet and crawled about, looking for the hair he had dropped. Instead of the hair he found a handbag of Lyn's, a brown leather one, fallen out of a chair between the back and the seat. But at last, after a long time, he did find the hair. He held it between his fingers, drawing it out like a bowstring. It was Lyn's hair and it was real. Or he thought it was real. If he went to Rip's Cavern now would he find Lyn's hair lying in the box with Marianne Price's and Ann Morgan's, or had the placing of it there also been a dream and an illusion?

If there was nothing on the news at ten he would go up to Goughdale and into the mine and look for the sack and the hair. Even if it were pitch dark, moonless midnight, he would go. The girl announcer's face swam on to the screen as he pressed the switch. His watch must be slow, he had missed the headlines.

He crouched on the settee, watching the President of the United States shaking hands with an African prime minister, union leaders talking about a projected rail strike, the search for survivors of an air crash in Turkey. There was going to be nothing, nothing, and he was mad. He shivered, clenching his fists.

The announcer came back. She moved a paper on the desk in front of her, said in that indifferent silky voice: 'The body of a third victim of the Vangmoor murderer was found this afternoon at the entrance to former lead mine workings near the village of Thirlton. The body has been identified as that of a journalist on a local newspaper, Harriet Jane Crozier, aged twenty-four . . .'

Stephen jumped to his feet and let out a crow of laughter.

17

It had been there since Saturday, its presence had prevented the cat from jumping onto his favourite place, but it was only now that Stephen really saw the book that was lying on the chestnut leaf table. *Muse of Fire, A Life of Alfred Osborn Tace*, by Irving J. Schuyler. Harriet Crozier had brought it to lend it to him as she had promised. He understood now. Lyn had gone and had left the back door unlocked for him and later, much later, Harriet had come with the book. There had been no one at home but by that time the storm had begun. The back door was not only unlocked but a little ajar and she had come in to shelter from the rain. There he had found her, dressed as Lyn often dressed, as a thousand girls did in summertime, in jeans and a tee-shirt, waiting for him, watching the storm.

And that brown leather bag he had found wasn't

Lyn's, it was Harriet's. He took it from the chair seat where he had left it and looked inside. The blue, green and white scarf was there, folded up, her reporter's notebook, a purse, a credit card and a cheque book, a jumble of pens and pencils, make-up and loose coins. Stephen couldn't help laughing again. It was so enormously funny. As far as his safety was concerned, nothing could have worked out better for him. He picked up the book. There was no inscription in it, nothing to show it had been the property of Harriet or the *Echo*. Filled with an exquisite relief, he took the book upstairs to bed with him and fell asleep over it, waking in the morning to find it still lying on the covers and still open halfway through chapter one, so deeply had he slept and without stirring.

It was late, after nine. There seemed something absurd in the idea of going to work. He made himself a large breakfast, eggs, bacon, tomatoes, fried bread, and he opened a can of sausages. It was the first proper meal he had eaten for days and when he looked in the glass he fancied he had lost weight. His face looked drawn and there were hollows under his cheekbones.

After breakfast — and after washing up, for though alone, he wasn't going to sink into squalor — he went up to his study, and because he was calm now and relaxed, knowing himself to be a sane rational man, he was able to mend the crack in Tace's head without difficulty. While the glue was drying he took out all his books and dusted and rearranged them. It continued to pour with rain and he had to have the light on.

Odds and ends of paint were kept in a cupboard under the sink. He found a tin of black undercoat, half-full. The paint itself was a very dark grey, not quite black. He spread old copies of the *Echo* out on the floor and set the bust of Tace on them and began carefully painting it with the undercoat, paying special attention to the mended head. While he was painting he noticed Harriet Crozier's name above an article about Three Towns girls cutting off and dyeing their hair and he started laughing again. To have made such a mistake! But of course it had been as dark as it would be now without the light on and he had never, either down there in the living room or in the old pony level, looked at his victim's face.

The painting done, he got out the vacuum cleaner and cleaned all the carpets and upholstery in the house. He dusted the rooms. At 1.30 he cooked himself the rest of the sausages with cheese on toast and then he took the car and drove through the rain down into Hilderbridge to shop for more food. The town was full of police, there were policemen and police cars everywhere, and when he came back into Chesney he saw that there were lights on in the gatehouse lodge and police cars parked outside.

The clean and tidy appearance of the house pleased him. From five o'clock onwards he watched television, later fetching himself a meal of cold chicken and precooked chips and packaged salad. For most of the evening he went on eating, chocolate bars, packets of crisps and nuts. He watched every news programme, switching from channel to channel to get all of them. There was an interview with the assistant chief constable of the county who had been censured by someone or other for his refusal to call in the help of Scotland Yard. There was an interview with a man called Martin Smith who said that he had been out with Harriet Crozier a couple of times. He would never forgive himself if he lived to be a hundred for not taking her out on Saturday afternoon instead of going by himself to the first football match of the season which was anyway cancelled due to the storm. Stephen didn't go to bed till midnight.

The following day passed in much the same way, pleasantly, peacefully, though without the painting or the shopping. The rain was sporadic and gave up altogether in the late afternoon. Stephen walked as far as Ringer's Foin and back and for the rest of the evening he watched television, eating pork pie and tomatoes and crisps and chocolate bars. It was years, not since he was a child, that he had eaten so much. Chief Superintendent Malm came on the BBC news at nine to say he was confident they would catch the Vangmoor killer this time. They were optimistic. A few more days or even hours would see the end of it.

Next day, having eaten heartily at breakfast, Stephen went back to work.

Dadda wasn't so far sunk in misery as to spare Stephen. He looked up with sunken eyes from the inlay he was working on.

'You've come back then. You've bloody condescended to come back. Had another one of your bloody viruses, have you?'

'Afraid I have, Dadda. Sorry about that. I always turn up like a bad penny, though, don't I?'

'Aye. Have you ever thought about your bloody future if Whalbys' goes bust? Noticed all the small businesses going bloody bust in the Three Towns this year, have you? Or d'you reckon I can do the lot on me own, a man with a sick mind like me?'

'Good Lord, Dadda, you haven't got a sick mind.'

Dadda turned and spat into the sawdust. 'You've got a wife, you want to remember that, you'll maybe have kids. What are you going to live on when Whalbys' goes down the bloody drain?'

'Actually,' said Stephen, 'I haven't got a wife. Not any more.' He gave a bright, strained smile. 'She's left me, we've split up. She walked out on me on Saturday.'

The table creaked as Dadda leant on it to heave himself up. He stood staring at Stephen with great arms hanging. 'What are you saying?'

'You heard me, Dadda. Lyn's left me.'

'I'll not believe it!'

'I'm afraid you'll have to. Good Lord, Dadda, we're not the first couple to split up. We'll get over, by or through it.'

Dadda said in a deep, dark, bitter voice, 'There's history repeating itself, there's the sins of the fathers visited on the children.'

It had happened almost before Stephen knew it. One moment he was standing next to Dadda, trying to avoid his eye, the next he found himself clutched in a bear hug, held in a crushing embrace, while Dadda murmured over him just as he had done all those years ago when Brenda first went away.

'Like father, like son,' crooned Dadda. 'We'll be all in all to each other now, all in all to each other.'

Stephen was more frightened by this now than he had been then. Then it had at any rate seemed natural, natural even to the child. Now there was something horrible about being embraced by this gorilla-like man who on his own admission was halfway to madness. As a child he hadn't wanted to hurt Dadda's feelings by protesting, later on he had given way to Dadda in everything for the sake of peace and not to offend. He had always believed he loved Dadda. Suddenly he understood how much he hated him. With this surge of hatred he pulled himself violently away, digging his elbows into Dadda's chest, bracing his back and jerking himself free, so that Dadda's arms flew wide and he staggered — huge, powerful Dadda actually staggered. He gave a low cry. Stephen ran upstairs and got behind the ranks of chaises longues and three-piece suites. He stood against the wall, listening, but there were no more sounds from downstairs.

After a while he crept to the top of the stairs and looked down. Dadda was sitting on a Hepplewhite chair with the whole of the upper part of his body prone on the table top, his head on the table between his outstretched arms. Stephen tip-toed away and went back to the Victorian love seat he had been working on in oyster-coloured velvet and to which he hadn't given a moment since the previous Thursday. At lunchtime Dadda was gone, though Stephen hadn't heard him leave. He went out himself and was crossing the square to the Market Burger House when someone touched his sleeve.

It was Troth.

'Oh, not *again*,' Stephen said. He felt enough confidence to say that, though if it had been Lyn who was dead he might not have. 'You don't want to talk to me *again*?'

'You don't know what we want,' said Troth in that tone of cunning triumph a stupid man uses when he thinks he has got the better of an adversary. 'I never said. I might be merely warning you about parking your car on a yellow line.' A fresh outcrop of acne made the near approach of his face offensive. Stephen slightly retreated. 'It could be just that,' Troth said. 'That's what an innocent man would presume.'

'Good Lord, I can read, you know, I can watch TV. Any bloke in my position would jolly well *know* you want to talk to me about this last murder. What are we waiting for? Let's get on with it, let's get going.'

Troth didn't say any more. They were only about a hundred yards from the police station. Stephen wasn't taken into an interview room this time but into an office with a desk and chairs and filing cabinets and a view of Hilderbridge roofs. Manciple, in a lightweight grey suit, his face burned to an even darker brick red by the previous week's sun, was sitting behind the desk and Malm was standing at the window against the light. Malm looked tired. The past weeks had aged him and whatever he might have said on television, he looked neither confident nor optimistic.

Manciple apologized to Stephen for bringing him there.

'We'll try not to keep you longer than is strictly necessary, Mr Whalby. We have to do our job, you'll appreciate that.'

Stephen shrugged. Manciple was looking at him in a way he didn't like, as if he saw into his mind. It was perhaps the most *intelligent* look any of these policemen had ever worn in all his encounters with them. It was a look of enlightenment. Stephen moved his eyes away.

Malm spoke. 'Your car was seen twice in Thirlton during the weekend, Mr Whalby, once on Saturday night and once on Sunday evening, both times parked outside the village hall. Would you like to tell us what you were doing there?'

Stephen blustered a bit at first. He said it was no business of theirs. But everything, of course, was their business in a murder case. He couldn't simply refuse to explain. After a while he admitted he had been to Thirlton and said he had been inside the village hall. It was a piece of luck for him, the merest chance, that when they asked him what had been going on there and he replied that it was a concert, he had guessed right.

Then Manciple wanted to know how well he had known Harriet Crozier.

'I'd met her three times.'

'Three times is ample to start a relationship,' said Malm, adding, 'at any rate, these days.'

Stephen wanted to laugh at that, it was so remote from any of the ideals or aims of his life, and he did feel a smile twitch his mouth.

'Something amusing you?' Malm asked.

'I don't have "relationships" with women. I've always been faithful to my wife.'

He felt that the dignity of this reply silenced them for a moment. Then Malm began talking of the nearness of Thirlton to the old pony level and Manciple, taking over from him, proceeded to give Stephen a straightforward and lucid account of how Harriet's body had been brought and left there. He described with perfect accuracy what Stephen had in fact done, from his placing the body in the tunnel, having first ascertained that no car was visible on the road in either direction as far as the eye could see, to his parking the car in Thirlton and returning on foot to cut off the hair. Stephen was alarmed. He had to keep telling himself about the difference in the blood subgrouping and that he was safe.

Manciple said in his diffident apologetic way, 'I don't suppose you can remember what music was played at the concert.'

Stephen knew nothing of music. Manciple's statement — for it had been a statement, though it required an answer — silenced him and blanked out his mind. But he must make some sort of reply. After a moment or two he said, for surely the work of these giants among composers must have been included, 'Oh, Beethoven, Bach, classical stuff.'

Their faces told him nothing. There was no derision

at the wildness of his response and no surprise at its accuracy, and immediately after that they let him go. Without a word about the future, without reassurance, without threat.

He came out into the street, telling himself he was safe, his blood made him safe. His blood was a clinging scarlet cloak, a magic cloak, that protected him. For two hours he had been with the police and for the first time no one had brought in coffee or biscuits or sandwiches. But Stephen had no appetite left. For a while he sat in his car as he had sat in it on Sunday evening, but the streets were filled with policemen, men in uniform and men who, though not in uniform, who wore as far as they themselves knew the clothes of the ordinary citizen, were nevertheless unmistakably policemen too. Stephen felt that they were taking particular note of this solitary figure in a parked car.

Dadda had gone. Stephen climbed the stairs, even less inclined for work than usual. On the horsehair padding of a chaise longue beside the love seat on which he had been working were two decanters in etched glass. Written on the sheet of paper on which they stood were two words: *From Dadda.*

Stephen felt anger well up and burn his throat. Dadda's gifts had always brought him more embarrassment than pleasure. He would have liked to smash the decanters and leave the broken glass for Dadda to find when he came back from wherever he had gone. Two things stopped him, a contemptuous impatient pity for Dadda that still survived and a regard for beautiful objects his upbringing had instilled into him.

But the presence of the decanters and the note bolstered, he didn't know why, a decision that had been taking shape as he sat in the car, crossed the square, climbed the stairs. He was going to stop working for

Whalbys'. He hated it, had always hated it, though never so much as he did now. Surely there was something else he could find to do, something more closely connected with the moor. If they gave him the chance to do anything else, if they left him at liberty . . .

He picked up the decanters, wrapped them roughly in newspaper and, holding them in his arms, went down into the street. The big double doors he closed almost ceremoniously and locked them, and then he turned his face towards the moor. There was scarcely a point in Hilderbridge from which it couldn't be seen, and now as he crossed the square towards his car a segment of it appeared between the overhanging fronts of the shops in Market Hill, the bluish peak of Hilder Foin.

Stephen hadn't been to church since he was a child, but there are two psalms the opening lines of which everyone still knows. He repeated tremulously under his breath, 'I will lift up mine eyes unto the hills from whence cometh my help . . .'

Freedom from marriage, freedom from work, should have lightened him, but he felt as heavy as lead. Every moment he expected the police to arrive again and begin their questioning or take him away for more questioning. The phone rang at about seven but it was a wrong number. That made him take another decision in his aim for total freedom. He sat down and wrote a letter to Post Office Telecommunications, asking them to disconnect the phone. What did he want a phone for? Who was there for him to call? He addressed the envelope and put a stamp on it and walked up to the green to post it, though it wouldn't go out until the morning.

Once more the gatehouse lodge of Chesney Hall was

heavily manned by police. Stephen felt a pang of real dread for Rip. With so many after him, surely he must be caught, there could be no final escape for him. It was like when he was a child, there in the lodge with his grandmother, and the Vangmoor hounds met on Chesney Green. He had pitied the fox then, pursued unfairly by so many.

And next morning, out on the moor, walking across the Vale of Allen towards the Reeve's Way, he met men in jeans and sweatshirts who told him they were police officers and asked his business. He recognized none of them but when, reluctantly, he gave them his name, he sensed that they knew it, that it was familiar to them in some unpleasant way. He couldn't guess why they were there or what they could possibly be looking for. They advised him to go home and Stephen agreed to this, it seemed simplest, but when they were out of sight he made for Pertsey and Tower Foin. He needed the moor, they weren't going to be allowed to take it away from him again.

Tace had been born ninety-eight years ago that day. Stephen thought about Tace and wondered if what the people who believed in reincarnation said was true, and if the novelist's spirit had entered into himself. He stayed out all day, walking, lying on the sun-dried, tilted, flat boulders of the foin, and when the sun grew hot, retreating into the shade of the powder house to sleep there in the cool dark. It was early evening before he got home.

A police car was parked outside his house and inside it were Manciple and Troth.

18

Manciple sat on the settee. Troth wouldn't sit down but
walked about the room, looking at things in what Stephen thought a very insolent way. He picked up Dadda's silver Stilton knife and examined the assay mark
and then he lifted up one of the decanters out of its
newspaper wrapping and tapped the glass to make it
ring. Stephen was glad he had taken Harriet Crozier's
handbag upstairs.

He didn't know why they had come. Not to arrest
him, certainly, not even to take him to the police station. Up to a point they were behaving as if making a
mere social call, yet they had refused his offer of a drink
or of coffee or tea. Manciple was doing nearly all the
talking. He sat with his legs crossed and one arm
stretched out along the back of the settee, giving Stephen a slow detailed account of how Harriet had been

missed at work on Monday morning and how, because she had told Martin Smith she was going for a bus ride on the moor on Saturday, a search party had been assembled and the body found at four on Monday afternoon. What she hadn't told Martin Smith but had told a girl friend was that there was a man she liked who was living on the moor, only he was married.

Manciple talked, not in an accusing or hectoring way, but as if perhaps Stephen were a criminologist who might be expected to be interested in such things. Troth walked about, examining ornaments like a valuer. After a while Manciple asked him to go out and wait in the car. Stephen thought Troth was going to refuse outright. He set down the chestnut leaf table which he had actually lifted up to scrutinize by the light at the window, turned and looked at Manciple with one eyebrow cocked up. Then he shrugged.

'Okay,' he said. 'Sure. If that's what you want.'

'Let yourself out,' Manciple said as Stephen moved towards the door. The front door closed, almost with a slam. Stephen stood where Troth had been, his back to the light. 'Stand if you'd rather,' said Manciple in his understanding, conciliatory voice. 'I won't keep you five minutes.'

Stephen sat down on the arm of a chair.

The social note was back in Manciple's voice. 'You know the introductory music to that Bleakland series on TV?' He hummed and pom-pommed a couple of bars. Reading from a scrap of paper he took from his pocket, he said, 'Vivaldi, part of the *Four Seasons.*'

'Of course I know it. Of course it's Vivaldi.' Stephen was always huffy when anyone questioned his intellectual pretensions, and huffiness prevented him seeing the trap.

'Funny you didn't remember that was one of the

pieces they played at the Thirlton concert on Saturday night.'

Stephen felt himself flush and the sweat start on his body.

'Strange when you're a descendant of Tace's and an admirer of his books and when you've got a TV set . . . It'd be a fair assumption you went to the concert just *because* they were playing that music. Only you didn't go, did you, Whalby? You went to the old Pony Level to cut the hair off a dead woman's head.' He took no notice of Stephen's gasp. 'We should like,' he said, 'to search this house first thing tomorrow. Okay with you?'

'Why should I help you?'

'Don't, if that's the way you feel. I can get a search warrant but I'm sure you'll let us in without. And don't run off, will you? That only pays when you're very rich and you've got friends in distant places.'

Stephen shook his head, saying nothing more. He closed the front door after Manciple. He *had* been shocked, he *had* been briefly frightened, but that was all. They had no evidence, they wouldn't be able to prove anything, it was all typical police bluff. No doubt they would come in the morning, though, and it would be unsafe to keep that book in the house.

The sun was shining, lying in golden bars and rectangles across the walls, the carpet. It was turning out rather a nice evening, the sky clearing over Big Allen. The idea of his running away made him laugh, to himself at first, then out loud. He? Run away? Where could he bear to go to? Where else could he live? What rotten psychologists the police were!

He put on his zipper jacket, slipping *Muse of Fire* by Irving J. Schuyler inside it, against his chest. At least he could get it out of the house and after that he could think how to dispose of it. A man followed him down into the village, or at any rate walked behind him down into the village. The man was young, he was alone, unknown to Stephen, and he might well have been a policeman. Or he might not. And when Stephen crossed the green and came to the gate into the churchyard the man also walked onto the green, got into a parked car there and drove off.

There was a police car with three men in it parked on the path that ran alongside the churchyard wall. He couldn't tell whether they were there to watch him or not. Two uniformed policemen stood outside the gatehouse lodge. But Stephen didn't feel at all afraid. Fear had begun to leave him that afternoon, had now entirely departed, and he felt, without knowing why, that it wouldn't return. He had said goodbye to fear, he felt invincible, full of power. It was like being in one of those dreams in which you have committed crimes that you know you cannot be punished for, no matter what you do now you cannot be caught and they can never reach you.

The book was cumbersome, a rigid block against his body, and he knew he must get rid of it without knowing how to do this, but it didn't worry him, he would find a way. The mine, of course, would be the place. But if it was true the police were watching him he didn't want to lead them to the mine. He owed it to Rip not to do that. The police car started, turned round, moved slowly off down the hill towards Hilderbridge. Stephen walked back across the green, pausing at the pillar box and pretending to post a letter. The evening was sultry and humid, the air quite still, all the trees that grew in the churchyard, that surrounded the vicarage, that concealed the Hall, hung down canopies of thick, dark, tired foliage. It was respite weather, in a hiatus between rain and rain.

The two policemen were back in the lodge. Stephen began heading in the direction of the path that led up on to Chesney Fell and Foinmen's Plain. Up there somewhere he would find a hole, a rabbit warren, a small cavern lipped by a stone, wherein to bury the book. He was approaching the Hall gates when a car came slowly down the drive. It stopped just inside the gates, the driver's door came open and Professor Schuyler got out and hurried back to the house.

Plainly he had gone back for something he had forgotten. On the back seat and floor of the car were a tumble of books, folders, two battered briefcases, a mass of manuscript held together with a clip. Stephen looked round quickly to make sure he was unobserved and then he pulled *Muse of Fire* out from the breast of his jacket and tossed it lightly among them. It made him chuckle. There was even another of the professor's own works among the books, a glossy jacketed memoir of Ford Madox Ford.

After that Stephen climbed the crinkle-crankle path with a light step, almost joyously. No one followed him. They wouldn't have the stamina, the lung power, to follow him up here or anywhere over the steep crests of the moor. He laughed as he climbed, throwing out his arms as if to embrace with wide heavens, the foins, the green fells. I will lift up mine eyes unto the hills . . .

There was no evidence of any kind against him. All they knew was that he had been twice to Thirlton by car during the weekend. They would look stupid when they had wasted time and manpower searching his house only to find nothing. Perhaps he should get himself a lawyer, though. Why? Why spend money on that, money down the drain, when there was no evidence against him? When he got home he would check on the car. There might be a hair or two in the car that by some scientific process they could tell wasn't Lyn's.

When they had finished with it, perhaps he would sell the car. What was the use of a car to him now he wasn't going to work any more? He wouldn't want to go anywhere but up here on the moor. The car was a useless encumbrance that would be as expensive to keep as a horse that never got ridden.

He came over the crest at the top of the path and stood looking across the plain to where the standing stones, the curious converging procession of them, stood out dark against a sky that was peach-pink and flecked all over with feathers of gold and blue. It was almost too gorgeous, too photogenic, too much of nature copying art, and art in this case the *Echo* calendar. A flock of birds passed overhead, flying very high, a hundred tiny black commas in formation. Stephen came slowly across the turf towards the gate in the railing. He thought he saw something move behind the Giant, but when he looked again there was nothing.

As he opened the gate he thought he smelt tobacco smoke. The air was heavy and humid. If someone had been up here smoking during the afternoon perhaps the smell would linger on that air for many hours. The two great comb-shaped shadows lay spread, between the stones and out beyond. Stephen walked along the shadow and caught it again, the whiff of smoke. The feeling of being alone up here had left him and now he turned back sharply to see who was following him.

The plain was deserted. Stephen blinked and closed his eyes against the dazzlement of the sinking sun. He turned away again and looked with screwed-up eyes towards the far end of the avenue and as he did so a figure moved out from behind the broad protection of the Giant and stood against the sky, the sun's rays gleaming on it with a brassy sheen. It was the figure of a very tall man with a bush of dark hair, a bearded man who wore dark trousers and a white or very pale sweater that the sun had dyed a fiery gold.

Stephen remained still. The man took the cigarette from between his lips, but instead of dropping it and treading it out, pinched it in his fingers and put the end into his pocket.

He began to walk down the avenue, between the bars of shadow. Stephen drew in his breath in a hiss. He went forward to meet the advancing figure, the godlike, bearded, golden figure, who was coming towards him down the aisle of a druids' cathedral.

The voice rang out like a bell. 'Stephen!'

It was part of the ritual, the magic, that this man in the pale loose aran, this man who was taller than Ian Stringer, taller even than Dadda, should know his name and address him by it. But Stephen himself couldn't speak. He simply stared and walked.

'I thought it was you. I reckon I still know your walk after all these years.' A long brown hand went up to the mass of disguising beard, the curly hair. 'You don't know me, do you, under all this? Peter. Peter Naulls.'

19

They sat on the Altar, watching the sun go down. It lay like a crimson ball on the horizon but only after it had sunk did the sky turn red, as red as the heart of a fire. Peter lit a cigarette, pushed the wooden matchstick deep into the earth.

'I used to dream about Vangmoor while I was on my travels,' he said. 'It gets you that way if you've been brought up here. I've been all round the world, walking mostly, going on buses, getting lifts, but the longer I was away the more I got to thinking about the moor and — well, missing it.'

'How long were you away?' Stephen asked.

'Years. I lived in Kathmandu, in the place they call Freak Street, for two years. I was a freak, I was all spaced out, I can tell you. There was a doctor there, he reckoned I'd die if I went on the way I was, so I came home. I've even got a job.'

'Here?' Stephen hazarded.

'In London. Hospital porter. Christ, Stephen, I sometimes wish I'd been bred up to a trade like you. What use is an English degree?'

Stephen looked at him in wonder. 'When did you come back from — Kathmandu?'

'Christmas, it must have been.'

'They've taken your picture away at Uncle Leonard's. Last time I was there it was gone.'

'Like I'm dead to them? You didn't think I stayed with them when I came up here, did you?'

'You could stay with me,' Stephen said.

'You're married, aren't you?'

Stephen shook his head vehemently. 'I'd like you to stay with me. I've got a big empty house, all those empty rooms. Whenever you want to come up to the moor you can always stay with me.'

It was a sidelong glance Peter gave him, one eyebrow raised. 'I've got a place to stay.'

'With me it wouldn't cost you anything. You could come and go as you liked, you'd be free.'

Peter didn't really answer that. He said, 'There's a girl I know in Loomlade, we've known each other since we were kids. It's her I come up to see.' He got up. 'Let's go. It'll be dark soon and I've got a long walk ahead of me.'

'But we'll meet again, won't we?'

'Sure. Why not?'

They walked along the avenue together. Stephen asked when Peter was going back. Sunday, not till Sunday. He wanted to ask about the girl, he wanted to ask if she had long fair hair, but he didn't quite dare so he asked her name instead.

'Stella. Stella Crane. Her dad keeps the electrical shop. You and me, when we were kids, we went in there once and bought a torch battery. Remember?'

Did he remember! Stephen's heart was full. He began to laugh with joy. He had to stand still and hold his sides, he was laughing so much.

'What's so funny?' Peter was looking at him oddly again, looking him up and down.

'I'm so happy,' Stephen gasped. 'Lord, I'm so happy it just makes me laugh, I don't know why. It's so terrific to see you, it's amazing. It's what I *needed*, d'you understand me?'

'I don't know that I do.' Peter closed the gate, stood at the point where the path divided, one branch descending the fell to Chesney, the other curving away over Foinmen's Plain. He said rather awkwardly, 'It's been good seeing you, Stephen.'

'Ring me before you go back? Say you will. I'm in the book.'

'Sure. Sure, I will, Stephen.'

'We mustn't lose sight of each other again.' Stephen put out his hand. He didn't know quite why he had done this, whether he expected Peter to shake it or hold it, and perhaps it was as well Peter didn't seem to see that outstretched hand in the gathering dusk. For a moment, though, it seemed to him that he had put out his hand in order to hold onto Peter and stop him going away. 'Good night,' he said, and wistfully, repeating himself, 'We'll meet again?'

Walking away, Peter laughed. His voice came very clear in the windless twilight. 'You know where to find me. Good night.' He looked back once and gave Stephen a wave. Stephen watched him until he was out of sight, and that was for a long time, for the Plain stretched more or less flat to the east of Ringer's Foin and in the dusk Peter's white sweater showed up as a moving glimmer.

They hadn't mentioned the mine or Apsley Sough. That was because they hadn't needed to, Stephen thought, or because what it meant to both of them was too deep for words at this their first meeting. Besides, Peter *had* referred to it. He couldn't have done so more delicately and subtly than by speaking of the day they had bought that torch battery in Crane's shop, the very day, Stephen remembered and knew Peter remembered too, when they had found the entrance to the mine. Perhaps Peter had been wise in refusing to come and stay in his house. Houses only trammelled people like them. It was up here in the open that such as they must meet. Probably Peter would phone him tomorrow. He would phone and then they would go to the mine together.

With nightfall the rain began again. It was a slow steady fine rain. Stephen went up to his bedroom, remembering that 'first thing' in the morning the police were due to search the house. On the foot of his bed, on the turned-back covers, was Harriet Crozier's handbag.

Slowly he emptied everything out of it onto the sheet. Every object was quite small, the largest item being Harriet's notebook and that was no more than six inches by four. Stephen reflected. He couldn't burn the things, there were no fireplaces in the house. Nor would he dare put the things in his dustbin. Lyn had probably asked her mother to send the rest of her clothes on to her but as yet Mrs Newman hadn't put in an appearance to do this and a great many of Lyn's possessions remained in the house. Stephen hesitated for a moment longer and then he put the empty handbag with Lyn's three handbags, the lipstick and eye liner in the drawer with Lyn's make-up, and the coins with the loose change in his own trouser pocket. Why not carry the rest of the things on him tomorrow? They would search the house but they wouldn't search him.

He slept soundly but he was awake early and up by seven. The police's 'first thing' was 8.30 and Stephen thought Troth seemed impressed by the sight of him standing at the sink washing up his breakfast dishes. A guilty man wouldn't be washing up when the police came to search his house for evidence to convict him of murder. From time to time, though not in the presence of Troth and the others, he patted his pockets and nearly giggled when he felt there Harriet Crozier's purse and notebook and cheque book and credit card.

But after an hour or two he felt so triumphantly certain they hadn't found anything and weren't going to find anything — after all, what was there to find? — that when he watched them poking about with his clothes and crawling about the floors it made him start giggling. Troth, picking at a pustule with the fingernail of his little finger, asked him where his wife was and Stephen said he didn't know, she had left him.

Troth's wedge face sharpened and his eyes came even closer together. It was all Stephen could do to suppress his amusement. He could see the way Troth's mind was working, the conclusion he was fast jumping to.

'*I* don't know where she is,' Stephen said, 'but my mother-in-law does. You've only got to go across the road and ask.'

The look on Troth's face, guarded disappointment, was such as to make Stephen let out a roar of laughter. It was very satisfying that Troth didn't seem to despise him any more. He looked as if he were scared of him or at least wary. They finished with the house by half past twelve and more or less put things back where they had found them. Troth said nothing about wanting to see him again or to expect a visit later in the day. He went into the Newmans' house but he was only there ten minutes.

Rain was still falling lightly. It had been raining all night and all the morning. The house felt defiled as a house is said to feel after burglars have been in it, but Stephen didn't feel like rearranging everything or getting the vacuum cleaner out again. He went into his study and composed an advertisement for insertion in the *Echo,* offering his car for sale. He put the advertisement into an envelope and a stamp on the envelope but he didn't like to go down to the post with it in case Peter phoned. Peter was bound to phone today or tomorrow because on Sunday he had to go back to that hospital porter's job of his.

What was he, Stephen, going to do about a job for himself? On the other hand, did he have to have one? The little bit his articles for the 'Voice of Vangmoor' brought in would be enough to buy his food, and without a wife, a car, without even perhaps a house . . . ? A new life was beginning for him and the prospect of it filled him with excitement. He wrote *For Sale, £1,200* on a piece of card, added *o.n.o.* for 'or near offer' and stuck the card in the rear window of his car with Scotch tape. There was just a chance of selling it that way before next week's *Echo* came out.

In spite of the rain, it was warm and he longed to be out on the moor. But he went back into the house and had some lunch and thought about the police finding blonde hairs all over his clothes and in his bed and in the car and reluctantly having to admit they were Lyn's hairs. He thought about Troth calling up some telephone number Mrs Newman would have given him. The idea of Troth expecting the person who answered to say he or she had never heard of Lyn, but in fact being answered by Lyn herself, made Stephen laugh again. He roared with laughter, shaking his head at the stupidity of the police.

In the afternoon the rain let up and when the sun came out everything outside began steaming. Stephen opened the french windows. Who would do the garden now Lyn was gone? A house and garden, he thought, were liabilities, more trouble than they were worth. If the phone didn't go by seven he would walk or take the car to Loomlade and find Peter at Crane's shop. He sat by the french windows, eating dry roasted peanuts and drinking tea. The phone rang at half past four. He answered it in his pleasantest voice, giving the number and then, 'This is Stephen Whalby speaking.'

His caller was Dadda.

Stephen didn't say any more. He put the receiver down. Of course he didn't want the phone disconnected before Peter could phone but they could cut it off as soon after that as they liked. It was a nuisance.

He was getting his supper, breaking eggs for an omelette, when the front door bell rang. His first thought was that it was the police back again but when he looked out of the window he saw no police car in the street, no vehicle at all. At once he knew who it must be. Very likely Stella Crane had no phone and for some reason he couldn't use the one in the shop. Going out into the hall to open the front door to Peter was the happiest moment he had known since the day he had sat in Rip's Cavern and eaten the biscuit and felt safe. His heart fluttered with excitement. He opened the door, smiling.

The man who stood outside, a middle-aged man who resembled Peter Naulls only in that he too had a beard,

Stephen recognized to his disappointment as Professor Irving J. Schuyler.

'Mr Whalby?'

Stephen nodded.

'I hope you'll excuse my taking the liberty of coming here.' His voice was rich and cultured with a strong transatlantic lilt. 'You can maybe imagine what I want to talk to you about.'

His immediate thought was of the book he had put into Schuyler's car. He wasn't afraid. After all, it was to him the professor had come, not to the police. Mrs Newman was watching from a downstairs window. Stephen moistened his lips. 'Please come in.'

'This is very good of you.' The professor stepped into the hall. He was wearing a tee-shirt and his Dr Scholl sandals. He brought his hands from behind his back where they had been clasped together and Stephen saw that he was carrying what was certainly the book in a large brown envelope. 'What a really charming village Chesney is. It's meant a great deal to me visiting with Mr and Mrs Southworth and really getting acquainted with the domain of Alfred Osborn Tace. Vangmoor — a most beautiful wilderness, is it not? So precisely as Tace has described it for us under the apt alias of Bleakland.'

'Do sit down,' Stephen said.

Schuyler looked approvingly round the room. The prospect of Big Allen seen in the distance above the garden fence brought a smile to his lips that was almost arch. He raised his hand to it as to an old friend spotted on the other side of the street.

'Lest you think we American academics lead lives of leisure, Mr Whalby, I should tell you I've been taking six months' sabbatical. A month here, a month at

Haworth, a little trip to the Lakes, and then back here to my kindly hosts. It's been quite a summer.'

Stephen watched the book being slipped out of its envelope. His cheeks felt hot. Schuyler laid the book in his lap and looked at it meditatively. 'Well, Mr Whalby, maybe I should come to the point and not take up more of your time than is strictly necessary. I don't know if you're aware that I interest myself a good deal in Alfred Osborn Tace. I teach him to my students and I've written one or two little works on him and *his* works.' He lifted up the book and wagged it. 'Viz,' he said facetiously, 'this one. My latest, *Muse of Fire*. As a matter of fact, I didn't know I had a copy of it with me in Chesney, but by a piece of luck this one was in my car. We academics have a well-deserved reputation for absent-mindedness, you may say.'

The relief was great. Whatever the professor had come about, it wasn't to expose a vital clue in the mystery of Harriet Crozier's death.

'I happened to read your article in the *Three Towns Echo* with which my hostess kindly provided me this morning. An interesting little piece, if I may say so. Now I expect you'll understand to what all this preamble is tending.'

Stephen nodded. 'Good Lord, yes. You mean about Tace being my grandfather?'

'Yes, indeed, Mr Whalby. Frankly, I'm fascinated. Though Mr Fowler wouldn't care for me to say so, I'm intrigued.' Schuyler began to talk of his knowledge of Tace, his researches into every aspect of the novelist's life. Without making too much of it, he must consider himself one of the world's leading authorities on Tace's life and works, and yet . . .

'The descent,' said Stephen, 'was, I'm afraid, on the wrong side of the blanket.'

'Pardon me?'

'Oh, Lord. I mean my mother was actually, well, il-legitimate.'

'What a most interesting expression,' Schuyler said. He seemed very much struck. 'The wrong side of the blanket. Yes, one sees how it must have originated. I must look it up in my host's copy of *Brewer's*. But, Mr Whalby, your mother being a natural daughter of Tace's, what an astonishing thing this is. I must confess to being astounded. One thinks of Tace's strict moral-ity, you know, that almost prudish rectitude of his. I confess to a certain dismay in finding my hero — shall we say blemished by hypocrisy? No longer quite im-maculate. Though still *sans peur*, no longer *sans reproche*. May I inquire the date of your mother's birth?'

'May 1925,' said Stephen. 'May, the twenty-fifth.'

'Well, more and more fascinating. The previous summer and autumn, of course, were those spent by your grandfather carrying out the famous lecture tour of the United States. I maybe have to check on my dates here . . .' The professor opened the book and leafed through chapter eleven. 'Ah, yes. The tour, as I should have been able to recollect without aid, began in the June of 1924 and concluded in some triumph for Tace through November. Your grandmother was perhaps an American lady? Or was she a companion Tace took with him — in great secrecy, I must say — on his trav-els?'

Stephen was silent. He took the book out of Schuyler's hands and read the dates. The print danced a little before his eyes. It was a matter of the greatest interest to Tace scholars, Schuyler was saying. If at some not too distant date he could trouble Stephen for chapter and verse, for a history of his grandmother, for any memoir of his own he could provide. They must discuss the whole subject. Any life of Tace, in view of this disclosure, would necessarily require amendment . . .

Stephen said abruptly, 'I'm sorry but you'll have to excuse me now. I have to go out.'

'Of course.' Schuyler jumped up. He was all apology, all consideration. 'I've taken up too much of your time as it is. Let me leave the book with you. We shall meet again. You can't imagine how excited I feel at the new prospects this discovery opens out, Mr Whalby.'

Stephen saw him out and closed the door. The sight of the book back again on the chestnut leaf table started him laughing, though he wasn't amused. He didn't know why he should laugh so hysterically when, in the space of ten minutes, a major motive for his continued existence had collapsed.

After a while he sat down on the settee and tried to read the relevant part of chapter eleven. He found it impossible to take it in. Somehow he didn't think he would ever read much again. Reading had had something to do with being Tace's grandson, not the descendant of Arthur Naulls. He felt thirsty and when he went into the kitchen to fetch himself a glass of water he stared almost without comprehension at the bowl of broken eggs, the whisk, the slices of bread on a plate. Had he been going to eat something? Eating seemed as remote and bizarre an exercise as reading.

He went upstairs. It wasn't possible to go out because Peter was going to phone. The sun was setting, staining a sky that was the wispy grey of wood smoke. Earlier and earlier it set, the autumn would soon be here. He saw the Newmans' front door open and his mother-in-law come out, cross the road. The doorbell rang. Probably she wanted to pack up Lyn's things. He ignored the bell and went into his study where he began typing a letter to Hilderbridge Rural District Council, informing them that as from the end of the month he wished to terminate his tenancy of 23 Tace Way, Chesney Moorside . . .

The doorbell rang again. He went down to answer it, knowing he would have to let her in some time. His caller wasn't Mrs Newman but Trevor Simpson. What was wrong with the car that Stephen was selling it so cheaply?

Once Stephen would have been indignant at that remark but tonight he didn't care. He shrugged. There was nothing wrong with the car, it had never given him a day's trouble.

'As a matter of fact, I'm getting out,' he said. 'I'm off to fresh woods and pastures new, making a clean sweep. There's nothing to keep me here. I'm giving up the house and I shan't need a car. You interested?'

Trevor was. He lifted up the bonnet, then sat in the driver's seat. Stephen made no objection when he said he would like to take it out on a test run but he wouldn't go with him. He had to wait in for Peter to phone. The letter was finished, signed and inside an envelope by the time Trevor came back, satisfied with his bargain. He would give Stephen a cheque for five hundred pounds and bring the balance on Monday.

'Good Lord, there's no hurry,' Stephen said expansively. 'The car's yours. I shan't let it go to anyone else, I shan't gazump you.'

Trevor gave him a knowing look and as he was leaving said, 'You can't run away from your own id, you know, Steve.'

It was dusk now, nearly dark. Peter wouldn't phone tonight, he would wait until tomorrow. From his study Stephen fetched the bust of Tace and from the living room, where the professor had left it, Harriet Crozier's copy of *Muse of Fire*.

He stepped out into the twilit garden. The sky was a deep violet colour. He had read somewhere why it is that the stars give no light but he couldn't remember why. The heavens were thick with stars and it was true enough they gave no light but appeared only as puncture holes in a dark velvet bag. He opened the cupboard by the back door where Lyn had kept the garden tools and got out a spade.

There were probably flowers growing in the border here. He saw them as a grey mass, a fuzzy fungoid growth, and he stabbed the spade in among them haphazardly. His fancy was playing tricks with him, for when he looked up he thought for a moment a face had looked back at him out of the gloom behind the kitchen window. He turned away and continued to dig. When he had dug a pit some three feet long and two feet deep, he laid the book inside it and then the bust of Tace.

For a long while he paused, leaning on his spade and staring down into the little pit, and then, slowly, he thrust his hand into his pockets, drew out all Harriet Crozier's small possessions and dropped them item by item into the grave with Tace and the book. The topsoil and the plants went back like earth falling on a coffin.

Stephen cleaned off the spade, restored it to the cupboard and went back into the house. He could have sworn he hadn't left lights on upstairs and in the hall. It took him a moment or two to realize what had happened while he was in the garden but he did realize when he walked into his bedroom. The wardrobe doors stood open and all Lyn's remaining clothes were gone. Mrs Newman had been in to fetch them.

Harriet Crozier's handbag was gone with them. Ste-

phen began to laugh when he thought of Harriet Crozier's bag being sent off to Lyn. He lay down on the bed
and laughed but when he put his fingers up to his face
because the skin itched, he found it wet with tears.

20

In the past days he had occasionally felt as if a cord
were tightly stretched inside his brain, stretched from
one side of his cranium to the other, from the eyes to the
occiput. At some time during the evening or the night
that cord had snapped and the freedom he desired had
come with it. He walked about the house, wondering
how he should dispose of his furniture. Dadda could
have it and sell it. Or it might go to Lyn. He bore Lyn
no ill will any more. He wrote a note to Dadda and a
note for Lyn and left them on the chestnut leaf table.
The sight of the notes there made him giggle, for it
looked as if he were about to commit suicide instead of
embarking on a new life.

There had been no sign from Peter. Of course there
would be, sometime during the day, but Stephen felt
impatient, he didn't want to wait. Perhaps he should

go to Loomlade and find Peter himself. The objection to that was that the girl might be there and Peter might not want the girl to know too much. He tried to reconstruct the conversation between Peter and himself in an effort to recall what Peter had said about the girl. And as he went over it there came back to him two things of profound significance Peter had said, though they hadn't registered with him at the time, though they had been lost in the generality of their talk.

'I've got a place to stay' and 'You know where to find me'. What a fool he was! What a fool he had been not to see what that meant. Of course he had a place to stay and of course Stephen knew where that place was. Peter had meant, I shall be in the mine, come up and meet me in the mine. He was going back to London on Sunday, so today he would be in Rip's Cavern, waiting . . .

Stephen felt almost unbearably excited. He was breathless and laughing with excitement. For a moment only his happiness was checked when it occurred to him that Peter might have been waiting in the mine all day yesterday, waiting in vain. But no. Yesterday had been Friday and he would have supposed Stephen to have been at work. Saturday was the day, all the pointers indicated it. Peter was probably making his way up there now, across the Vale of Allen.

Stephen's laughter became rather shocked and awed when he walked about the house, looking at things and realizing he might never come back there. He wouldn't waste time going into the village to post the letter to the council. Might as well leave it with the notes for Lyn and Dadda. What should he take with him? A change of clothes, of course, and a blanket for the night. There was food enough in the cavern. Later on, say on Monday after Peter had gone back, it would be his turn to stock up with food and drink. A sleeping bag would have to be bought and a mattress for himself. He would make the cavern welcoming and homelike for Peter's return . . .

The last he saw of Tace Way was the pram on the bright green square of the Simpsons' lawn and the last he heard was the urgent crying of Joanne's baby. I am shaking the dust of this place off my feet, he said to himself, shaking it off my feet. The expression pleased him and for a while he walked in a prancing way, shaking his feet as he lifted them, repeating what he had said, and then, as he crossed the Jackley road, lifting up his eyes to the hills.

His rucksack, containing the rope, the big torch, candles, clothes, was on his back. Under his right arm he carried a blanket, rolled up and tied with string. He had decided to grow a beard like Peter's; he had shaved for the last time. There was no one following him, he was as alone as he had ever been when out on the moor. Behind him a car passed along the road, going towards Jackley, then after a moment or two another heading for Hilderbridge, but Vangmoor itself where there were no roads was stripped of people. It was empty and silent and now at the end of summer no birds sang.

In the Vale of Allen there was here and there a golden flower on the gorse. It was a curious thing about gorse that although the season of its flowering was springtime, there was always blossom on it even in the depths of winter, even if it were just one solitary bloom. He should have written about that for the *Echo* but it was too late now. He didn't think he would ever again write the 'Voice of Vangmoor'. Someone else would have to take over, for he, though not far away, would nevertheless be removed from such activities.

Pleased with the idea, he understood he was making himself into an outlaw, a modern Robin Hood. He and Rip together would be a kind of robber band, though it was not robbery they would come out of the hills to commit.

The mist which enclosed the moor, which almost since sunrise had been shot with gold, should have lifted by now, but instead it seemed to be closing in, growing colder, whiter and more autumnal. He could see the foin only as a vague blurred shape, rising out of the flat land ahead. The coe and the windlass were invisible, and when they did appear it was to loom up like men advancing.

He fastened the rope to the lip of rock and clambered down Apsley Sough. The sides of the shaft were moist and slippery but not running with water and there was no water lying in the chamber at its foot. Stephen felt relief. There had been times in the past days when he feared a flooding of the mine.

All the rain seemed to have done was intensify the sour chemical smell. He made his way along the winze, wondering if Rip were here already and if the sound of his footfalls might be audible to him through the rock walls. The atmosphere felt colder than usual, laying a thick chilly breath on his skin. His throat tightened with excitement but he walked slowly, he walked with measured tread, to give Rip a chance to know that he approached.

The end of the winze, where it opened out into the doorway to the chamber, he saw as he rounded the slight bend in the passage, was in darkness. If Rip had come he was there no longer. Unless he sat waiting in the dark. Stephen remembered that Rip didn't know he was called Rip, that was only his own secret name for him, and he called in a loud clear voice, 'Peter! Peter, it's Stephen!'

There was no answer. He hadn't come yet. Stephen had a sudden feeling that Rip might have been alarmed by the discovery of the third girl's hair and have emptied the cavern for safety's sake. *He* didn't know, couldn't then have known, the identity of Harriet Crozier's killer. Stephen raised the torch. The light leapt across the rocky walls and showed him everything as it had been before, the boxes, the bottle of cider, the clothes, the bedding, the candles in the bottles and the candle in the candlestick.

Being in the cavern, the cavern as he had always known it, made him feel happy again. He sat down on the mattress, unrolled his blanket and lit all the candles. Like someone who, though long intimate with a friend's house, has always been a visitor, he had now taken a room there himself or moved in to share and might take liberties that were previously forbidden. He lit the calor gas burner. The kettle, he found, had been filled with water. It would take a long time to boil but eventually he would get himself a cup of tea. Into the box where the tins were and the biscuits Rip had put two packets of cigarettes, and Stephen seemed to smell again the scent of tobacco that had come to him as he opened the gate on Foinmen's Plain.

The gas burner gave a little welcome warmth. Stephen ate biscuits while the kettle boiled. There was only dried milk for the tea but he didn't mind. Doing without, making do, added to the fun of picnics. He saw before him a vista of future picnics with Rip, hard-won tea, the sweeter because it took so long to brew, biscuits softened with keeping, meat dug out of a tin. He had slept badly the night before, after he had buried Tace. He lay down on the mattress and covered himself with the blanket and fell asleep.

When he awoke his watch told him it was the middle of the afternoon. In the mine all times and all seasons were the same and the silence was the same. He sat up, feeling stiff and rather cold and listened to the silence. The candles had burnt down a long way but there was still a new one in the candlestick and he had brought four spares with him. He lit the new candle and that made him look at the candlestick and fancy he recognized it. In his own home surely when he was a small child? Or in the gatehouse lodge — yes, that was more likely. It must have been Helena's, passed on to Leonard, then to Peter. It gleamed like gold in the dimness of the chamber.

It was after four. Surely Rip would come before dark, surely he wouldn't wait till nightfall? To pass the time he undid the flaps on top of the secret box. He was almost certain the three hanks of hair lay exactly as he had left them. Did that mean Rip hadn't looked in the box since then, that he didn't know the third girl's hair was in there? What times he and Rip would have together! Sharing this place, hidden here, descending sometimes from their mountain fastness like wolves on the fold. He closed his eyes and saw them as wolves, grey, shaggy, powerful and fleet of foot, a victim held between white and red jaws. The first victim perhaps should be Stella Crane who could easily be lured from her sanctuary in Loomlade.

He laughed at the thought, though by now his teeth were chattering. His watch showed five and he got up and walked about, rubbing his hands and stamping his feet. It seemed to be growing colder all the time but he didn't want to light the burner again and use up all the gas in the canister. They would need it for tea in the morning. He decided to go for a walk, take some exercise. That was another thought to make him laugh, the notion of taking exercise down here in the bowels of the earth. He walked back along the winze and when he came to the fork continued a little way along to where the bad air began. And there he saw he had been wrong about the unlikelihood of flooding in the mine. Here the floor of the passage which had always been wet was lying under water. The level of water in the lake called the Bottomless Pit had risen up the walls of the cavern it filled and the water was spreading out to cut off the passage. Stephen shone his torch up ahead and whistled at what he saw. It was impossible to tell exactly how deep the water was but it had come so high as to leave a gap of only a foot or so between its ruffled black surface and the coffin-curved roof of the winze.

Ruffled, not still. It was rising as he watched. Was it raining again outside? Had it perhaps been raining all the time he had been asleep and before and since? For the first time Stephen realized how steeply after the fork the two branches ascended, the one to Rip's Cavern, the other to the egress chamber. It would take a long time for the water to get up there, perhaps it never would, perhaps whenever there was heavy rain the mine flooded like this and then afterwards the water gradually seeped away again to be sucked up by the moor.

An awareness that he might be in some danger struck him with a chill. He felt less fear than irritation at this threat to his and Rip's happiness. Was that why Rip hadn't come? Because it was raining once more as it had rained on the day of the storm? Stephen thought he would go up and see. He would go up the shaft and see if it was raining.

It was at this point that his torch battery failed. Of

course he hadn't been so imprudent as to come without a spare and he went back to Rip's Cavern to fetch it from his rucksack. Should he take the rucksack and the blanket up with him? Not yet. It might not be necessary at all. Rip would come. So great was his faith that he would come back and Rip would come that he left the candle burning in the brass candlestick.

Back to the fork he went and along the winze to the egress chamber. Water was running in thin trickling rivulets across the floor out from the mouth of the shaft. But it wasn't these runnels of water that made Stephen stare and then dash forward across the wet shale.

The rope had gone.

He moved the torch beam aside to give the effect of closing his eyes. Then he shone it again on to the shaft opening. The rope wasn't there. He went to the shaft and stood in it, looking up. A big drop of water splashed on to his forehead. He imagined it raining hard up there, the water draining off the hillside, over the stones and into the sough. Could the rain have been heavy enough to have washed the rope from its anchorage? If that had happened it wouldn't have disappeared altogether, it would have dropped down the shaft. Someone had unfastened it.

After his first couple of visits to the mine he had found himself so agile at climbing the shaft that he could have done without the rope. Now was the time to prove that. Should he go back for his rucksack? Of course not. He didn't mean to stay above ground, he intended to come back into the mine. The torch, however, he would take with him. He hooked it over his arm.

The first steps he took were encouraging. Down here

there were prominent ledges of rock for footholds and the streaming water made little difference to the purchase obtained. But after the first five or six feet the walls grew smoother and the shaft became a slippery gullet. When he had calculated that he could do without the rope he hadn't reckoned with the results of heavy rain. He lay against the wall of the shaft about six feet up, unable to find a secure hold for his hands, and until he could do so, scarcely daring to move his right foot. But he did move it, his hands grasping shale and nearly liquid mud. Both feet slipped and he slid back down all the way he had come, grazing chest and arms and hands on the sticky gravelly surface.

He tried again. He tried twice more and had to give up when he twisted his left ankle. His clothes were covered in mud, his hands were bleeding and he had cracked the glass in the torch. It was stupid to struggle like that and get in a state over it, stupid to risk injuring himself, for there was no chance of his being trapped in the mine. Rip was coming. Rip would bring his own rope with him.

Holding the torch, which still gave a powerful light in spite of its cracked glass, Stephen limped slowly back along the winze. At the highest point he had reached in the shaft before sliding down again he had fancied he could hear rain, a roaring overhead like the sound of the sea. But down here was the same eternal deep silence. He could hear his own footsteps and that was all.

He stopped dead. He froze, he was utterly still, and yet he could still hear footsteps. Very faintly, ahead of him, reaching the fork perhaps from the other direction and pattering along the passage that led to Rip's Cavern.

Rip had come at last. Stephen couldn't tell how he had come, by what means he could have entered the mine, but he had come and must now be in the cavern where the candle still burned. Stephen would have run on then in his anxiety to reach him but for his ankle. It was starting to hurt to put it to the ground. He limped as fast as he could up to the fork and turned down the other winze. Before he reached the bend and saw the light from the candle he smelt the sweet aromatic cigarette smoke. He called out, 'Rip, I'm coming,' and stumbled up to the entrance to the chamber.

The figure which had its back to him, which was bending over the box that contained the hair, cast on the wall a grotesque and monstrous shadow. It remained bent there as if paralysed and then it turned slowly round to face him. Stephen let the torch fall, it smashed and went out.

The man in Rip's Cavern was Dadda.

21

There was everything to say and nothing. They said
nothing for a long time. Stephen staggered over to the
mattress and half sat, half lay on it. He saw it was his
own aran Dadda was wearing, an old one he had left in
the house in King Street when he got married. He remembered the candlestick too. It came from Whalbys'
stock of antiques.

Dadda had been looking in the box where the hair
was. He was holding Harriet Crozier's hair in his hands
and now he looked long and hard at Stephen. He took
the cigarette out of his mouth and ground it out on the
floor. It had always been his way to smoke only when
he was happy.

Stephen forced himself to speak. 'Did you take away
my rope?'

'Aye. Didn't know it was yours, did I? Didn't know it was you.'

Stephen shivered. 'Then how did you get into the mine?'

'Same bloody way I always do. Down Apsley Sough.'

'But that's Apsley Sough, where my rope was.'

Dadda lifted his great shoulders. 'Years ago you came home and said you'd found a way into the mine. Apsley Sough, you said. When I — needed a place I looked for a hole and I found a hole, that's all.'

There *were* two ways in then — and two ways out. Stephen got to his feet. Pains shot up his left leg from his ankle but he hardly felt them. For the first time he noticed how wet Dadda was, up to the waist he was wet as if he had been immersed in water.

'I'll go,' he said. 'If you'll tell me the way you came I'll go. This is your place, I won't come again.'

He felt, though, that he had come to an end, the end of his life perhaps. If he tried to climb out of it, as he had tried to climb out of the mine, he would only slide back and break himself in pieces. Dadda threw the hair from him. It fell in gleaming coils, bright as the candlestick.

'We'll both go,' Dadda said, and he added in a low wondering voice, 'Like father, like son . . .'

He handed Stephen the candle and switched on his own lantern. Stephen left the rucksack and the blanket behind. Dadda didn't speak again until they were at the fork, Stephen limping along behind him. Then he pointed ahead.

'It's up there we go and it'll be wet, I'm warning you. When I came in I was wading up to my belly in it.'

Stephen objected, 'The air's bad up there. You can't keep a match alight.'

'Can't you, lad? I never tried. I breathed it all my comings and goings and I'm still here — worse luck.'

Half a dozen yards farther on and the water was over their ankles. It rose rapidly after that and it was icy cold. Stephen felt it like pain mounting up his legs, past his knees, to his thighs. When the water was up to his waist the candle flame began to sink. He pushed on through the water, Dadda's back ahead of him like the back of some great ox, and he watched the flame sink and quiver and die.

He said like a child in the dark, 'Dadda, I can't see. My candle's gone out.'

A wave of black water rippled over his chest as Dadda turned round. It was light again from the yellow beam of the lantern. The air Stephen was breathing smelt worse than coal gas, it was like inhaling vapourized metal. He began to cough.

'Does it get much deeper?'

Dadda didn't answer. Perhaps he didn't know. His face, haggard and ghastly in the yellowish gloom, told Stephen how much deeper the water was now than when he had come in.

'Stephen,' he said, 'I'd best go on alone, lad. I've got the height. When I get up top I'll drop your rope down.'

Stephen meant to say yes, all right, but the words came out as a choked sob. He cried out, 'I'll be left in the dark!'

'Aye, there's no help for that.'

He stood in the water up to his shoulders, watching the light move away from him. Dadda couldn't swim and neither could he. The faint receding light filled the narrow space between the surface of the water and the coffin curve of the roof and against it he could see Dadda's head, a silhouetted head as black as Tace's. There was a bend in the winze and the light went out.

Stephen shuddered, he wanted to scream, there in the dark, in the black water. He only whimpered a little. He began to wade and thrust back the way he had come, a blind man in an invisible flood.

The silence was total and the darkness absolute. In the space of seconds he had been deprived of his principal senses. That of touch remained, though the cold of the water was numbing his limbs, and he could smell the metallic sourness of the air. But he struggled slowly on back. If he could only make it without succumbing to panic, without losing his foothold, without breaking out into screams in this black silence, rescue awaited him at the other end. Even now the lifeline might be dropping down the shaft of Apsley Sough. He ground his teeth against his whimpering. and imagined his hands at last grasping the rope.

Into the silence came a distant rumbling sound. It wasn't very loud, a muted roar very like the noise the thunder had made when he lay among the Foinmen on the day he killed Harriet. Without having experienced such a thing before, he knew it was a rock fall he had heard, a fall somewhere inside the mine. As the reverberations died away something told him, some sense heightened by the deprivation of his other senses, that the fall was a threat to him, a danger to him. Instinctively, he flattened himself against the coffin curve of the wall and clung with his fingers to the tool ridges. He did so just in time. The tidal wave swelled and rolled the water up to his face and over his head, engulfing him. If he hadn't been holding on it would have swept him away. Under the water, up against the rock, he thought that this was what drowning must be, and then the wave passed. He threw up his head and gasped in a breath of the leaden bitter air.

There came a second wave, a smaller one. It swept a heavy object past his face. He reached out for it and, feeling its shape and its hardness in the dark, knew it for Dadda's lantern.

The water subsided and lay still. He began to push back through it once more, one hand on the wall, the other holding the lantern. The level sank to his waist, to his knees, until he was free enough from it to shiver and feel once more the pain in his ankle. Almost on dry land now, he came to the branching of the passage and there he flung the lantern on to the floor and heard it shatter against the rock.

There was no object now and no hope in taking the left-hand passage, for the rope would never come down the shaft. He was enclosed in the mine for ever. He began to make his way along the tunnel to Rip's Cavern and after a while he fell on his knees and crawled like an animal, thinking that there would be light there for a little time. There was nothing left now but an hour of light before the perpetual night time and, longing for that light as he had sometimes longed for the sun, he crawled and dragged himself towards it.

In the implacable rain Goughdale was as grey and unearthly as it had been in the mist. Men were advancing from the Reeve's Way up between the crushing circle and the coe. They carried ropes and picks and a ladder and through the shrouding downpour they looked like the shades of those lead miners of old. Malm walked ahead of them with Manciple.

'A piece of luck for us,' Malm said, 'that woman seeing him bury that stuff last night.'

Manciple nodded. 'Let's hope he'll tell us who killed the first two.'

'If he knows.' Malm pulled up his coat collar, shivered in the wet. He kicked at a stone. 'You'd better be right he's down there.'

'I'd bet a good deal on it.' They had come to the shelf at the foot of Big Allen. Manciple stared at the rain pounding on the boulders and running down the hillside. He said in his diffident way, 'I reckon I can find the place, though it's years and years,' and then, his eyes bright as if those years and years had fallen away, 'I was just a kid. I was up here on the moor and I spotted this rope going down a hole, so I looked down and there was this boy climbing up . . . Ah, here it is and a rope lying ready and waiting for us!'

'Go down and take him,' Malm said.

About the Author

Ruth Rendell, whom the *Los Angeles Times* calls "the heiress apparent to Agatha Christie," is the author of *Death Notes, Lake of Darkness, From Doon with Death, Sins of the Fathers, Wolf to the Slaughter, The Best Man to Die, Vanity Dies Hard,* and many other mysteries. She received the Current Crime Silver Cup award for best crime novel of 1976, the Crime Writers Association Gold Dagger for best crime novel of 1975, and the Mystery Writers Association Edgar for best short story of 1974.

Ruth Rendell lives in London.

From Ballantine